living with Regret

Sometimes the simplest choice has the power to change your life.

RIANN C. MILLER

Copyright © 2016 Riann C. Miller
Editing by Edee M. Fallon
Cover Design, Formatting and interior design by Jersey Girl & Co.

First Edition: April 2016

ISBN-13: 978-1532767142 | ISBN-10: 1532767145

10 9 8 7 6 5 4 3 2 1

introduction

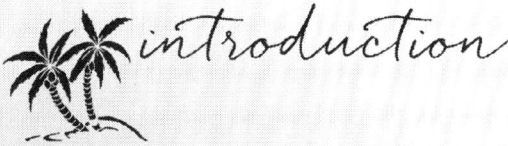

Sometimes the simplest choice has the power to change your life.

Chase

Ten years ago, I turned a hard decision into a simple one. I allowed others to decide my future ...then I lost the best thing that ever happened to me. I let go of the girl I loved in exchange for a life I was told I wanted.

Then one day I woke up with no recollection of my reality and instead I believed my life had turned out how I had once dared to imagine. Now everyone is waiting for me to remember the day I ruined my future as I struggle to recall a life without the person I so carelessly tossed away.

Somehow, I was gifted a second chance with the woman I love, and I'm going to fight like hell to keep her.

Jordan

Your brain has a funny way of convincing you what is real and what is not; even if your heart never lets you forget the truth. After Chase Adams broke my heart, my life moved forward, even though the light I once felt had extinguished. Then I received an unexpected phone call that changed everything.

Every day we make choices, but most of the time they don't affect the rest of our lives. I wanted to love again. I wanted to trust the gift I was given, but every choice has consequences. Now I have to decide to let go of the past for the sake of my future...or risk living with regret.

by riann c. miller

Unlikely Love
Beneath The Lies
Living With Regret

Jordan

I woke up already knowing my life is about to change, and I couldn't be happier. I met my boyfriend Chase Adams when I first moved to Oak Cove, Florida almost two years ago. Once he broke down every wall I had built around my heart, we became inseparable.

In this part of the world, Chase is a legend. There isn't a person within a hundred miles that doesn't know and love him. More importantly, everyone is banking on the day that Chase's talent as a quarterback takes him all the way to the NFL. For me, none of this matters because I know the person that Chase keeps hidden from the rest of the world, the one that could do almost anything with his life.

I grew up a military brat, moving from one Army base to the next. After my father retired, we moved to Oak Cove to live near my grandparents. For the first time in my life, I knew I would be staying somewhere long enough to invest in friendships. What I wasn't expecting was to be the center of attention. New students at Oak Cove High are few and far between. When I first moved here, it felt like everyone was seeking my attention in one form or another.

When Chase first made his intentions clear—that I was going to be his—I blew him off like I had everyone else. I didn't need or want a boyfriend, let alone the local hero. However, Chase didn't take no for an answer. Annoying as it was, he followed me around until I finally broke down and agreed to go on a date with him. That night changed my life. Away from everyone else, Chase isn't a football legend. He's just a beautiful person both inside and out, and I knew after only being around him for a few hours that I would be stupid not to give him a real chance.

Tonight is a warm late-July evening, almost seven weeks after we graduated high school. More importantly, it's the night before Chase leaves for Ohio State. This morning, right before I snuck out of his parents' house, he asked me to meet him at our park.

Halfway between my house and Chase's is Cove Park. The two of us have been meeting here since the night of our first date. This place is ours. This is the place I want to bring our children to one day because it was here that I first discovered I was in love with Chase.

Tonight, though, I have butterflies in my stomach at the idea of meeting him. My mother and friends have convinced me that Chase asked me here to propose. We've talked about marriage, about making our future official, but knowing we're about to take that leap is still scary ...in the best possible way.

When I arrive at the park, Chase is sitting at the picnic table with his feet on the bench, nervously tapping away. His arms are resting on his knees and his face is pointed down.

As I get a little closer, he whips his beautiful face up towards mine and I instantly know something's not right.

His shoulders sag, his eyes look worried, and his smile is forlorn. Whatever is going on, he doesn't seem like a guy that's about to propose.

When I get close enough, I reach out to grab his hand. "What's wrong?" I question as his eyes flash with some unknown emotion before he jumps to his feet while reaching out for me. "Chase? What's going on?" I ask again as my hands begin to tremble.

He slowly closes his eyes, almost as if he's in pain, before opening them and sighing. He pauses and carefully watches me before he shatters my world. "This isn't going to work. I mean—you and me—being together. I think …I think it's best for both of us if …we go our own way."

My mouth drops open as all the air escapes my lungs. This is a joke. It has to be a sick and twisted joke. But when I look at him again, I can tell …I can tell it's not.

I take a deep breath and step away from him as my thoughts run rampant. The one thing that stands out the most is: This isn't my Chase. My Chase is strong, dominant, and possessive enough that he would never toss me to the side while he moved on with his life. This is his parents talking. They've never accepted our relationship. As far as Steve Adams is concerned, I'm a distraction. Chase needs to focus on what's important, which is his football career.

I could stand here and yell at him for breaking my heart, for not standing up for us, for not believing that together we could beat the odds, but I'm not going to. I can tell he's already made up his mind and I'm not going to stoop so low that I have to beg him to take it back. It's already too late. The damage is done.

"What was last night about?" I breathe out, trying my best to hold back my tears.

Last night, Chase had called, begging me to come over. His parents were out of town for the night and he wanted me to stay with him. I made up a story about staying with a friend then went to him.

Looking back, last night was different from any other night we had spent together. Chase and I have been having sex for over a year now, but last night he was beyond gentle. He showed me with his body that words weren't necessary because I could tell with every brush of his lips how much he loves me. But now ...less than twenty-four hours later, he's crushing my heart ...he's crushing our future.

"Last night was a goodbye. I wanted us to have one more night filled with lasting memories," he quickly says before turning his face away from mine.

I'm trying my hardest to be strong but I can't hold my tears back any longer. "You don't think I had the right to know what last night was about?" I allow the bitterness that's filling my body to take control.

"If you had known last night then things would have gone very differently. I wanted ...no, I needed last night. God, I'm sorry. I know this is hurting you and I promised myself that I would never ever hurt you, but . . ." He trails off and turns his face as I brush my tears away and straighten my shoulders. Tonight isn't going how I expected but I refuse to act weak. I refuse to give him and everyone else in this town something to gossip about. He wants a life without me, and like it or not, that's exactly what I'm going to give him.

I clear my throat and wait for him to finally look at me. He's chewing on his lip and his eyes are glassy. He's clearly in pain but that does very little to ease my own.

"Beyond your outside layers is a wonderful man. I hope

as you go through life you'll stay true to him because you deserve nothing less than an amazing life. And when . . ." My voice unwillingly cracks. "When you do find a woman you want to spend your life with, I hope you don't settle."

Panic takes over Chase's face as he quickly responds, "I don't mean forever. God, Jordan—I can't—I just think while we're both going to different colleges that we shouldn't be tied down. Hell, we'll hardly see each other. Taking a break makes sense but we belong together. I won't have to settle because it's you. It will always be you. One day, we'll be together again."

I didn't think it was possible for my heart to break any more, but I was wrong. He's dumping me while he goes off to play the role of superstar—which I know will involve other women—and he actually thinks I will be waiting for him afterward?

"I—I can't . . ." I shake my head, allowing myself a few seconds to collect my thoughts. "The man I'm going to spend the rest of my life with won't need a break from me. He'll know from the moment I enter his life that I'm worth keeping. That's the type of man I deserve to be with and I'm not going to settle for anything less." Chase's eyes flare with anger but otherwise, he doesn't respond as I slowly close the distance between us.

I bring my hands up and place them on each side of his face. I see the anguish in his eyes as my lips slowly find his. When our mouths meet, I close my eyes and allow myself to think of happier times, a time when our love was all we needed to survive. All too soon, I drop my hands and step away.

The agonizing look on Chase's face is one that might haunt me for the rest of my life because I know in my heart that tonight wasn't his choosing, but the end result is still the same. If he's not willing to stand up for us then it's best I find out now.

"That's how you say goodbye," I softly say as I turn and walk away.

"Wait, can I—I don't know...call you sometime?"

I stop and turn back towards him. With a half-smile, I give him the only answer I can. "No."

"No?" he asks as his eyes wildly take me in.

I swallow, pushing down the lump in my throat. "You're my first love, and you'll always hold a special place in my heart, but unfortunately, our story is over."

He can't have it both ways and that's something he doesn't seem to understand. I know he wants me ...wants us, but he allowed his desire and maybe even fear of the future to override everything we've shared. There's not a doubt in my mind that his father convinced him that his dreams won't happen if I'm involved, but now it's time he lives with his decision.

I give Chase the best smile I can muster before I walk out of Cove Park, a place that up until tonight held so many beautiful memories, a place I always felt safe in, but that's not the case anymore. Now it's the place where my heart was broken into a thousand pieces, a place, after tonight, I never plan to visit again.

I knew today was going to change my life; I just wish I had predicted the real outcome and not allowed myself to dream about a fairytale ending that was never going to happen.

ten years later...

chapter 1

CHASE

My head doesn't hurt. Actually, it feels better than it has for a very long time and that is why I'm tuning out everyone.

"Hello? Chase? Are you even listening to me?" an annoyed voice says, bringing my attention back to the people sitting around me.

I'm not a mean guy, but I'm big and am used to intimidating men almost twice my size, but nothing I do or say has Dr. Mark Wallace backing down.

"Chase, you're one serious concussion away from altering your life."

I sigh and roll my eyes. This is a conversation I'm sick of having. During the playoffs last season, I was sacked. The God's honest truth is I was more than sacked. I had my ass handed to me.

At the age of twenty-one, I was a first-round draft pick for the NFL. Now, depending on who you talk to, at the age of twenty-eight, my professional football career might very well be over. However, that's not a reality I'm willing to accept.

"Chase, you have two serious concussions documented. This last one was relatively minor, but medically speaking, I don't think you'll recover from another severe blow to your head."

I turn my face away, not wanting to listen to the same ol' crap. Dr. Wallace started this song and dance after my concussion last year. During preseason this year, I was sacked during a game I never should have played in the first place, but I got up and walked off the field without a problem. Then three weeks ago, I was tackled and I was slow getting up. If I had a concussion, it was minor, but a concussion is a concussion, or so I'm told. I haven't played a game since.

"Doctor, I understand your concern but if my son is one concussion away from retirement, then I think it makes sense for him to wait it out. For all we know, he may never suffer another in his life or, God forbid, that does happen, I don't see why he shouldn't keep himself in the game until then." My father's voice, like normal, is firm, almost demanding.

Without a doubt, my NFL career means more to my father than it ever has to me. Don't get me wrong, I'm living the life I always dreamed of, but during my twenty-eight years on earth, I've learned that there is more to life than just football. My dad, however, didn't get the same memo.

"Mr. Adams, I didn't say anything about your son retiring. If, or realistically, when Chase suffers another concussion, the best-case scenario is early retirement, but no one in this room other than myself seems to be concerned about the long-term effects of another concussion." The doctor takes a deep breath then looks back at me.

"Chase, I'll sign off on your clearance papers if you'll look at me while I explain to you why I don't think this is in your best interest."

I heard Dr. Wallace's request but I didn't respond fast enough to keep my father from kicking my leg to help garner my attention. After giving my father a go-to-hell look, I turn and stare Dr. Wallace in the face.

"Chase, concussions with athletes, especially football players, is a very common occurrence, but hardly anyone wants to talk about the lasting effects." The doctor clears his throat. "I have personally cared for athletes that have suffered from both short and long-term brain damage. I've seen everything from losing control of their basic motor skills to severe emotional problems. I have a patient that spends hours each day confused about things he learned to do as a small child. Other patients deal with anything from headaches, nausea, depression, and I have even seen cases of amnesia. For some, these symptoms can go away relatively quick, but I've also seen patients dealing with symptoms even decades later." The doctor pauses before sighing. "Chase, I need to know that you understand the risk you're taking by being on the field."

I heard every word that came out of Dr. Wallace's mouth, but I can't walk away from the only thing I know ...the only thing in my life worth having. I'm in my sixth season with the NFL, but I'm only in my third as a starting quarterback. I have the rest of this season and next year before my current contract is up. If I take the proper time off to allow my brain time to heal, I might as well kiss my football career goodbye.

"I understand what the risks are, Doctor," I say in a tone that lacks any emotion.

"And even understanding those risks you're still willing to go back out on the field?"

I look around the room, first at my agent, then his assistant, and finally my father. They're all waiting for me to say one very simple word. "Yes," I answer.

At this point, I really don't care what, if any, long-term effects I may suffer because the only solution the good doctor has offered is to give up football, and that's not an option. That will never be an option.

"Will you please go out with me?" After my fifth request of the day, the most amazing pair of blue eyes move up towards my face.

"The answer is the same as the last five million times you asked me. No."

Jordan gives me a frustrated sigh before pushing her dark hair over her shoulders and turning to walk away.

"Hey, where are you going?" I ask as I run to catch up with her.

"To class, like everyone including you should be doing."

It might sound cocky, but I could date any girl in this school I choose, and that includes the ones that have boyfriends. But until I met Jordan, I never even considered giving a girl the time of day.

My family owns and operates a citrus grove and when I'm not at school or practicing football with my personal trainers, I'm expected to pull my weight. My father employs hundreds of people during peak season, but I'm always expected to do my part. Honestly, now that my mind is completely consumed by the beautiful Jordan Taylor, I know this is exactly why my father has tried his hardest to keep me so damn busy.

Everywhere I go, everything I do, she's all I can think about. Her first day at OCH, she walked into class and my brain and heart stopped at the exact moment my eyes landed on her. When I was finally able to regain my composure, I looked around the room and noticed that I wasn't the only male that had that same reaction. I knew right then and there if I wanted any chance with Jordan, I had to act fast and make sure my impression was the only one she remembered.

"Give me one solid reason why you won't go out with me and I promise I'll stop asking you out ...at least for a few days." I give her what I hope is my friendliest smile. I want her to feel safe and comfortable with me, and I know asking her out every few hours is probably not the best way to accomplish that.

Instead of answering me, those piercing blue eyes penetrate straight through me. "I'm serious, one good reason. Do I smell funny? Do my looks offend you? Do you ...have a boyfriend back home where you came from?" Out of all the things I asked, I really hope the last one isn't the reason she continues to turn me down flat.

"No, I don't have a boyfriend, but that doesn't mean I'm looking for one, either." Jordan's sass and attitude are another reason I want her to say yes. Any other girl in this school would die for me to ask them out for the sole purpose that everyone expects I'll make it big one day. But right now, whatever my future holds doesn't seem to matter to this girl.

"Well, the good news is I didn't ask to be your boyfriend. I only asked for a date. Just one. If you hate it or me afterward, I promise I'll leave you alone for good."

Jordan jerks her head a little to the side like she's trying to decide if she should believe me or not. "I don't know . . ."

Holy hell, that wasn't a flat out no. I'm finally wearing her down. *"That's okay. You don't have to have all the answers. I'll pick you up, we'll go out to dinner, and then afterward if you're ready to ditch me I'll take you home. If not, I know a local place that I think you'll love."*

The way Jordan looks at me, it's unlike everyone else. Her eyes take in everything I do, and when she looks straight at me, I swear she can see past the heavy armor I always wear.

"If I go on a date with you, you promise afterward you'll let go of this crazy idea you have that we should be together?" She tilts her head, waiting for me to answer.

I need to choose my words wisely. I'm not a liar and I'm not about to form that habit, but I'm not positive I'm capable of walking away when it comes to Jordan Taylor.

"I promise that if you absolutely hate our date that I won't ask you out on another one." And I plan to do everything in my power to ensure that she loves every moment we spend together. And if for some crazy reason she doesn't, then I'll stop asking her out, but that doesn't mean I'll stop taking every opportunity I can find to talk to her. My promise probably isn't what she's looking for but it's all I can give her without running the risk of becoming a liar.

"Okay. I'll need to ask my parents first, but if this is all it takes to make you stop asking me out every five minutes then it should be worth it," she says with a breathtaking smile on her face.

I never would have guessed that being annoying would actually pay off, but in this case it did. Big time.

"Saturday night. Get your parents' permission and I'll pick you up at seven o'clock." The small smile that still lingers on her face is the last thing I see before I turn and walk in the opposite direction before she has the chance to change her mind.

"Man, it's good to have you back," Jake says, bringing me out of my thoughts.

"Thanks, it's good to be back." Most of my teammates appear happy to see me, but I know a few don't think I can cut it. I haven't played a game for three weeks and my replacement did a stellar job in my absence, which was great for the team but not so much for me if I want to keep my starting position.

"I heard Wallace wasn't going to allow you back on the field for the rest of the season, but I guess that was just fucking gossip. I swear guys in a locker room are just as bad as any chick I've met when it comes to talking about shit that doesn't concern them."

That's just it ...my return and the condition I'm in does affect everyone in this room, but I know Jake is trying to ease the blow that my teammates have been talking shit behind my back.

"Wallace didn't have a medical reason to keep me from playing. He gave me his spiel about how I should rest my brain and blah, blah, blah but he's just making sure he's covered his own ass," I add before tossing my bag into my locker.

"Well, I hope you're right. Now let's go kick some ass." I wish I had half the enthusiasm that Jake Girard has. Jake is probably the only friend I've made since I've left Oak Cove.

Between college and the NFL, I've hung out and partied with a lot of different guys, but when the time comes that we part ways, they never seem to be guys I hear from again. Jake, however, called, text, and even stopped by my house a few times during the last few weeks to check on me. I think I can finally place him in the true friend category.

As a kid, I often dreamed of making it to the NFL, but never once in any of those dreams did I feel lonely, which is the exact word I would use to describe my life.

Every day I'm surrounded by people, but none of them actually gives a damn about me. Even my own father, who I know loves me, is always looking out for what he feels is my best interest, but that's not something we often agree on.

When women want to date me, or guys want to be my friend, it's always about what I will bring to their life and never because they want to know me, the real me. The guy that I keep locked away tight, the guy that only one person has ever really known.

"Are you a hundred percent ready to be out there today?" I look up and see Jack Jones, the offensive coordinator, looking at me with concern.

I resist the urge to roll my eyes, knowing that won't go over well. This is football, players are tackled, it's a part of the game and I don't understand why everyone is fussing over me.

"I'm fine. I wouldn't be here otherwise."

He doesn't say a word but he slowly nods his head. I can see the doubt he has about me playing. Until the time comes that someone tells me I can't go out on that field, I'm not going to give up the only thing in my life that I love... no matter the cost.

chapter 2

Jordan

"Take the shot and stop bitching!" I curse under my breath as I resist the urge to slap my best friend. I'm tired and ready to go home, but somehow agreeing to meet Lacey for a couple of drinks has turned into an all-night drink fest—and I should have known better.

"Seriously, take the damn shot then let's go talk to that guy over there about taking you home and fucking your brains out."

I bite my lip and give her a go-to-hell look. She's annoying me and she knows it. "Lace, I don't need you picking up guys for me. If I want to take home a complete stranger, I'm sure I could find one without your help."

Lacey rubs her hands together. "Well, if that guy fucks anywhere as good as he dances then the woman he takes home tonight is in for a treat!" I follow her eyes to the dance floor where there is a man that definitely knows how to move, but I'm not looking for a casual hook up, at least not tonight.

"Lace, I'm good. I have a lot of work I need to get done tomorrow. I'm heading home," I say in a firm tone that leaves no doubt about how serious I am.

"Okay, I'll let you ditch me but only if you finally agree to go out with Caleb." I grab my purse off the table and shake my head.

"For the last time, no."

If you met Lacey out at the bar, you'd probably guess she's a crazy alcoholic. In reality, she's a very successful lawyer, in New York City, no less, which makes that statement twice as powerful.

Caleb is a man Lacey used to hate. The two of them were offered an internship at the same time. The firm they worked at pitted them against each other but somehow they were both offered a partnership. Afterward, they decided they made better friends than enemies.

"I'm not dating a guy you work with. That's a recipe for disaster if things don't work out. Why would you want to put yourself in that position?" I ask as I push my shot back in front of her.

"Because if you two hit it off, then you'll both owe me forever and if you don't ...then, whatever. I like Caleb, but no matter what happens, I'll always have your back."

I can't help but smile at her. When I left Oak Cove for NYU, I met Lacey during freshmen orientation and we hit it off immediately. I was still recovering from a broken heart and Lacey was exactly what I needed in my life. When I broke down one night and confessed what happened only weeks before, she went straight into the role of my best friend slash protector, and it's a role she takes seriously.

"I'll think about it," I lie.

"Bitch, that's what you said last time. I'm giving him your number and you can deal with him yourself. I think he might already be half in love with you after he saw a picture of the two of us in my office."

Her comment turns my stomach and it's one of the main reasons I'm on a hiatus from dating. The last few guys I tried to start a relationship with started out wonderful, but I slowly became arm candy for them when they needed to be seen in public.

Being the CEO of a large company in New York, I typically date successful men. However, none of them cared enough to make me a priority in their life, and I can't imagine a lawyer being any different.

My actual fear regarding the type of men I usually attract is that I never feel like their equal. I earned a business degree from NYU with honors and I'm the CEO of Natural Cosmetics, but I received that title by default, not because I earned it.

My mother's side of the family started Natural Cosmetics generations ago. My grandparents had every intention of my mother taking over the company one day. However, my mother wanted a life outside of their empire. She married my father less than six months after she met him and I was born a few months after their first anniversary. Because of my father's military career, my mother and I moved around a lot in order for our family to stay together. There is no way she could have stepped up into the role her parents offered her and still make a marriage work with my father. For my mother, there was never a choice to make. She loved my father and couldn't picture a life that didn't include him.

My grandfather was secretly hoping that I would one day take over his company, but he learned the hard way not to push. However, once I learned about my acceptance to NYU, the same city that houses Natural Cosmetics' headquarters, he swooped in and started grooming me for my future role as the CEO.

"Are you sure you'll make it home okay?" I ask Lacey as she gives me one of her typical mean girl stare downs, but her bitchy powers no longer work on me.

"Yeah, I'll be okay. If you're going home alone, then make sure you give your vibrator a good work out. God knows you need to loosen up."

Again, this is where any rational person would want to slap her but I know she means well, and a night with my BOB sounds pretty fantastic compared to doing something with a man I know I'll later regret.

"Okay, I'm out of here. Good luck with whomever you decide to spend the rest of your night with." An evil smile takes over Lacey's face before she turns and disappears into the crowd.

Once again I'm heading home to an empty apartment. This is something that should make me happy because I suck at relationships and the last thing I need in my life is a man distracting me. But I can't let go of the idea that one day I'll meet a guy that will sweep me off my feet, and I'll find a love as powerful as the one my parents share. However, the closer I get to thirty, the more I think I should settle for a man that will at least treat me good. I'm positive that deep down my heart knows I've already met the man that had the power to love me the way I desire, even though he was able to toss me away without a second thought. I need to do what I've said for years and that's face reality and let go of the silly fairytale that promises a happily ever after.

"Sweetheart, he's here."

My mother's comment causes my stomach to drop. When I came home from school the other day and told my dad that a boy asked me out on a date, I was positive he would refuse to allow me to go. However, he easily agreed. I think my dad feels guilty that I'm sixteen and I don't have any friends. He knows his job is the reason. Either way, I wasn't expecting him to say I could go out with a boy. I think it helped that Chase's family is well-known and well-liked by everyone in the area.

I have no idea what Chase has planned for tonight but I decided to wear a pair of white shorts with a dressy tank top. Casual, but not too casual. I close my door, head down the stairs, and come to a complete stop when I see Chase and my dad talking like they've known each other forever. My dad even stops and lets out a huge laugh, something that is rare for him.

I'm not sure what catches Chase's attention but he stops in the middle of his conversation and looks over at me. My dad's eyes follow Chase's and now they are both watching me. I instantly feel uncomfortable with the attention.

"Um, here, I got you these." *Chase hands me a bouquet of wildflowers, looking nervous. He's acting completely different from the overly confident guy I've seen at school.*

"Thank you."

"Here, honey, I'll put those in water for you. That way you two can get going." *I hand the flowers to my mom before glancing back at Chase.*

"Are you ready?" *I ask.*

"Absolutely." *At school, I swear Chase stares at me as if he's trying to undress me with his eyes, but here in front of my parents, it feels like he's doing that plus so much more, which makes me extremely nervous.*

"Make sure you have her home by eleven, Chase."

"Yes, sir." *Chase holds his hand out for me to take, and once*

I do, he leads me to the passenger door of the truck I've seen him drive to school. He opens the door for me and waits until I'm inside before he closes it and walks around, hopping in the driver's seat.

I'm so nervous I think it's possible I could puke at any moment. While I'm trying to get myself under control, Chase places his hand on top of mine, causing my breathing to become labored. I bring my eyes back up to his.

"Thank you," he says with a smile.

This right here is why I'm so nervous; it's the way Chase is watching me. No one has ever looked at me with the type of passion I see in his eyes. I'm not sure what exactly Chase is expecting from me but I hope he knows I'm not the kind of girl that's going to sleep with him.

"Thank you? For what?" I mumble.

Chase gives my hand a squeeze before answering me. "For tonight, because I already know it's going to be the best night of my life." He smiles at me one last time before starting his truck.

That was the first crack in the wall I'd built around my heart, a wall that I later learned didn't stand a chance against the powerful determination of Chase Adams.

"Ms. Taylor, here's your schedule for the day," Silvia says from the chair across from mine.

"Thank you." I think it's possible I have the best PA known to man. I inherited Silvia when my grandfather retired, and I don't know how I would've survived without her.

"Mr. Winters, the manager of the plant in Westwick, is waiting for your final approval before the new line can go into production.

"Also, you're receiving about two calls a day from Mr. Brooks's secretary requesting you accompany him to the annual art gala a week from Saturday."

I sigh and roll my eyes. Geez ...his freaking secretary?

I think it's safe to say the man will never learn. This is the exact reason why I broke up with the self-centered prick in the first place.

I casually dated Derek Brooks for almost six months last year. After having more conversations with his secretary then I ever did with him, I politely told him things between us weren't working out, but he didn't seem to care. Now, anytime he needs to appear at a red-carpet event and thinks he might be photographed, he calls me trying to score a date. I'm not about to go anywhere with the man if he's not willing to pick up the damn phone and ask me himself.

"And finally, I'm sorry to bother you with this, but a woman has been calling the office multiple times a day requesting to speak with you. When she first informed me that her call regarded a personal matter, I told her she needed to contact you on your private number, but she hasn't given up. I just want to double check that I should continue to refuse her calls."

When I first filled the role as Natural Cosmetics' CEO, I started receiving calls from people I've never heard of before hoping to gain something by being my friend. There were days when I didn't get any work done because I was constantly answering or returning unnecessary calls. A few months with my new title and I gave Silvia a list of people that are allowed to call me. If they aren't on that list, then they don't make it past her. No exceptions ...until now.

"How long has she been calling?" I question.

Silvia sighs. "The last couple of days, usually three or four times per day." That's definitely persistent.

"Who did you say it was?"

"I didn't, ma'am. The woman's name is Donna Adams." My entire body goes solid with tension as Silvia waits for my response.

I only know one Donna Adams and I can't begin to imagine why she would be calling me. I exhale loudly. "Put her through the next time she calls, Silvia."

"Yes, ma'am. Will that be all?"

"Yes." Silvia picks up on the change in my mood but she's smart enough to know I won't talk to her about my personal problems. With a half-smile, she stands up and leaves.

Chase's parents—Steve and Donna Adams—were never rude or mean to me, but they made their feelings about me dating their son apparent. I was a distraction he didn't need. I was the girl that would single-handedly keep him from achieving his dream of playing professional football.

I hated how they viewed my role in Chase's life, but even as a teenager, I knew they had their son's best interest at heart. It wasn't until they convinced Chase to crush any chance we had of a future together that I truly began to hate them.

In the last ten years, I've never once returned to Oak Cove. When I first moved to New York, my parents would visit me every few months, leaving me with no reason to make the trip down to Florida. Within a few years, my parents moved up north so they could be closer to me.

When it came to Chase, I allowed myself to suffer much longer than I should have. I was convinced after a certain amount of time he would come to his senses. I was waiting for him to call me—even though I told him not to—and tell me he made the biggest mistake of his life, but he never did. After six months of living in limbo, the only thing I had to show for myself was a semester of crappy grades.

With a new year and a new semester, I decided it was time for a new me. I purchased a new phone and number, deleted all of my social media accounts, and good, bad, or otherwise, started to live life again.

I would be lying if I said I never think of Chase Adams. There was a time when I would avoid going anywhere during football season if I thought someone might be watching a game he would be playing in. But that's not the case anymore. Chase Adams is just a guy I dated in high school. He's just a faint memory, and I hope like hell that Donna Adams doesn't do or say anything to change that.

chapter
3

CHASE

"I love coming out here with you," Jordan says, staring up into my eyes.

"Yeah, well, I love going anywhere as long as you're with me, baby," I tell her, pulling her body even tighter against mine.

Never in my wildest dreams did I imagine I would find the girl I'd spend the rest of my life with while I was still in high school. I might be young, but I know Jordan is the girl I'm going to marry one day—hopefully soon.

"What do you think it will be like when we leave for school?"

"We'll be fine. We love each other and that's all that matters," I firmly state. I hate having this conversation and lately it's all Jordan talks about. For the next four years, the two of us will spend more time apart than we will together, but I have no doubt that we'll be fine.

Will it be hard? Sure. Will I miss her like crazy? Absolutely. But I know we can weather the storm and come out a stronger couple in the end.

"Nothing and I mean nothing will keep us apart. I love you." I turn Jordan's head back towards me. When I see her *beautiful but watery blue eyes, my heart speeds up even more.*

I could name hundreds of things about Jordan that I love, but it's the beauty below the surface that truly captured my heart. Other than her obvious good looks, I'm not sure why I was immediately drawn to her. But from the day I first set my eyes on her, I've undoubtedly wanted her in my life. And nothing, including going to separate colleges hundreds of miles apart, is going to keep me from the only person my heart plainly desires.

"I love you, too. I'll love you forever."

Beep. Beep. Beep.

My head is fucking killing me and I want that fucking beeping noise to stop. My eyes slowly open and I start to panic when I see that I'm in what looks like a hospital room.

The walls are crisp white, I have a machine attached to my arm, and I can see what looks like a clipboard at the end of the bed.

Fuck me. I don't remember what I did or what happened to land me here, but more importantly, I don't know where everyone is.

I turn to the IV machine that's attached to my arm and I push the help button. The fucking thing starts screaming, causing the pounding in my head to increase.

Oh God. Make it stop. Someone please make that horrible noise stop. As that mantra continues in my head, I hear the sound abruptly stop, which causes me to slowly crack an eye. I first notice a woman, who appears to be a nurse, and then I spot my mother standing off to the side with a worried look sketched across her face.

"Hey, Ma," I say with a scratchy throat. After hearing me talk, my mother's face relaxes a little and she steps closer to my bed.

"Hey, sweetheart. How are you feeling?" she asks in a soft but concerned voice.

"Like shit. My head hurts. Where is everyone else?" I ask while my eyes are still scanning the room.

"Oh, your father is off somewhere trying to flag down a specialist we were told about. He should be back soon."

I'm trying my best to patiently wait for her to tell me about the person I was actually asking about but she remains silent. "Ma, where is she?"

Ma gives me a confused look before she appears to know whom I'm asking about. "Oh, the nurse? I'm sure she'll be right back." My mother isn't one to beat around the bush.

"Cut the shit, Ma. You're really starting to make me mad. Where the fuck is Jordan?" I snap out in a rather harsh tone.

My mom drops my hand and moves a few inches from the side of the bed. "Jordan? What—who—Jordan who, sweetie?" I close my eyes and take a deep breath, willing myself to relax. When I open them, I see my mother still carefully watching me.

"Ma, you know exactly who I'm talking about. Jordan. My wife." This time, my mother jumps away from my bed like I'm on fire and she's about to get burned.

My eyes narrow at her strange behavior. Between Ma acting weird and Jordan not being here, added to the fact that no one has told me what the fuck is going on, I'm at my breaking point.

"Get my wife and the fucking doctor NOW. I'm serious, Ma. I don't know what game you're playing or why but I'm done fucking playing it with you," I growl out while my head feels like it's about to explode.

"Sure. Yeah. I'll just ...go . . ."

My mom takes off and out the door at a speed much faster than I'm used to seeing her move. I know something's not right. For starters, I can't remember what happened to land me in a fucking hospital, not to mention the fact that both Jordan and my dad are nowhere to be found.

Waking up to her beautiful face would have been nice, but I know since she's not here then there must be a good reason. I just hope wherever she is, she gets here quick because I want her. No, scratch that ...I need her.

Jordan

"Ms. Taylor, Mrs. Adams is on the phone for you. Shall I put her through?" I swallow and push down the nervous lump in my throat.

"Yes, Silvia, thank you." My skin prickles as I watch the light on my phone flash. Ever since Silvia mentioned Donna has been calling, I've tried to think of every reason she would have to contact me, but I came up empty. I guess I'm finally about to find out.

Taking a deep breath, I push the flashing light.

"Good morning. This is Jordan Taylor, how can I help you?" I say in the most professional voice I can muster.

"Jordan? Um . . ." Donna pauses then clears her throat. "This is Donna Adams. Chase's mother," she nervously mumbles.

"Yes, Mrs. Adams, my PA informed me who was calling. I hate to be rude but I'm very busy. Could you please get straight to the reason you're calling?"

If it weren't for the light on my phone, I'd wonder if she hung up. The silence stretches for a few more seconds before she finally decides to speak up, only now her voice sounds weak.

"Chase is hurt." I hear her sniffle. "He's in the hospital and I was hoping you'd come to visit him." Now I'm the silent one. I'm repeating what I think I heard her say over and over in my head but it doesn't make sense.

"Chase is hurt?" I repeat.

"Yes." My heart instantly sinks. No matter what life has dealt us, I never wanted anything bad to happen to him.

"Oh. I'm ...I'm very sorry to hear that, Mrs. Adams. I hope he gets well soon. Was there something else you needed?" I question because I'm still quite confused as to why she's called me.

"Yes. I want you to come here and see him." Donna's tone was sharp, almost the tone a mother uses when she's scorning her child.

"Mrs. Adams, I—"

"Donna. Please call me Donna. You never called me Mrs. Adams before."

Before. She couldn't have said that better. I did a lot of things differently ...*before.* "I called you by your first name ten years ago when I was dating your son because I felt comfortable around you and in your home. That is no longer the case. But it does make me wonder, Mrs. Adams, why in the world would you ask me of all people to visit Chase?"

The phone is silent again, however now I can hear her lightly breathing. "Mrs. Adams, I'm sorry—"

"PLEASE. I'm begging you. Please." The desperation in her voice is clear, but I just can't understand the reason behind it.

"You're going to have to give me more than a please. I'm sorry that he's hurt but this is not my problem. Chase made it clear that I wasn't going to be a part of his life when he dumped me and then left for college. That was ten years ago, Mrs. Adams, and I haven't heard from him since. And to be honest, I think I'm the last person he'd want visiting him."

She sighs heavily before saying, "I wasn't positive, but I was hoping maybe you had seen him over the years. This really is our fault." Donna huffs out a breath before continuing. "We convinced him it was best for you if he allowed you to go off to college and experience what life had to offer. If you two had stayed together, you would have held each other back and that wasn't fair to either of you."

I remain quiet, not wanting to relive the past with a woman that just willingly admitted to playing a role in the demise of our relationship.

"Jordan, he never wanted to break up with you, and after he did ...well, as his mother, I knew we made a monumental mistake. He wasn't the same without you. And right now he's lying in a hospital bed after suffering a blow to his head. He's confused and for whatever reason he thinks the two of you are married."

My heart drops to my stomach. *Married?* He thinks the two of us are ...married.

"He woke up several days ago and he's gone from worried

to upset because his wife hasn't shown up to see him. Last night he had to be sedated, and no one knows if or when he'll get his memory back, at least, the correct one. But..."

My hands are shaking and my heart is slowly breaking as I listen to her. I can't believe this has happened to him, and now after ten years, he's somehow involved me in his life.

"His doctor said it's possible if he sees the grown-up version of you, it might spark his memory, especially if he hasn't seen you in all of this time. At this point, I'm willing to do anything because watching him wonder where you're at is just too much. It's breaking my heart." She sniffles again and I can hear the tears in her voice.

She's waiting for me to give her an answer, but I'm not sure I have one. Years ago, I heard that Chase was drafted to the Arizona Cardinals. Other than that, I've made it a point not to know what is going on in his life.

"I know you must be busy with work. Congratulations, by the way, with everything you've achieved. But, please, I'm begging you to come here and see him."

"Where is here, Mrs. Adams?" I say as I close my eyes in defeat.

"He's at Phoenix Medical Center."

I silently curse myself for even considering what she's asking me. "I'll need to think about this, but you can leave your number with my PA. If I decide to make the trip, I'll let you know."

"Oh, Jordan, please. I'm begging you. He's so confused and upset, and I think you're the only one who can make things right."

"I'll think about it. I have to go." Before Donna can get another word in, I transfer the call back to Silvia. I'm staring down at my desk when I see a drop of water then another before it finally dawns on me that I'm crying.

Chase is someone I think I could handle accidentally running into. A quick *"How are you doing? That's great. Well, I got to go"* conversation, but not this. Why in the world would he think we're married? Does that mean he thinks about me? God ...I could be opening a huge door if I make the trip to see him. At the same time, he might take one look at me and snap out of it once he remembers all the reasons he was able to let me go so easily.

I don't even know what Chase looks like these days. Ten years ago, Chase had a body that put any other guy I knew to shame. His father made sure he worked out for hours every single day and it paid off in a way that made it impossible not to notice him. He had short, dark brown hair, alluring hazel eyes, but none of that mattered to me. What truly sold me on Chase was the beauty I saw on the inside, the beauty I saw after I got to know the boy he kept hidden from everyone else. The boy that would mow his neighbor's yard when she got too old to do it herself, the boy that put money on Gunner Brown's lunch account to make sure he'd always have at least one good meal every day. The boy that pulled over to the side of the road to help a dog that someone else hit with their car.

The list of amazing things Chase did was never-ending, and more importantly ...he always did things because it was the right thing to do and never because he was looking for credit for his good deeds.

Knowing the kind of person Chase was only added to my devastation when he broke up with me. I wasn't prepared for him to break my heart because he promised me we'd be fine. Then he went back on his word, and that was something Chase never did. He let me go without a second thought, which left me to wonder if our entire relationship was one big lie.

chapter 4

Jordan

"You can't be serious. Get your ass on a plane back to New York, now!" I breathe out a sigh as Lacey hollers in my ear.

When I got home last night, all I could think about was Chase. I owe him nothing yet I couldn't get Donna's plea out of my head. Caving to my curiosity, I looked up Chase's name on the internet. At first, I didn't even recognize him. According to the most recent photo I could find, his brown hair is long and wavy on the top with curls framing his ears. Over the years, he alternated between a clean-cut look to a full beard. No matter, his hazel eyes popped in almost every picture I looked at. He looks older but not old by any means. Time has done nothing to take away from his gorgeous looks.

The articles I read were ones that reminded me of the Chase I once knew. I saw pictures of him with sick children in the hospital. He volunteers both his time and money at a local animal shelter. But what finally sold me on the idea of jumping on a plane to see what I could do to help him was the lack of females he's been photographed with.

During the last ten years, I've pictured Chase as a man whore and maybe he is. If he is, at least he's smart enough not to be photographed with a different woman every weekend. He's never been married, no children and no pregnancy scares, at least, none that were made public. From everything I could find he appears to be a great football player and an overall good guy.

Maybe Donna was telling me the truth. Maybe Chase broke up with me for some noble reason, which is why I bought a plane ticket to Phoenix.

I knew Lacey would blow up—and rightfully so—if she knew where I was going. She's the only person that truly knows what I went through after Chase broke up with me. She held my hand and reminded me on a regular basis what a douchebag loser he was, and even though she's never met him, I know she hates him on principle alone.

"Calm down. I'll be back in three days, Lacey."

"Three fucking days? What the hell, Jordan? You don't owe this guy shit. He broke your fucking heart. Please tell me you haven't forgotten that!" she screeches in my ear, causing me to pull the phone away until she's done ranting.

"Argh, of course I haven't, Lace. Look, I just arrived at the hospital. I'll call you tonight when I make it back to my hotel room. Please do not worry about me."

"Whatever," she says before the line goes dead. Geez …Lacey never hangs up on me. I think she might be on a whole new level of crazy at the moment. I guess it was a good call to wait until I arrived in Arizona to tell her what I was doing.

When I called Donna to tell her I would make the trip today, she asked me to send her a text when I arrived at the hospital. Visitors aren't allowed anywhere near Chase's room without a family member's approval. The only thing I know is that Chase is on the eleventh floor.

After sending Donna a text, I take the main elevator up to his floor then wait for her by the elevator banks. That's when Mr. Adams spots me.

I give him a polite and extremely fake smile but he looks angry. Livid might be more appropriate. Steve Adams's anger seems to be aimed straight at me.

"What in the hell are you doing here?" *Um …what?*

Steve narrows his eyes. "Do you really think this is what my son needs right now? Huh, do you? You almost destroyed his chance to play football before and he sure as hell doesn't need you here to do it again."

I shake my head, trying to clear my thoughts. My mouth opens only to immediately close. Stunned is the only way to describe my reaction to Chase's father. As the words he just practically screamed at me sink in, I turn around and push the down button on the elevator.

I don't know what I was expecting when I arrived, but I know I didn't sign up for this. I'm astonished that Donna asked me to come knowing how her husband would react to seeing me. What's worse is that she didn't feel the need to at least give me some heads up.

Mr. Adams always discouraged Chase from spending time with me when we were dating, doing everything from giving him endless amounts of chores to unexpected trips out of town. However, he never came right out and told me he didn't want me around his son, but that was clearly the case.

I'm nervously tapping my foot on the floor, watching the lights on the elevator. When it opens, I rush forward without looking where I'm going and run straight into a very large man.

"Whoa there, gorgeous." The man lightly grabs ahold of my arms to keep me from losing my balance. All I want to do is run and hide, even more so once I see how attractive the man is. It's not until he opens his mouth that my overwhelming need to get the hell out of here returns. "Hey, Steve, how's our boy doing today?"

You have got to be kidding me. I step out and around the man in time to see the elevator doors close again. I push the down button repeatedly, hoping by some miracle it will open. But, of course, I'm not that lucky.

"Steve, I think you've been holding out on me. How about you introduce me to the beautiful lady?" I rub the bridge of my nose, praying like hell I can get out of here, and quick.

"Jordan?" I hear Donna say. Good Lord, luck is not on my side today. I take a deep breath and turn around to face the woman that has gone to extreme lengths to convince me to come here. "Were you leaving?" she asks in a concerned voice.

I clear my throat and straighten my shoulders. "Yes, Donna, I'm leaving. A little heads up regarding this asshole over here would have been nice." I can practically see steam coming out of Steve's ears.

"What did you call me?" he growls.

"Be quiet, STEVEN!" Everyone within hearing distance stops and looks in our direction. I don't really know Donna but I get the impression based on both Steve and the big guy's reaction to her outburst that this is not normal behavior.

"We've tried it your way and that hasn't worked. Now we're trying it my way and my way includes help from

Jordan. You can either shut up and deal with her being here or you can leave."

"Wow, Mrs. A., I didn't know you had that in you!" the big guy says with laughter in his voice.

"Not now, Jake. I'm not in the mood."

Whoever Jake is mumbles "Clearly" before turning his breathtaking smile towards me. "In case you didn't already know, I'm Jake. You must be Jordan." He gives me a wink and another gorgeous smile. "I've heard a lot about you on many drunken occasions, but I have to say you're even more beautiful than I imagined."

I blink a few times, trying to remember if I've seen this man before but nothing comes to mind. "Why would I know you?"

"Because I'm Jake Girard." And just like that, his good looks vanish and all I can see is an arrogant douche.

"Jake, cut it out, please." Donna turns her hard look towards me and softens it some before speaking. "Jordan, Chase's doctor would like to talk to you before you see him."

Jake drapes an arm over my shoulder. "We're not accomplishing anything standing in front of the elevators so let's get the gorgeous babe to Dr. Wallace."

Steve grunts out his displeasure while Jake continues smiling at me in an unnerving way. With a slight pull, I start walking with him.

Jake removes his arm once we arrive at a warm looking office where the three of them make themselves at home. Jake grabs a candy dish off the desk and starts eating away while Steve and Donna continue their strange standoff due to my arrival.

Minutes pass before a nice looking older man walks in.

He takes a look around then heads to the desk in the center of the room. "Hello. I'm glad to see everyone. I take it you must be the famous Jordan."

"Yes, Dr. Wallace. This is Jordan." Donna speaks up before I have the chance to say anything.

"Good, I think having you here will be very valuable. Has anyone filled you in on what's going on, Jordan?"

"Yes. I mean kind of." Dr. Wallace shakes his head as if he was expecting my answer and then he starts talking again.

"Chase is recovering from a serious concussion. This concussion has caused his memory to differ from reality. His CT scans look very promising and I was hoping his memory would have corrected itself by now. But, for whatever reason, he's holding on to the thought that the two of you are married. He becomes aggravated more times than not at the idea that you haven't been in to see him." The doctor pauses while Donna sniffles and Steve grunts his dissatisfaction.

"In a nutshell, Ms. Taylor, when Chase woke up, it was to an altered state of mind. From what I can tell, Chase recalls everything that has happened in his life, but now, somehow, the last ten years of his memory includes you."

I take a nervous breath of air. The doctor practically told me the same thing Donna already has, but it seems more serious while listening to him.

"Have you seen or spoken to Chase lately?" the doctor asks, keeping his eyes locked with mine.

"No, I haven't heard a word from Chase for over ten years."

"Right. That's what Steve and Donna said, so this works perfectly."

I let out a loud sigh, scan the room, and then look back at the doctor. "I'm going to be honest, Doctor Wallace. Right now I would rather have a few teeth pulled than be here dealing with those two and"—I point in the direction of the big guy who's still munching away on candy like he's at the movies—"him. But against my better judgment, I'm here, so please get to what it is you want or need from me or I'm going to get up and take a cab straight back to the airport and head home."

This Jake person makes a drawn-out whistling noise before adding another unnecessary comment. "Man, for such an exquisite creature, you sure pack a lot of attitude. Did you have this temper back when you belonged to my boy?"

I'm compelled to really show him my attitude when Dr. Wallace speaks up. "Jordan, I think it's possible when Chase sees you the reality that the two of you aren't married will set in. If he hasn't seen you or a picture of you in ten years, then your appearance alone should jar the reality he's, for whatever reason, allowed himself to believe is true."

Donna speaks up first and asks the question I think we're all wondering. "What if it doesn't?"

The doctor nods his head. "Jordan, if Chase continues to believe you're his wife then whatever you do don't burst his world. I'm not asking you to lie or even pretend that the two of you are married. Instead, ask him questions. When he calls you his wife, ask him when and where you were married. The more he's forced to face this new reality he's created for himself, the better chance we have that his brain will start to see what's real and what's not. Do you understand?"

I feel like I've stepped into an insane world, and maybe I

have …a crazed world that Chase has somehow created. "I don't think this is a good idea," Steven says.

"And I told you we're done doing things your way. If you don't like it, then there's the door," Donna snaps back.

"This is what he needs. To get better, this is what he needs," Jake adds as he finally puts the candy dish down. "You mean something to him and I think you always have. Now, my dear, it's show time." Jake gives me what I think is supposed to be a panty dropping smile, but it's not working on me. I just want to get this over with and get out of the hell Chase has created for me.

CHASE

I can't stand looking at these bare white walls anymore. And if one more nurse comes in here acting excited to see me then I might just say fuck it and throw a bouquet of flowers at their head.

I'm going fucking crazy. I can feel it. All I want to know is why. Why isn't she here? I'm officially desperate to see her, and I'm sick and fucking tired of listening to everyone's bullshit excuses about where she is.

She'll be here soon.

She's busy.

She's out of town.

Her cell phone isn't working.

It's one excuse after another and the only thing I know

for sure is everyone is lying to me. I just can't figure out why.

I click the TV off then stare into space before noticing someone out of the corner of my eye. Like every other day since I've been in this hellhole, I'm expecting it to be some ecstatic asshole who's just 'oh so happy to see me,' but it's not. It's her ...It's finally her. My breath catches in my throat as my heart thumps like a kettledrum.

She's standing right inside my door. Her dark hair is down around her face. Her beautiful blue eyes are taking me in while she nervously bites her lip.

The first thought that travels through my head is how peaceful I suddenly feel by just setting my eyes on her, but then my pleasant thoughts are taken over by the disappointment I've felt as I waited for her to finally come to me. I'm her husband and I've been lying in this bed attached to machines waiting to hear if the doctor thinks I can ever play football again while she's been where? Doing what?

She takes a step further into my room and gives me a hesitant smile. I watch her closely but don't say a word.

"Hi," she nervously breathes out. Oh God. Just the sound of her voice has me the most spirited I've felt since I woke up here all alone. "How are you feeling?" she adds as she takes a step closer.

"Okay. Mad. Confused," I say with a sigh.

Jordan slowly approaches my bed. Then her tongue darts out, tracing her lips. Fuck me. My eyes follow the path of her tongue and my dick stirs. In one sense, this is good because even with some of the most erotic looking nurses I've had this week, not a single one of them have aroused any interest from my lower half, to the point that I wondered if I broke my dick the same time I hit my head. Evidently, that's not the case.

"Those are some mixed emotions. Maybe we should start simple. How's your head feeling?" She gives a sweet, almost shy smile, something I remember her doing when we first started dating.

"It's fine now. When I woke up, it hurt like a bitch, but you would have known that if you were here." My voice is harsher than I meant it to be, but I can't keep the anger that's simmering from boiling up to the surface.

Jordan doesn't react to my comment. If anything, she appears timid, almost uncertain, and if anyone has the right to be suspicious it's me.

"Where have you been?" I question.

She exhales loudly. "Well, um, I've been working."

Working? She's been working. I was lying here worried out of my goddamn mind and she was—wait ...Oh shit. My heart drops to my stomach from fear. I know my memory is foggy at best. Is it possible her weird demeanor is from something I said or did?

"You'll have to forgive me. I don't ...I don't remember what happened the day of my accident. Did we have a fight? Is that why you haven't been here?"

She starts shaking her head no but there's a slight panic in her voice when she finally speaks. "I—No. No, we didn't have a fight. I was working in New York and ...and I didn't hear about your accident until yesterday." Her words turn the blood in my veins to pure ice. I've been going out of my mind, and no one fucking called her.

Truthfully, the whole situation is a little bizarre. If she were out of town for work, why wouldn't she have called home just to check in with me? I sigh in frustration. She's my fucking wife and I can't remember something as simple as this. I don't know where she went or why, but the fact that she wasn't here is the classic work of my father, who has never approved of our relationship.

"I'm sorry my parents didn't call you sooner. I'm sure you were freaked out when you finally heard."

Jordan is chewing on her bottom lip. This is a habit I don't remember her having, but again her behavior is offbeat in general today, leaving me to wonder if she's not being truthful about us fighting. "The call was definitely unexpected." She turns her head away towards the door like she's nervous or waiting on someone.

"Jordan, would you please look at me?"

She slowly brings her head back towards me. She takes her time but when her eyes finally lock with mine, I feel a jolt in my chest, almost like someone knocked the wind out of me.

How is it possible after all of these years to be this enchanted by her beauty and charm? Having her in the same room as me soothes me in a way nothing else has this whole week.

"I'm sorry." And I am. I'm just not exactly sure what I'm sorry for. All I know is that my beautiful girl isn't too excited to see me and with my head this fucking cloudy it leads me to believe that I did something to make her act this detached.

"What are you sorry for?" Her stunning blue eyes turn glassy as she does exactly what I feared: asked me for a detailed answer.

"For everything. For everything I've ever said or done that's hurt you. But more importantly, I'm sorry for making you sad. I hate seeing you upset. When I get out of this fucking place, I'll do everything in my power to make you happy again."

I vow to do everything in my power to fix whatever fractured our relationship, especially the piece that currently has tears falling down my beautiful girl's face. Jesus, I'm so pissed that I can't seem to remember something that feels important, something that everyone else seems to know. Something I'm sure I did but for the life of me can't seem to make myself remember.

"Knock knock." Both of our heads turn towards the door.

Awesome, the doctor is fucking here and unless he's here to tell me I can go home, then he can turn right the hell around and go fuck off.

"How are you feeling today, Chase?" he asks in the same chipper voice he uses every time he comes into my room.

"Perfect. Amazing. Wonderful. Ready to go home. How about you, Doc?" I ask, barely taking my eyes off of Jordan.

"I'm doing fantastic, Chase, thank you for asking." Dr. Wallace is giving Jordan a questioning look, and when I look back towards her, I see her lightly shake her head no. This is the exact fucking reason I know I'm missing something because this isn't the first time I've seen odd looks and hushed voices pass between the people that have been visiting me. There's something that no one wants me to know and as much as I hate feeling left out, I can't get over the alarming sensation that I don't want to know.

"How's your visit going with Jordan?"

Visit? That's an odd choice of words seeing as she's my wife. I glance back and forth between them. Whether it makes me a coward or not, I just want him to fucking leave, to leave us both alone so that I can make good on my promise to her.

"We're fine. I'm doing fine. Again, I'm ready to go home," I say a little more firmly, hoping he gets my point.

"I know you are, Chase, and I want you to go home. I just want to make sure your head is completely healed, that's all."

"What did my scan show?" He said he'd have the results first thing today but he hasn't shared them yet.

"Your scan looks good, Chase. I'll tell you what. How about you talk to a colleague of mine, set up a rapport with him, and then I'll sign off on your release papers."

I'm already shaking my head no. The words talk and rapport is bullshit code for talking to a fucking shrink, and that's not going to happen. Fuck him for even suggesting it. When I'm about to tell the prick exactly what I think of his idea, Jordan speaks up, halting my response.

"Please, Chase, talk to this doctor. Do whatever you need to do to be healthy enough to go home." Her eyes are pleading with me to do what I've been asked.

I fight the urge to smile because I know there isn't anything this woman could ask me that I wouldn't do for her, which now includes talking to a quack doctor.

"Okay. I'll talk to him, but you better start working on those release papers."

"If you're willing to talk to him then absolutely. Jordan, could I have a word with you?"

My heart speeds up as a panic sets in at the idea of Jordan leaving. "NO!" I shout. "I mean, I don't want her to go." They both appear shocked at my desperate outburst, but I don't care. I have this sinking feeling that if I'm not careful Jordan could disappear from my life and I may never see her again.

My heart continues to beat wildly in my chest while I wait for her to agree not to leave me. Jordan looks sad as she turns away from me. Dr. Wallace motions for someone by the door to come in. Seconds later, I see Jake and my nurse push past them.

"Well, you can fuck me sideways, dude. I haven't seen you look this happy in...well, a long fucking time." Jake plops down in the chair next to my bed while Jordan and Dr. Wallace move even closer to the door.

"Jake, I'm going to step outside with Jordan for a second. Why don't you stay with Chase until we get back."

Before I have a chance to protest, Jordan is gone and I see the nurse shooting something into my IV. My fear, irrational or otherwise, takes over as I feel whatever crap that woman gave me already taking effect.

"Jake," I desperately plead his name until he jumps to his feet then moves to stand over me. "Make sure she doesn't leave. Make sure whatever happens, she's here when I wake up. Please."

Jake, who is always a comedian, turns serious when he hears my request. I think he can see and hear my fear and knows now is not the time to joke around.

"I promise. No matter what, she'll be here."

Hearing him and knowing that Jake never makes a promise he doesn't keep allows me to relax. Whatever drug the nurse gave me lulls me away from Jake and into a world where everything is peaceful.

Jordan

"Jordan, you're aware of Chase's memory problems but Mrs. Adams has granted me permission to fully discuss his medical condition with you. I'd like you to know that this information hasn't been made public. Mr. Girard is the only other person outside of Mr. and Mrs. Adams that knows about Chase's condition."

After leaving Chase's room, Dr. Wallace asked me to visit with him for a few minutes. When we arrived at his office, we walked in on Steve and Donna in the middle of a very heated argument.

"I understand. I won't say anything."

Dr. Wallace gives me a reassuring smile. Everyone's eyes follow Steve as he grunts his displeasure about me still being here.

"Chase has an unusual case of retrograde amnesia. He knows who he is, who his friends and family are, and he even knows that he plays football for the Arizona Cardinals. However, somehow his brain has made up a role for you in his life and Chase believes he has the memories to support this. I was hoping that once he saw you that it would dispute his memories to the point that he remembers you're no longer a part of his life, but that doesn't seem to be the case."

Dr. Wallace taps his fingers on his desk. "One or all of us could go into his room and confront him, tell him the truth, demand that he listen, demand that he shows proof of this reality he feels he lives in. However, I feel blindsiding him with this information will send his mental state spiraling out of control.

"I believe, for whatever reason, Ms. Taylor, that Chase was thinking about you before his concussion, or it's possible before he regained consciousness he was dreaming about you. Either of those situations could have tricked his mind in to believing his thoughts are real."

Steve makes another rude noise but this time everyone ignores him.

"Since Chase didn't immediately know after seeing you that his new reality doesn't actually exist, I think we should give him a little more time. I would like Chase to talk to Dr. Matthew Stein. He's a colleague of mine that happens to be one of the best psychologists on the west coast."

Steve jumps to his feet. "My son doesn't need a quack doctor. He's not fucking crazy!"

Mr. Adams appears to be done listening and pretending to be respectful because next he turns his vile attitude on me.

"Were you calling him? Were you talking to him?" He shakes his head in anger. "Lord, I knew—hell, everyone fucking knew—you were a huge distraction for him and now you've finally done it. Instead of paying attention during a goddamn game, he was thinking about you and now ...fuck! Now he may never get to play again. I hope you're fucking proud of yourself."

My heart sinks and my anger spikes. The only thing I ever did to Chase was love him. It was Chase that broke my heart, even though I now have a better understanding of why he did.

I do my best to push my anger down as I stand up. Steve and Donna got their wish ten years ago, but I'm no longer the teenage girl they can treat however they want.

I give Dr. Wallace the nicest smile I can manage to fake. "I wish you the best of luck on Chase's recovery." I turn to walk out of the office but Donna is already up on her feet, running after me.

"Please don't leave. Please. He needs you. He wants you here. I'm begging you, Jordan, please don't leave my son."

I never questioned Donna's ability as a mother, and her concern for her son right now just proves what a wonderful mother she actually is. She's clearly going against her husband's wishes and the Donna I remember always agreed with Steve.

"I'm sorry, Donna. I really am." I reach out and give her hand a big squeeze before I turn back towards the door.

"Don't be sorry. Stay and give him time. That's all he needs. Just a little bit of time, please."

I breathe out a sigh and decide to try a different route. I move towards Mr. Adams and look him directly in the eyes. "Why exactly do you hate me?"

Steve's face shows a frenzy of emotions before he decides to answer me. "I don't hate you. I just don't think you're what my son needs."

I hold his stare. "If you don't hate me, then maybe you shouldn't act like you do. I didn't ask to come here. I didn't ask to be pulled into his mess. And it's time that you stop treating me like I'm a despicable person that's out to ruin your son's life because I'm not and I never was."

"But you already have."

I gasp loudly as Donna hollers, "Steven!"

I'm not one to throw around the word hate often but I'm almost certain that's the feeling I have for Steve. I take a step closer, invading his personal space. "I don't know the way it works in your world, but in mine, when someone acts like a pompous asshole, then that's exactly how I treat them. Which means I'm going to ask you the question that both Donna and Chase have been too fucking chickenshit to ask." The room goes quiet while I stand toe-to-toe with Steve. He straightens his back and glares at me. He doesn't appear to be backing down any more than I am which is fine.

"Why does Chase play football? Have you ever stopped for even one goddamn second at any point in your life and asked Chase what he wants? Was it his dream to play in the NFL or was it yours? You had trainers working with him before he even started school. You may have fooled everyone including Chase that this is his dream, but you never fooled me, and that's the reason you've always hated me. I'm the only person who's ever crossed your path that had the power to undo all of your hard work. But guess what? That happened anyway and I didn't have a damn thing to do with it. Chase may never play football again, and if you want to stand here and blame me for Chase thinking about me when I haven't spoken to him for over ten years, then you're only proving what I already know: that you're a huge jackass."

The room is deathly silent to the point that I can hear my heart pounding in my ears. Then someone behind me starts clapping. At the same time, all four of our heads turn to see Jake standing inside the door with a huge smile on his face.

"Damn, girl, you pack quite the punch and you're entertaining as hell." I'm not positive but judging by the way he's smiling at me, I think that was a compliment.

However, Donna speaks up before I can. "Jake, not now."

Without another word, Steve pushes past me and out of Dr. Wallace's office, slamming the door shut as he leaves. I have no idea if I've made Donna mad and I'm not about to apologize if I did.

"Looks like I made it to the party a few minutes too late. Are you always this dramatic, sweetheart?" Jake's eyes are dancing with amusement.

"You know what? You can all go screw yourselves. I have a life, a very busy life, and I don't have time for this." I grab my purse and move towards the door when Jake steps in front of it, blocking my exit. "Excuse me," I say, trying my best to maneuver around the beast. But instead of moving, Jake continues to stand in my way.

I roll my eyes and glance up at him. Instead of the jokester he's been since I arrived, he looks concerned, almost worried.

"I promised my boy that you would be here when he woke up. And I never go back on a promise." The sudden change in Jake's behavior has me rattled. Before I can think about it further, Donna is back to begging me to stay.

"Please don't listen to Steven. He's mad and upset and wants someone to blame, but none of this is your fault. I know that and deep down so does Steve. And you're right. Every single word you just spoke is closer to the truth than Steve is willing to admit.

"Jordan, I know my son truly cared about you when you two were in high school, but it wasn't until after he left for college that it became clear to me that he was in love with you. He changed and not for the better. Being away from you, it broke something inside of him, and while I never predicted the condition he's in now, I'm also not the least bit surprised that he allows his mind to believe you two are together."

My back is to Donna while my glassy eyes are cast to the floor. "You came before football, at least to Chase. And I know you think he had a choice but he didn't. Not really. He was forced to sacrifice the one thing he was told he could live without." Donna takes a deep breath and sniffles. "Sweetheart, he was eighteen, and right or wrong, parents can influence their children into doing things they don't really want to do. Ten years ago, I played a part in Chase's decision to let you go, but I refuse to stand by and do that again.

"He loves you. He never stopped loving you and you might not be in love with him anymore but I'm begging you ...please stay and help him."

Tears streak down my face while I wonder what I should say. I don't want to think of Chase suffering but I'm not sure I'm strong enough to handle this. Because, hell ...I'm being asked to save the man responsible for destroying me. And if I'm not careful, history is liable to repeat itself. Only this time, I know in advance that I'm about to sacrifice more than my heart can handle.

Instead of answering Donna, I turn to Dr. Wallace. "What exactly do you want from me?" I quickly brush away my tears, hoping no one else witnessed them.

"Only what you're willing to give, Jordan. I'm not up to

date on the history you share with Chase, but it's evident that being here is hard on you." His voice is filled with compassion.

I was hoping he'd act like an ass like Steve so I'd feel justified in my choice to leave. Instead, he acts concerned about me.

Can I really agree to do this? Can I put my life on hold to help Chase? But the bigger question is: Can I go back to New York with this on my conscience? Go back to living my life wondering and worrying about him even if he isn't my burden to carry? And that's the problem ...I don't think I can. Like it or not, I'm involved and from what Dr. Wallace has said, my involvement plays a large role in his recovery.

I square my shoulders and clear my throat. "One week. I'll stay and help Chase work out his memory, but I have a life back in New York and I'm not willing to put my life on hold indefinitely. One week, that's all I'm willing to give."

Donna sags with relief as Dr. Wallace speaks up. "Chase might not be able to appreciate what you're doing for him at the moment, Ms. Taylor, but when he does, I know he'll be very grateful."

God, I hope he's right. I can't help wondering how grateful he's going to be when I get on an airplane next week and disappear from his life.

CHASE

"What the hell is your problem, kid? Are you deliberately trying to get yourself killed out there? Fuck."

A day doesn't go by that I don't think of Jordan, but today is worse ...much worse. No matter what I do, I can't get her out of my head and I know why. Today is her eighteenth birthday and I don't even know where she lives, let alone have a way to wish her a happy birthday. Not that it matters since I'm sure she probably doesn't want to hear from me.

Cutting her off and out of my life is what's best for both of us, or at least, that's what I was told. If that's the case, then why do I feel horrible all the time? I'm anxious and I can't concentrate for shit. So far, my coaches seem extremely let down that the golden boy isn't cutting it.

"Adams, I'm only going to tell you this once. Figure your shit out and bring you're A-game to the next practice or scholarship or not, your ass will be cut! Now get out of my fucking office."

Karma is officially a bitch. I dumped the girl I love for football and football is about to dump me. Now I have to decide if I care enough to do anything about it.

I come awake with my heart pounding from the dream I had, only to find that I'm still in this God forsaken hospital. As I look around the room, I start to panic when I don't see her. She can't be gone. She just can't.

My mom jumps to her feet. "Honey, what's the matter?"

Shit, it's not that I don't want my mother here. It's that I need *her* here. "Ma, where is she?" I frantically ask, hoping the last time I saw her wasn't just a dream.

Ma starts to relax. "She'll be back, sweetheart. Probably any time now. She was tired so I told her to go and rest her eyes awhile."

My panic turns to concern. I never thought about how any of this is affecting her. I've only thought about myself and getting out of this hellhole.

"Oh, yeah, I'm sure she was tired. Thank you, Ma. Why don't you go and get some rest, too? I know you must be beat."

Ma gives me a half-smile and squeezes my hand. "I will soon. I promise. You have an appointment today with Dr. Stein. I met him already. He seems like a wonderful man."

"Ma, why do I have to see him before I can go home?" Something is bothering my mom. I don't know what it is but she looks stressed all the time and she's careful when she talks to me. Almost like she's afraid at any moment I'll go insane.

"You know that your head is still a little unclear about what happened and Dr. Wallace thinks Dr. Stein will help you put the pieces together, that's all," she says as she looks away from me.

"But I don't need the pieces. I don't care what happened that day." I exhale loudly. "I understand that I may never play football again, but none of that matters, not anymore. Not as long as I have you, Dad, and Jordan in my life."

Ma looks like she's in agony, which I would have expected from my father, but I'm telling the truth. I'll survive fine without football. I have a shit ton of money in the bank and a college degree. I'm more than ready to start a family with my beautiful wife. If I have to talk to this man to get out of here, then so be it. But talking to him isn't going to change anything.

I hear a throat clear by the door. "Hey." I look and see Jordan once again acting hesitant. She watches me closely for a few seconds until she finally cracks a smile, and just like that, my world feels right again.

"Hey yourself, beautiful. Did you get a chance to rest?" Jordan takes a few steps closer to my bed.

"Yes, I did. You look really rested yourself." I would give anything to jump out of this bed and wrap my arms around her, to take even an ounce of the pain away that I see in her eyes.

As much as I want to leave, I start to think talking to this Stein guy may not be a bad idea. I've fucked something up with Jordan and he might be able to help me figure out what I did and what I need to do to fix it.

"Ma, when is my appointment with Stein?" I ask, taking my eyes off my wife and returning them to my poor, rundown mother.

"Two o'clock. A nurse will come and get you and take you to his office." Good, it's already close to two and I'm ready to figure this shit out.

"Babe, do you want to come with me?"

Jordan's eyes are huge and I don't know if it's from me calling her babe or from my request to have her come with me.

"Do you want me to go with you?" she softly asks.

"Of course I do. You're my wife. I don't have anything to hide and once I figure out whatever I'm missing, I'll fix it and we'll be fine again." Both of the women in my life are staring at me with looks of anguish on their faces. I want to be pissed at them for keeping whatever secret they share but I have a nagging feeling in my gut that keeps telling me to let it go, that I don't really want to know …that it's better I don't.

"Well, I'm going to head out for a while, get some rest. I should be back around dinner time."

"We'll be fine, Ma. Take however long you need."

I know my mother has to be overwhelmed by being here practically twenty-four-seven and now that I have Jordan, it's not necessary for her to camp out in my room.

"Love you. Be back soon." As she passes Jordan, she gives her a light squeeze on her hand before walking out and leaving the two of us alone.

"Do you want to lay down with me?" I ask as I pat the spot next to me on the bed.

"What?" Her voice cracks and her eyes look panicked. I want her back. I want us back, and I hope she knows I won't stop until I fix us.

"That's okay, you don't have to, but will you please go with me to my appointment with Dr. Stein?" I ask, ignoring the way she reacted.

"Yes, if you want me to and he says it's okay, then I'll go."

"Jordan, I'm not stupid. I know I'm missing something, but whatever it is, it's not important. You and me, together we can weather any storm that comes our way, but only if we stick together." Her lips part but she doesn't say anything. She looks as lost as I feel.

"I know it's a shitty thing to do …to ask forgiveness when I'm not sure what I'm asking you to forgive me for, but I love you. I always have. I always will. But I need to be honest with you about something . . ." My heart feels like it's about to pound out of my chest.

"I'm scared." My voice shakes. "I'm scared when I figure out what I'm asking you to forgive that I won't be able to forgive myself and I can only hope whatever I've burdened you with is something I can atone for." I'm looking down at my lap in fear of what I might see on her face.

Jordan reaches out and places her hand in mine. "We'll work through this. Together." Her voice is as soft and soothing as her touch. I feel like I'm finally able to breathe for the first time since I woke up in this place because she said exactly what I needed to hear.

Together...that word gives me a strange peace. A peace that, for whatever reason, I think has been missing from my life for a long time.

chapter 6

CHASE

A nurse—who only last week was dying for my attention—pushes me in a fucking wheelchair to Dr. Stein's office. Thankfully with Jordan here, the nurses' advances aren't nearly as obvious. Still, Jordan trails slowly next to us, acting unsure of her place, which bothers me.

"Mr. Adams is here for Dr. Stein," the nurse says over my head to a receptionist. Before she says anything, the doctor's door opens and a man who looks to be in his early fifties steps out.

"You must be Chase. I'm Dr. Stein, but if you feel more comfortable, you can call me Matt." He reaches out and shakes my hand.

"Nice to meet you, Doctor. This is my wife, Jordan." I grab Jordan's hand, looking for any sort of comfort.

"Nice to meet you, Jordan." The two of them shake hands then everyone's eyes focus on me.

"Chase, why don't you allow me to talk to you for a few minutes then we'll add Jordan into the conversation," Dr. Stein says, motioning for Jordan to take a seat in his waiting room. I'm not sure why, but anytime I know I'll be separated from Jordan panic takes over my whole body.

Jordan squeezes my hand. "Hey, it's okay. I'll wait right here and when it's time I'll come in with you."

I exhale slowly and shake my head. I need to get this done so I can get out of this hell. I give Jordan a tight smile as she takes a seat. "Thanks," I mumble as I hop out of that damn chair and follow the doctor inside his office. Once the door closes, the doctor starts in. "Make yourself comfortable." As I look around his office, I see a couch, a recliner, and a small bed.

I'm not sure what his patients usually choose but I head straight to the couch. Dr. Stein takes a seat in a chair across from me and gives me a warm smile that does nothing to calm my nerves.

"What would you like to start off with? Any questions or concerns?" My stomach turns. I don't want to talk. I just want to go home. Instead of answering, I shake my head no.

"Let's start with something simple, Chase. Why are you here?"

I laugh but it lacks any humor. "I'm in this hospital because I hit my fucking head. I'm in your office because I was told I couldn't go home unless I talked to you, and honest to God, Doctor, I will do just about anything to get out of this place. I want to walk out that door, grab my wife and"—I expel a frustrated sigh—"just fucking go home."

The doctor doesn't react to my outburst. Instead, he just gives me a half-smile and carries on like I didn't just beg him to release me from this hell.

"Chase, can you tell me anything about the day you played in the game against Pittsburgh?"

"No," I quickly reply, giving him an answer I'm sure he already knew.

"How about the day before?"

"No," I say again, slightly firmer.

"Why don't you tell me the last thing you remember." A small grin crosses his face like he thinks he finally got one up on me.

"I remember a lot of things. Workouts, practices, but nothing seems to be in order. I can't remember if one event came before another."

"That's fairly standard given your case. How about your personal life? Your family and friends? What is the last event you remember doing with them?"

Do you think it's possible to take the rest of the year off and return as a starter next year?" I ask my dad after a lousy practice. I couldn't concentrate worth a damn and the whole time I kept wondering if maybe Dr. Wallace was right.

"Are you out of your fucking mind? Of course you won't be a starter. For crying out loud, Chase, you're only twenty-eight! If you start acting like you're fucking injured, then you can kiss the chance of getting another contract goodbye. Grow the fuck up and act like a man!"

"Yes, I remember talking to my dad about if I should be playing or not," I say, looking away from the doctor. That memory is only one of many I can recall. With my dad, everything is always about football.

"Any other conversations or events that come to mind?" he asks after I remain quiet.

I look around the locker room at my teammates. Most of them seem happy to see me, but not all of them.

"I heard Wallace wasn't going to allow you back on the field for the rest of the season, but I guess that was just fucking

gossip. "

"I remember talking to Jake. I think...I think he came over to my house not too long ago."

"Dude, you're almost out of beer. We better get more because I can promise you this isn't going to be enough."

"Good, very good. Do you remember anything else?" I try to focus but nothing else comes to mind.

"No. Can Jordan come in now?" God, I hate being separated from her.

"Yes, in a minute. First, tell me a little bit about Jordan."

Talking to a stranger about my wife feels awkward. What does he really expect me to say, anyway? After a few seconds, I sigh and give him what he's looking for.

"She's the best thing that's ever happened to me." That's the only way I can or ever will describe Jordan.

"Wow, that's a pretty amazing woman. When did you two get married?"

God, he's asking me questions that he already knows the answers to and the part that's pissing me off is he also knows I have no fucking clue.

"I don't know, but you already knew that ...It's why I'm here. I can picture what my life looks like, but anytime I force myself to come up with details, I can't and that pisses me off because I want to. I should be able to remember them."

"Good."

"Good?" I repeat. Surely this man earns enough money to come up with a better answer than just good.

"Chase, you're missing a part of your life and if you weren't a little upset over that, then I would be very concerned. A person's subconscious can work in strange ways to protect them from something they truly don't want an answer to, but you're claiming the opposite."

A panic takes over because he's wrong. "Wait. Only a fool wouldn't remember marrying his wife. Especially a wife he loves. I don't want to be a fool, but I know something's not right, even if I'm not sure I want to know what's wrong." Answers might make my fear a reality and that's Jordan disappearing from my life.

The doctor takes a deep breath. I think my last statement left him a little disappointed. "I think it's time to allow Jordan to come in, if you're still comfortable with that."

"Yes, I want Jordan with me," I quickly say. Moments later, Jordan is sitting on the other end of the couch, looking awkward and uncomfortable.

"Thank you for joining us, Jordan."

"You're welcome."

A strange silence takes over and it seems like everyone is waiting for someone else to speak up.

"Jordan, Chase claims he wants to know what's going on in his life. He wants to discover the pieces he's missing but he's also worried that he might not like the answers he'll uncover." The doctor pauses. "Chase, there's a reason your subconscious is keeping you from moving forward, and I feel confident that it has nothing to do with the last game you played. I believe your memory problems stem from the choices you've made and the people you've kept in your life. Once you learn everything, you might be upset, or you might be relieved. Whatever you're feeling, I'll be here to walk you through every step you need to take to be healthy and successful once again. Right now, I want you two to go home and live your everyday life, and as questions or concerns come up, you can call me. I'm going to leave you both with my personal cell and I don't want you to be afraid to use it."

I've been waiting for someone to tell me I could go home and now that I can, I find the idea of it scary. I'm not sure what waits for me outside of this hospital, but I'm about to find out.

Jordan

Dr. Wallace agreed to release Chase as long as he agreed to continue treatment with Dr. Stein. Chase went from nervous, to happy, to acting a little apprehensive, but ultimately I think he was willing to agree to anything if it meant he was allowed to go home.

While the nurses and Donna fussed over Chase, I returned to Dr. Stein's office where I was given a quick rundown on how I should handle the situation with Chase. When it came down to it, his instructions were easy.

"Don't lie to him and don't give him information he hasn't asked for. He's not going to ask you anything he doesn't want an answer to. As his mind starts to heal and the fog in his memory begins to lift, he'll begin to ask you serious questions. Questions that will require you to give him detailed answers, answers that more than likely won't match the life he's created in his mind. That's why it's important you don't lie. We don't want him any more confused than he already is."

Sounds simple, but the reality is I'm just as confused as Chase. I want to hate him. I want to be pissed that I'm here. I want to be mad that he's involved me in his life, but

I can't seem to find the anger I once felt towards him.

"We're here." Chase gives my hand a tight squeeze before hopping out of the car his mother arranged for us to take to his house. As I step out of the car, my breath catches. Chase's house is in the outskirts of town on a beautiful hillside that looks down over the city. The view is incredible, but his house looks more like a resort than a home.

I stopped picturing the kind of life I thought Chase lived years ago, but when we were kids, we talked about the house we'd have together and it was nothing like this.

Chase unlocks the door with a key his mother gave him and walks inside without a care in the world.

"God, I'm so fucking glad to be out of that hospital."

I roll my eyes as I place my bag down by the door. Chase spent fourteen days in the hospital but he was awake for only half that time. You would think he was there for years by the way he's been complaining.

"You know I've been thinking, since I'm not returning to the team, at least not anytime soon, then we should make the most of it. Go on a few of those vacations we've dreamed of." Thankfully, my back is turned to him so he's unable to see the pained look that crosses my face.

"Name a place you've always wanted to go." We're naked, I'm lying across his chest, and I've never been happier. The last thing I want to think about is traveling. Chase can't wait to go places, to see new things, while I grew up moving every other year. Our view on this topic couldn't be more opposite.

"I told you already, I don't like traveling."

Chase brushes his hand up and down my back. "No, baby, you don't like moving. There's a big difference. You want a stable life and that's exactly what I'm going to give you, but that doesn't mean we can't see the world while we're building a life together."

I can feel the butterflies in my stomach flutter. Chase seems to always know what to say to make me feel better. "I guess you're right, and when you put it that way, there's a lot of places I still haven't seen. Hawaii, Paris, maybe Vegas." I smile into his chest, picturing myself traveling to new destinations with him.

"Then we'll go there, plus hundreds of other places. As long as we're together, baby ...that's all that matters."

"Jordan?" I'm snapped back to the present when I hear him say my name. I have no idea how to answer him. Since that conversation, I've traveled to all three places, but of course he doesn't know that.

I clear my throat. "I think we should wait until your mind is back to normal before we make plans to travel." Chase nods his head and wanders further into his living room.

Chase looks around with a confused expression before he stops and stares at his couch. His eyes widen in horror.

"Is something wrong?"

He's already shaking his head no. "Everything is fine, it's just . . ." He opens and closes his mouth several times with a look of panic on his face. His eyes scan the rest of the room, almost with a look of distaste.

He seemed happy when he first walked through the door but he's anything but happy now. I wonder if someone else picked out this place for him? Maybe an old girlfriend or, hell, it could have been his dad. Money and prestige definitely matter to Steve Adams and that's exactly what this house screams.

"What are you thinking about?" I ask softly.

Chase shakes his head like he's trying to clear his mind of

a bad memory. "I just ...this place ...it doesn't seem right. Not with you here, and I want you ...to be here with me."

Ah, so this is the real reason he wants to take a trip. It appears being in his house for only a few minutes has jarred his subconscious. He knows I don't belong here, which means if I want him to remember his life—the one that doesn't include me—then this is exactly where we need to be.

"Maybe we'll take a trip in a few weeks after you've had time to rest." The smile on my face disappears when I see the look he's giving me.

"Please don't treat me like I'm incompetent. I can handle that from a lot of people without giving a shit, but not from you. Never from you." Crap. His voice sounds lost and sad, and never once did I think my comment would make him feel incompetent of anything.

"I'm sorry, I never meant—"

"I know you didn't," he interrupts. "I want to be the one who's protecting you, not the other way around. I'm almost certain I've done a really shitty job of protecting you in the past, but let me now. Please. Give me the chance to show you I can do better."

Oh ...my ...God ...The eighteen year old me would love to forgive him. I want to go back to the night in the park, only this time, Chase would ask me to marry him and all would be right in the world.

God, I don't know what in the hell I was thinking agreeing to this fucked up brand of torture. This isn't real, he isn't really apologizing, and I need to do my best to remember that before I break down and actually forgive him for breaking my heart.

CHASE

I hate this fucking house. I can't even remember why I bought it in the first place ...why we bought it, but I know I don't want to be here, and I'm almost certain I know why our relationship is strained.

When I looked at the couch, I had a vision, or God forbid a memory. Either way, I saw an unfamiliar female and she was taking her clothing off ...for me. The idea that I might have cheated on Jordan is more than I can stomach, but it does explain why she seems tense, almost guarded around me.

Oh God, what have I done? How could I have cheated on the only woman I'll ever love? That has to be why she was in New York, why she didn't show up until the other day, and why I haven't seen a lick of anything in the house that belongs to her. No matter what, she's here now. She came back to me and that only proves how much she truly loves me. If God is going to gift me with a second chance, then I'd be a real fool not to take the time to remind her why we belong together.

"Oh, hey, there you are." I glance up from the chair I'm sitting in that overlooks the hillside. I came out here to drink a beer while Jordan took a shower because I didn't trust myself to be in the house while I knew she was naked and wet. Naked. Shit, all the blood runs from my head to my other head and now I'm trying my best to hide the rather large erection I'm sporting.

"Um, yeah, I came out here for some fresh air and to enjoy the view." Jordan turns and looks out over the deck and her eyes go wide as she takes in the sight before her.

The view from the deck isn't what I'm looking at anymore. Instead, I'm sitting here staring at Jordan in a tank top and some rather short shorts that have my cock painfully hard. I wonder how long it's been since we've had sex because my body is reacting to Jordan the same way it did when I was a horny teenager.

Jordan turns towards me with a smile that's more medicating than anything Dr. Wallace could prescribe, then gestures with her hand towards my dick as she asks, "Should you be doing that?"

Fuck no I shouldn't allow my dick to grow painfully hard if it doesn't have any chance of getting some relief, and I'm just about to comment something along those lines when she asks another question. "Did Dr. Wallace say it was okay to have a drink?" I look down and see that I've been using the beer in my hand as a way to cover up my erection.

"Oh." I laugh under my breath. "He said I shouldn't get drunk but a beer here and there is okay." Jordan nods then takes the seat next to me and goes back to looking out at the hillside.

"I think this is my favorite part of this house," she says as her eyes scan the hills. I definitely agree with her. The view from the deck is immaculate and I've never grown tired of sitting here. For some reason, I can't remember being here with Jordan and she's definitely acting like this is the first time she's been out here. I sigh and shake off my thoughts.

Jordan is taking in the view but I'm devouring Jordan. I love how after all these years she's kept her dark brown hair down to the middle of her back and how her blue eyes still sparkle just as much as the day I met her. It couldn't have been that long ago that I saw her, but it feels like it's been forever. I want to break this friction between us and explore every inch of her delicate body. I'm brought out of my illicit thoughts when I hear a song playing from inside the house. Jordan perks up and glances in my direction.

"Oh, sorry, that's my cell phone. I thought I had it on vibrate." She makes no attempt to get up to go see who is calling her.

A peaceful silence lays over us. I love sitting here with Jordan. I could easily forget the outside world exists and shamelessly lock Jordan away forever. I'm sure if I voiced my thoughts, Jordan, along with Dr. Stein, would be frightened, but sitting here, I feel raw and unguarded. Even with my memory in a haze, I know this is the most real I've felt in a long time.

"I'm surprised your friend Jake hasn't been out here," Jordan says, breaking the silence.

"He's gone. The team left last night for San Francisco. He won't be back until Monday, and I'm sure he'll be out here as soon as they're back."

"Well, we better enjoy the peace and quiet while we can." I think she's joking but I'm not a hundred percent sure.

"Do you not like Jake?" Jordan draws her feet up on the seat of her chair then wraps her arms around her legs as she shrugs.

Everyone likes Jake. He's funny, easy-going, and for the most part, he gets along with everybody. That fog in my head is thick again because I don't remember Jake and Jordan disliking each other, but then again, other than the hospital, I can't remember an exact time when I was with both of them at the same time. I hate feeling invalid and not being able to remember if your wife and your best friend like each other is definitely a sign of that.

"I think I'm going to go to bed." I stop feeling sorry for myself the second I hear her talk about being in a bed because that's exactly where I want to go ...with her. "Goodnight, Chase. I'll see you in the morning," she breathily says before she turns and walks back inside.

Fuck. I've clearly been dismissed for the night. I guess I'll go take a shower myself and find some much-needed relief from my hand.

chapter 7

Jordan

Damn, it's hot. I can feel the sweat dripping between my boobs. When I try to bring my hand up to wipe it away, I discover that I can't because my arm is trapped. It's stuck because I have a man lying behind me, with a leg draped over my legs, and an arm wrapped tight around my chest. Shit, no wonder I'm burning up.

I'm the type of woman that will never talk about the amount of guys I've slept with. I am by no means a whore and have had my fair share of booty calls. I have even had sex with men that I had no intentions of dating. Let's face it, women can get just as horny as a man can, but I think it is tacky to discuss it.

As long as the man is single, then sometimes you need to scratch an itch. But there is another number I know ...the number that stands out in my head is zero. That's the amount of times in the last ten years I've allowed a man to sleep in the same bed as me.

You may find it crazy, but I feel sharing a bed with a man is more intimate than having sex. When you're asleep, you are vulnerable and unsuspecting of the doors that could get opened. The ones I am not ready for.

When I went to bed last night, I was alone, but somewhere between then and now, Chase decided to join me. Chase is the only man I've ever spent the night with, but even those times were few and far between as we were forced to lie to our parents about where we were really staying. The last night we were together, the night before he shattered my heart, was the last time I slept in the same bed with a man ...until now.

"God, you're so beautiful." Chase's greedy eyes travel down my naked body while I lie on his bed, waiting for him.

"I know you're planning on staying the night, but don't plan on getting any sleep. Tonight . . ." He bites his lip as a worried expression crosses his face ..."Tonight you're all mine."

As I lie here thinking about the most incredible night of my life, a night I've never forgotten, Chase's hand starts moving around my chest. His fingers cup my left boob then he stops moving.

Against my will, my nipples harden at his touch, causing me to fight back a groan. God, I would love it if he would flip me over and fuck me the way my body desperately needs, but I'm sure that's crossing some crazy professional line. I know I'm not a doctor, but I still have knowledge that Chase doesn't, and until he knows the truth—that we aren't married and never have been—then I can't or shouldn't do anything that could harm his recovery.

His hand starts moving, brushing back and forth over my hard nipple.

"Chase, what are you doing?" I finally ask when I can't take any more. "Um." I have no clue what he just mumbled.

"Chase, why are you in my bed?" I try again.

"Ugh, why are you talking this early?" He nuzzles his

face into my neck.

I crack an eye to look at the clock on the wall. Chase isn't kidding. It's early but my body belongs in a different time zone and it's a few hours later for me than it is for Chase.

"Why are you in bed with me?"

If it weren't for the fact that I can feel his heart beating a little faster against my back than it was a few seconds ago, I would have thought he went back to sleep, but I know better.

"Because you're my wife and I love you. I fucking tried sleeping in the other room but I couldn't. Not when I knew you were in here, so I gave up and joined you, and until you decided to get all chatty before the sun has come up, it was the best night's sleep I've had in a long time."

I feel rested myself and I'd be lying if I didn't say other than the heat that's generating from being tightly tucked into is body, I love how he appears to be drawn to me no matter where I'm at.

When his breathing evens out again, I softly lift his arm off my boob and slide out from under him because I'm wide awake. After I use the bathroom, I head to the kitchen in hopes that he has coffee somewhere, and I'm in luck. He actually has a fancy machine that looks like it could do a lot more than just brew coffee.

As I'm pouring my first cup of the day, my phone starts to ring and I can tell from the ring tone that it's Lacey. I ignored her call last night and if I put her off much longer, she'll be on a plane out here, ready to kick my ass.

"Hello," I cheerfully greet her.

"Hello? That's all I get after days of nothing? Are you fucking kidding me right now? Jesus H.—No! No, this is fucked up and I'm going to cut a bitch. Seriously..." Oh geez. I think she actually sat the phone down while she physically attacks something in her apartment.

I love Lace, I really do, but she could use a healthy dose of anger management. She cusses—a lot—and if she held her anger to only words, then I probably wouldn't worry that much about her. But everyone once in a while she gets on a kick and her anger spills over, then Lord help us all, especially those in her path.

"Why the fuck are you still out there? I mean, okay, whatever, the guy is a fucking head case and thinks you're his wife, but then you say *No, douchebag, I'm not your mother-fucking wife because your dumbass dumped me without a fucking care in the world!* But did you say that? Fuck no you didn't. Oh. My. God. If I didn't love your stupid ass so much I would hire one of the low-life fuckers I've helped get off on murder charges to kill you."

I slowly close my eyes and sigh. Yes, a healthy dose of anger management could do Lacey a world of wonders. "I'm just trying to help him, Lacey. Why are you making this into a bigger deal then it needs to be?"

There's a long pause before I hear her voice crack as she answers, "Because he hurt you, and I don't ever want you to be hurt like that again. Maybe you've forgotten what he did to you but I haven't."

Just like that, I'm no longer annoyed with Lacey. She might be more than most men could ever dream of handling but once you find it, Lacey has a heart of gold, and right now her craziness stems from her need to protect me.

"Believe me, I haven't forgotten what he did to me, but I came out here to help him ...to help him remember the truth."

"And what happens in the meantime, huh? He thinks

you're his wife and I'm sure he's acting like he's your husband. How are you going to keep yourself from falling for it? He broke your heart once, promise me you won't let him do it again."

Oh God, if she only knew that I woke up today with him wrapped around me and telling me that he loves me. But she's right. If I'm not careful, I could easily fall in love with him all over again, and I'm not sure where that will leave me once he remembers that I'm not a part of his life.

"I'll be fine. I promise. Look, Lace, I need to go but I'll call you in a day or two."

"Yeah, you better. Love you." Her voice sounds defeated and she appears to be giving up, at least for now.

"You too."

CHASE

Believe me, I haven't forgotten what he did to me, but I came out here to help him ...to help him remember the truth.

A knot forms in my stomach when I overhear Jordan on the phone, because that confirms my worst fears. I hurt her, but right now this gives me an advantage. Her goal is to make me remember and my goal is to make her fall back in love with me.

"Is that coffee I smell?" I ask, startling her out of her thoughts.

"Oh God! You scared me." Jordan places her hand over

her heart and takes a deep breath. "Yes, I brewed a pot. I hope that's okay," she says before biting her lip again.

"Why wouldn't that be okay? What's mine is yours, my love. Oh, I was wondering, do you have your passport with you?"

She stops moving, her coffee mug halfway to her mouth, and gives me a questioning look. Yes, I know my question was out of the blue, but if I want my plan to work, we have to get out of this fucking house.

"No, I don't have it with me. It's back at my . . ." Her place. She's trying her best not to force me to remember how she doesn't live with me anymore.

"Oh, I think your mother may have been here while we were sleeping because there was a bag in the living room with your stuff in it when I woke up. I saw a cell phone on top of it and it matched a charger I found in the kitchen so I plugged it in for you."

My eyes go straight to where I charge my phone and there it is. Shit, until this second, I had forgotten I even had a cell, but I knew instantly where I charge it. I have no idea where I used it last, but if I had to take a guess, I would say I left it behind in my locker when I left the game in the back of an ambulance.

"Well, go clean up and pack a bag. I have somewhere I want to take you."

"Chase." Her tone is sharp, making it clear she doesn't want to go anywhere, but unless she refuses and tries to leave, then I'm not going to take no for an answer.

"Jordan, are you here with me because you're trying to help?"

Her teeth start chewing on her lower lip again while she tries to decide how to answer me. I'm desperate and I'm willing to stoop low if it means I get to keep her in the end. "Jordan, this is what I need. Give me this and if you do, then I promise even if I can't remember, or if I do and I hate myself for the things I've done, I'll let you leave. I'll let you go back to whatever world you exist in without fighting you, but I need this. Please," I beg.

This woman inspires me to do and say some of the dumbest crap possible. When she finally nods her head yes, I know everything I just said was worth it.

"Okay, go clean up and then we'll head out."

Jordan grabs her phone and coffee then walks out of the kitchen and down the hall towards the bedroom we slept in. I quickly run over to my phone to check outgoing flights to Hawaii. That's a place Jordan said she always wanted to go and I want to take her somewhere warm, somewhere she won't be wearing much of anything. Without a passport, that doesn't leave me with many options.

When I open my phone, I see tons of missed calls and texts and quite a few of them are from numbers I don't recognize. Mom, Dad, and Jake are the only three names I know, and my heart drops when I see that I don't even have Jordan listed as a contact. Did I get pissed off at her to the point that I didn't even want to keep her number? God, I hope not.

As I'm trying to open a search engine, a text comes in from a person named Carrie. I have no idea who Carrie is or why she would be texting me. I click on the message only to instantly regret it. This isn't a text message. It's a picture ...a picture of tits. Just tits. Oh, fuck. Is this the girl from the couch or am I that much of a cheating bastard that this is another chick?

I immediately delete the picture and hope like hell there's

not anymore on my phone when Carrie sends an actual text.

> **Carrie:** I hope you're feeling better, big boy. If not, I know exactly what to do to make you feel much better. Call me.

Um, no thank you. Good Lord. I'm giving my phone number out to random women who are sexting me. No wonder my marriage is practically non-existent. If I saw a text like that on Jordan's phone, I would go batshit crazy then fly to wherever she lives and beat the ever-loving shit out of the douchebag.

I need to get a new phone number so I don't risk Carrie, or whoever else has this number, interfering with my goal to win Jordan back. But first I flip back to the internet and check the outgoing flights. I quickly purchase two first-class seats to Honolulu. Next, I book, as well as pay for a resort that offers private bungalows that claim they are perfect for those looking for their own private getaway, which is exactly what we need.

I hear the shower turn off so I head to the room that Jordan has claimed as hers. When I see the unmade bed, it makes me smile. I want to spend every night wrapped around her the way I did last night.

I really did try to sleep in the master bedroom, but I had never felt more alone then I did lying in that huge bed all by myself, especially knowing the other half of my heart was across the hall. After I got up and snuck into Jordan's room, I immediately felt better, but it wasn't until I climbed into bed with her that I knew without a doubt I was exactly where I was meant to be.

"Hey." At the sound of her shy voice, I turn and swallow

my tongue. Jordan is standing in the doorway with a small towel wrapped tightly around her irresistible body. I swallow a few more times, willing my wanton thoughts away before I say or do something that sets us back.

"I came to tell you to pack up whatever you brought with you because our flight leaves in a few hours."

The entire time I was talking my eyes unwillingly remained on the swells of her breast that are peeking out of the top of the towel.

"Chase, my eyes are up here." I snap my eyes up, thinking from the tone of her voice that I pissed her off. But from the sparkle I see in her eyes, I can tell she was joking, and thank God because I plan to do a lot more than just stare at her exquisite tits.

"Yes, I know exactly where your beautiful blue eyes are, but that doesn't mean I don't love looking at your tight, sexy body."

Jordan nervously chews on her lip and her face reddens at my comment. After ten years, I still have the ability to make her blush. I guess a perk to my lack of memory is that I get to discover this magnificent woman all over again.

Jordan

I had no idea where Chase was taking us, and I was even more confused when we made a few stops before we finally arrived at the airport where we boarded a flight to Honolulu. I didn't tell Chase that I've vacationed in

Hawaii, but I never made it to Honolulu. Therefore, he still managed to take me somewhere new.

The place he reserved for us is beautiful and intimate ...very intimate. We're staying on the beach in a fancy modern day hut. Each hut is spaced a half a mile apart, giving the illusion that you have your own personal beach.

Inside, the hut is just as breathtaking. Other than the bathroom, the whole place is one open room. This is where you'd go to get away from the world or a place you'd take someone you want to spend some very personal time with. I'm guessing with Chase it's the latter.

I told Donna and Dr. Wallace that I would give Chase one week and in the two days I've spent with him, Chase isn't any closer to remembering the truth. If anything, he seems more determined to win me over than uncover the life he really lives, the one that doesn't include me.

I wander out to the beach, taking in the view while Chase deals with the bellhop and our luggage. It's beautiful here. My life in New York is fast paced and hectic at best. Being here gives me a sense of peace I didn't know I was missing.

"I hate that I can't remember where we went on our honeymoon." Chase's voice is right above my ear, startling me out of my thoughts.

"If we want ...if you're willing to let go of the past, we could treat this trip like it's a new beginning. I know I need to remember what I did before I can ask you to forgive me, Jordan, but honestly ...I'm not sure I'm strong enough to handle the truth." Chase turns me around so I'm facing him. He watches me closely while his warm eyes are pleading with me to believe him.

"Whatever I did ...I'm sorry." His voice cracks. "God, I'm so fucking sorry because it made you leave me and that's a world I can't imagine living in."

I clear my throat, fighting the urge to cry. Dr. Stein didn't prepare me for this. Don't lie and don't give him information he's not ready to handle, that's what I was told ...but what about me? He's doing everything in his power to make me fall in love with him again, and if I open my heart for even a second, then that's exactly what will happen.

We live two separate lives on opposite sides of the country, lives that haven't once in ten years included each other. What happens if I open my heart to him and then he remembers? He remembers the life that I don't belong in, a life that he might love, a life he wants to return to.

That leaves me in the exact same place I was in ten years ago and I don't think I can survive losing Chase a second time, but ...what if? *What if this time he chooses me?* His parents aren't here to remind him of what an awful person I am. Even if they were, I get the impression that they don't wield the same power over Chase that they once did.

I'm completely caught up in my own thoughts when I hear Chase talking again.

"I remember the first day you walked into Mr. Wilbert's homeroom. When I looked up and saw you, my world as I knew it changed. I've never been able to tell you or anyone else why. Why you? All I know is I feel a pull towards you, only you. Maybe it was love at first sight, maybe you're my soul mate ...fuck, I don't know. I'm not sure if I even believe in any of that crap. All I know is that from the moment I laid my eyes on you, something changed inside of me." Chase reaches out and laces my fingers with his.

"Give me a second chance. Give us a second chance and I promise you won't regret it." His voice is strong and primal, and in my heart I believe he means every word.

"How can you promise me your future when you don't remember your past?" I sniffle as I mentally come undone. "Once your memory comes back, everything could change. You might not want the life you're asking for now."

He's looking at me the same way he used to, the same look that once told me how much he loves me. A look I tried for years to forget.

His voice shakes as he says, "I'm the one who broke us, correct?"

My heart drops to my stomach. Being this close to him and thinking about the day I thought he was going to propose only to be told goodbye causes my eyes to tear up. Instead of speaking, I nod my head in agreement.

"That's what I thought. Whatever I did, is it something you can forgive?"

I sigh and step away from him. "Ugh, Chase, it's not as simple as a yes or no." From the second I opened my mouth, I lost my battle with holding my tears at bay. Chase closes the gap between us and places his hands on my face then tilts my head back. His eyes are gazing into mine as his thumb brushes away my tears.

"Make it that simple. Tell me ...do I have the power to fix us?" he boldly questions.

I feel like the roles have reversed, like I'm the one who's done something wrong because I'm keeping a secret from him, one that has the power to change everything, but if he can get past that and still want me, then . . .

"Yes."

chapter 8

CHASE

Yes. She said yes. I've never heard a word sound sweeter, especially coming from her exquisite lips.

Jordan gave me the power to fix us and I'm not about to let this opportunity pass by without giving it everything I have.

Today we wandered around the beach, acting almost like a couple. We held hands a few times. Talked about things we might like to do while we're here, but we kept our conversation light. I know I don't have the power to snap my fingers and magically fix us but I'm beyond nervous I'll say something that slams the door I've recently opened.

Tonight I had our dinner brought out to our private bungalow and we ate beachside. We're enjoying a traditional Hawaiian meal that leads to a long conversation about times we both tried strange food. As much as I love hearing her talk about herself, I also hate that nothing she says triggers a single memory.

"College was hard, wasn't it? I mean ...I mean, being apart?" I fumble my words as fear crashes through me.

I remember being brave, trying my hardest to make her feel that everything was going to be okay, but I had my doubts. Not doubts about us, but I was afraid I'd hold her back from things she wanted to explore and learn when she moved away for school. I was also afraid that one day Jordan would grow to hate me for keeping her from an easy life, one she deserved. That was a fear that my dad definitely played on.

"You'll ruin that girl's life and one day she'll hate you for it. Where will that leave you, huh? Don't fuck up her life and your chance to play football over some damn puppy love. There'll be plenty of girls at school, Chase, you'll see."

There are times when I have such detailed flashbacks and then other times I try so hard and I can't remember anything, like now. No matter what I do, I can't remember much about my time at college.

Jordan nervously swallows before answering, "The first semester was the worst. The second one was a little better and from there it got easier over time." She turns her head away from me to gaze out at the ocean. I sense this is a topic she'd rather not discuss, and while my fear of upsetting her hasn't gone away, I know we have to move past this conversation if a future for the two of us exists.

Jordan's tormented eyes glance quickly at me before she frantically looks away again. Maybe learning about who Jordan is today is a safer tactic. "I think it's safe to say that we don't live together. I heard you say something about New York. Is that where you're living now?" I hold my breath, waiting for her to answer. I hate the idea of us not living together, but it's hard to stomach the thought that she lives so far away.

She blinks at me a few times before nodding her head,

but that's it, that's all I get from her. I hiss out a frustrated sigh before trying again.

"What do you do in New York?" Her features relax.

"I work at a company called Natural Cosmetics." Cosmetics? Nothing about that sounds right. Jordan is naturally beautiful and she doesn't wear a lot of makeup, yet she's working at a company that sells them.

"Is that your dream job or is it just a job that pays the bills?"

She stops to think about her answer. "Well, I didn't grow up dreaming about working in that industry, but I do enjoy my job. The people I work with are great and it's in New York, which I love."

"You won't consider moving back to Arizona?" I rush out.

Whatever is going through her mind has her thinking about how she should respond. "I love New York. That's where I've lived for the past t—" She bites her bottom lip before continuing. "I've lived in New York for a while now. That's where I consider home to be, and yes I have a career. Those are all reasons why I'm not sure things between us could work."

I want to ensure her we'll be fine, but she's right. If she lives in New York and I live in Arizona, then there will be a good chunk of time that we'd have to spend apart. On the flip side, I'm not sure if or when I'll be released to play football, or if I even want to. If someone made me choose right now between Jordan and football, then it would be Jordan hands down. And that tells me everything I really need to know about the future I want.

"Do you ever go back to Oak Cove?"

She quickly shakes her head. "No. My parents moved

and my grandparents have passed away since we were in high school. How about you, do you go back very often?"

My chest tightens after learning about her grandparents. They were the reason she moved to Oak Cove in the first place, and I don't recall hearing about their passing.

"I'm sorry about your grandparents. And to answer your question, yes. I think." I groan as I rub my hands over my face. "God, it fucking sucks that I can't remember certain things. My parents still have their house in Oak Cove, and if I recall correctly, I usually spend time there during the offseason."

As I say that out loud, I wonder how long Jordan and I have been apart. Telling her I go to Oak Cove feels right, but wouldn't she know that?

Jordan must sense I'm about to lose it because she gives me a brilliant smile and changes the subject. "Do you want to go for a swim?"

She's watching me carefully, waiting for me to respond, but my mouth is dry and words won't form, so I nod my head yes.

"Okay. I'm going to go put my suit on." I would love to tell her she doesn't need to wear one, but this beach isn't completely private and it would be just my luck that someone would walk by and see her delectable body.

As Jordan hops to her feet, I clear my throat. "I'm going to call guest services and tell them we're done with dinner."

Jordan gives me another quick but beautiful smile before turning away and heading inside. After I call the front desk, I step inside. Jordan is in the bathroom with the door shut. I grab my swimming trunks and quickly drop my pants and briefs. I barely get them on when the door opens and Jordan steps out, provoking a surge of indecent thoughts to travel through my head.

She nervously chews on her lips as she watches me watch her. Her long dark hair falls over one shoulder. Her tits are barely covered by two very small pieces of fabric. And her tanned legs ...fuck, they go on forever. I don't know how long it's been since I've seen her this way, but this is exactly how I remember her.

I swallow and clear my throat. "Jordan." Her name comes out as a plea, a plea for so much more.

"Are you ready to go?" Her voice shakes with the same nervous energy that's coursing it's way through my body.

I nod my head. "Come on, let's get in the water before I toss you down in the sand and show you how much I like your swimsuit." Her face turns red again before she spins around and heads out to the beach, leaving me to follow behind her.

We wade out into the water but neither of us knows what to say until Jordan breaks the silence.

"What made you decide to buy a new phone?"

I look at her and shrug, unsure of what I should say. I could be honest with her and tell her about the text. More than likely I wouldn't be in a huge amount of trouble, seeing how Jordan lives in New York and has for a while. It is entirely possible whatever I did with that woman happened after she left. But at the same time, I risk bringing up a topic that has the power to destroy us, and right now it's not worth the gamble.

Dr. Wallace and Dr. Stein are the other reasons I changed my number. I'm skipping my appointments with both of them this week. I made a deal with Dr. Wallace that I would take my post-care seriously if he allowed me to leave the hospital, and within a day I went back on my promise.

Maybe I should snap a few pictures of Jordan in her bikini so he can get the big picture. That being here with her is better than any medicine he could prescribe me.

Jordan waves her hand in front of my face. "Hello, Chase? I asked you a question."

"Oh, yeah, sorry. Looking at your enticing body could render any man speechless." She gives me another shy smile but she doesn't blush nearly as much as she has at my past few comments.

"People I don't remember meeting have my number. I'm sure everyone that has it is someone I've met at one time or the other, but I don't like that." I shake my head. "Actually, I hate it. I hate that my brain is playing tricks on me. I don't like games, I don't like dishonest gestures and I don't want someone in my life because they're hoping to get something from me. And how do I know if they're real or not if I can't even remember meeting them before?"

We're standing in the water, letting the waves slowly rock us back and forth, but were not enjoying the scenery because our eyes are locked.

"That would be a pretty freaky feeling. Looking at someone and having no idea how well they know you. Wondering about everything you've shared with them." She understood what I meant, that I was talking about other women, but she doesn't appear mad, just receptive to my feelings.

How is it this woman beckons me on a level I've never known without her? She captivates me in a way I haven't felt in ...Shit, my brain almost let something in and then it was gone, like a door slammed shut. I was just about to say it's been forever but that's not possible.

"Chase, are you okay?" she softly asks, taking a step

closer.

"I don't know. It felt like I was about to remember something but then my brain shut off." I shrug but I can't shake off the strange feeling I'm left with.

Jordan reaches out and brushes her hand up and down my arm. Her touch is more healing than a thousand appointments with Dr. Stein could ever be. God, I love this woman.

"You didn't remember because you're not ready to, not yet. Whatever thought you almost had will come back when you're equipped to handle it. And when that happens, I'll be here with you."

Just moments ago I felt weak and exposed, but Jordan's words give me the strength I need. This woman ...damn. She inspires me in ways I didn't know were possible. And right now I want to show her without words how much I need her in my life.

I pull her tight against my body and lean down. Then I do what I've been waiting days for ...I kiss her.

Jordan

His lips move against mine, his tongue politely seeking entry into my mouth, which has me giving in and allowing him to take over. This kiss brings back a thousand forgotten ones and my body inflames, causing me to groan softly into his mouth.

"Do you want to go back to our room?" I hear him ask

as I slowly open my eyes, peering up at a man I desperately want. My body is fully awake and I'm ready to impale myself on him.

I shouldn't. God, I shouldn't do anything with him, but knowing that and doing it are two entirely different things.

"Yes," I softly beg. Chase pulls away from me but keeps his eyes locked with mine. I can see lust and possibly even love shining back at me.

"No, I want to be very clear. Jordan, I'm asking you if you're okay if we go back to our room so I can make love to you."

I was pretty confident that's what he was asking but it feels strange, almost awkward that he laid it out for me because ...now I'm making a choice and not just acting in the heat of the moment.

Right or wrong, I want everything he has to offer me. I only hope I don't regret it later. "Yes, Chase, that's exactly what I want." The fire I see in his eyes burns even brighter with my answer.

"Then let's go, beautiful."

Before I have the chance to move, Chase leans down and picks me up, causing a slight scream to slip past my lips. "You're not afraid I'm going to drop you, are you, baby?"

"No. Never." My answer is like a whisper and a plea all in one because whatever happens from here on out, I hope that Chase Adams never drops me again.

"Never. We may not always end our day in the same bed, but we will always end our day in each other's hearts."

Inwardly I scream like a girl, but on the outside, I'm trying to keep myself under control. He just soothed every irrational fear I've had about the two of us. Right or wrong, I want him to do exactly what he just promised me.

When we get back into our room, Chase slowly places me down on my feet and then stands back to take me in. My hair and swimsuit are wet. I'm sure what little makeup I have on is smeared, but the way he's looking at me, I don't think any of that matters.

Chase licks his lips then reaches behind me and pulls at the knot that was keeping my top tied in the back. When he lets go, my top pops up and exposes both of my breasts. The longing in his eyes heats even more as he unties the knot at my neck and allows my top to drop to the floor.

He slowly slides my bottoms down until gravity takes over and they fall to the floor. I step out of them. As Chase stands, his hands run up my body and stop at my breast. His fingers pinch one of my nipples as his mouth latches on to the other.

Lust shoots straight down my spine and spreads throughout my body. I didn't realize I had my eyes shut until Chase steps away from me and I'm forced to open them to see what he is doing. He's stripping himself of his swim trunks, leaving him just as naked—and standing directly in front of me.

My mouth waters as I take in the adult version of the boy who captured my heart. He's much bigger than I remember, but then again, a lot of things are different about the teenaged boy I once knew.

He steps towards the bed and motions for me to join him, and I do without hesitation. I lay down as Chase crawls up the bed above me. I'm staring into his perfect eyes as he brushes my hair away from my face.

"Why does it feel like it's been forever since I've touched you like this?" My heart speeds up. *Don't lie; don't lie . . .*

"Because it has been a long time," I say as my eyes water.

"Never again. We belong together. We've always belonged together. You're mine and I'm yours. Forever." A tear slips out and down my cheek, but Chase quickly brushes it away.

If only a week ago someone had told me that I would be here with Chase, I would have thought they were crazy. But somehow, in a matter of only a few days, we've sealed the gap that's kept us apart.

"Before we do anything else, I want you to know that I love you."

I gasp for a breath of air. Oh God ...My voice cracks as I say, "I think deep down, even during the darkest of times, I've always known that you loved me."

He smiles down at me. "Good, because you're worth everything I have and I will sacrifice it all in order to be with you."

Before I have the chance to say anything else, Chase is kissing me again. As his mouth moves against mine, his hand travels down my stomach and stops between my legs. He deepens our kiss as his fingers find my clit. He starts rubbing me in a perfect, light circle that's sure to bring me to a climax, but then he slows his movements as he pushes a finger inside of me. My hips start to move as he begins to fuck me.

Chase adds another finger while his thumb continues moving in perfect circles. He pulls his mouth away from mine while I groan from the magic he's making my body feel.

His eyes shine down into mine. My body starts to tingle as I grasp a hold of his upper arm then moments later I'm shamelessly coming on his fingers, riding out the amazing orgasm he's given me.

Ten years ago, Chase made my body feel things it never

had before. Tonight he showed me the adult version of the boy I once dated. He knew exactly what he was doing and he lit my body on fire. It's only because of how incredible I feel that I won't allow myself to think about how he's learned his new skills.

"I know you think I brought you here for this but I really didn't. I wanted us to be alone, away from anything that could affect us negatively; but I didn't bring you here for sex, therefore . . ." He stops to clear his throat. "I didn't bring any condoms with me. I know we're married but I'm still confused where we are in regards to each other. At the hospital, I had a full health screen so I happen to know for a fact that I'm clean. But..." He trails off as his eyes continue to consume mine.

I wonder how he'd react if I told him it's been over ten years since he last had sex with me. I won't, though, because right or wrong, I want this more than my next breath.

"I'm on the pill and you don't need to worry. I'm clean, too."

A look of relief washes over him and I don't know if it's from me giving him the okay or the fact that I know I'm clean. Like maybe I'm clean because I haven't been with anyone else, which couldn't be further from the truth.

"Are you ready for this?" I slowly nod my head. I'm not sure I have the strength to actually form words. He holds my eyes as he fills me inch by glorious inch.

As I feel the burn from my tightened walls being stretched, I know I will be sore, but I don't care. I want to commit every detail to memory of our second first time. I bite my lip as I feel the pain followed by pleasure. I close my eyes for one split second to memorize the feel of him inside me once more.

"Jesus, you feel—I can't. God, you feel pure. Perfect. Mine." His eyes flare with lust. "Yes, mine. Forever mine," he mumbles as his eyes gloss over with desire. Chase starts rocking back and forth, his hips slamming into my body with a force that shows the need he has to consume me, and already I'm on the verge of a second climax, but Chase pulls out and flips us around so I'm on top.

"I could feel you tightening around me, but I want to watch you. I want to see exactly what your face looks like when you come." I smile as I reach between my legs and grab a hold of his dick, which is silky and wet from being inside of me just seconds ago, then I slowly sink down on him, causing both of us to groan from how amazingly well we fit. "Oh, fuck, that is ...You feel . . ."

I start bouncing up and down on his shaft and the tightening feeling within my walls is already back. Another tingle travels throughout my body and then I explode, riding out my wave of pleasure. During all of this, Chase kept his eyes glued to my face, watching me, memorizing every second we've been joined together.

I start to slow my movements as I come down from the second best orgasm of my life. Chase digs his fingers into my hips and begins to pump his cock deep inside of me. His face looks on the verge of pain as his mouth opens to that perfect O and then he finds his own release, spilling inside of me.

As Chase's movements slow, he never once takes his eyes off of me, then the most satisfied look I've ever seen takes over his beautiful face. "I love you."

My stomach flutters from his words. I've waited forever for someone to love me the way it seems only this man is capable of. "I...I love you, too. I've loved you forever," I whisper back as a beautiful smile takes over his relaxed face.

"Let's do that, let's plan on forever," he says, rubbing his hands up and down my arms.

"Forever," I repeat.

"As long as we love each other, then none of the other shit matters. Everything else will work out. I'm positive. All you have to do is trust me, trust us, and we'll be fine."

I'm glad he's feeling this confident because one of us needs to be if we're going to make it through the mountain of crap waiting for us when we return.

chapter 9

CHASE

Last night was proof of how much we belong to each other, but it also brought out another emotion. Because deep down somewhere, I know at some point along our journey through life we've been with other people and I hate it. I know I never want to be at a place in my life where that happens again. I want to bottle up whatever magic we're making here on this island and I want to keep it with us forever.

"Have you seen my phone?" Jordan asks as she digs through her bag.

As a matter a fact, I have. Last night as she started to drift off to sleep, safely in my arms, I heard her phone buzzing away. I'm not kidding when I say the thing didn't stop. After I was positive she was out for the night, I moved her off of me and went in search of the damn thing. When I found it, the fucker was locked and I didn't know the code—even though I tried every combination I could think of—therefore I had no idea who was calling. On the one hand, I'm hoping it's her work and not a man or someone back home who's wondering where the hell my beautiful wife is at. On the other hand, I don't want her to lose her job and hate me for being the reason she did. Either way, I powered the thing down and hid it in the bag I use for my bathroom shit, hoping she wouldn't look there.

"Yes, but I've decided this should be a phone free zone."

"A phone free zone?" she repeats while stilling her search to look over at me.

"Yes." She's looking at me like she can't decide if she wants to kiss me or slap me, but I'm hoping it's the first.

"And why is that?" she questions.

Well, shit, if I tell her it's because the damn thing wouldn't shut up, she'll want to check it even more and I can't have that. "We need to rekindle what we've lost and how can we do that properly if the outside world is trying to break in?"

She's suspicious and rightfully so. "Is your phone off limits, too?" she fires back.

"Of course, but that doesn't really matter. You and Ma are the only two people in the world that know my cell number."

"How do I know your number?" she questions, narrowing her eyes.

"Because I'm giving it to you when I give you your phone back." Jordan is trying to fight a smile. She would love to appear pissed off but she's not fooling me.

"And just how long do I have to go without my phone?"

I'm half-tempted to say forever. Let's ditch the rest of the world and just be together without outside interference, but I know she needs to address the life she's been living without me.

I desperately want to resolve this mess we're in and move forward. I want to remember our wedding and I want to do it all over again, making new incredible memories, memories I won't spoil by acting like a jackass.

"Well, this is only a suggestion, but how about we spend the next few days here in our own personal paradise then head back to Scottsdale and check in with Ma and my doctors. After that, we keep heading north until we hit another place you've always wanted to go."

She's trying to think of where I'm referring to when I see the light bulb go off. "Vegas?"

"Yes, Vegas. We can ask my mom to go and your parents if you want, and while we're there we can renew our vows."

An uncertain look crosses her face, which in turn has her disconnecting from our conversation. I suspect this has everything to do with what she knows, what I have yet to remember, but I don't care. However, the last thing I want is for her to pull away from me.

"We don't have to. It was just an idea."

Jordan gives me a half-smile but it lacks the confidence she had moments before.

"I want that and I want that with you, but I think it's important that you regain all of your memory before we make plans for the future." I hate how reluctant she feels to move forward until I'm a hundred percent healed. I know I'm missing pieces of my life, and any normal person would probably be turning over every stone possible until they learned what's going on in their life, but not me.

I know at some point in my life I hurt Jordan. I know that at some point in our lives we weren't together, and I know that when I hit my head and woke up in a cold, lonely hospital room, she was the only person I wanted and she came ...for me.

Maybe I'm too eager to move forward when I don't have

all the pieces but maybe I don't need them. Maybe all I need is the love of my fearless woman to make it through life, at least, that's all I feel I need to survive.

"Chase, the parts of your life that you're missing ...they might mean more to you than you realize. What if you wake up one day with all of your memory back and I suddenly don't fit in your life?"

"Never. That could never happen," I growl out, shaking my head no.

"How can you be so sure?" she asks as her beautiful blue eyes water.

"Because I regret it. Whatever I did ...I regret it because it made me lose time with you, and living life without you doesn't seem possible, not anymore."

Her face is shining with approval. I don't remember what I did, and again I shouldn't ask forgiveness for something I don't remember, but if it puts that look on her face, then it is worth it.

"I just hope when you do remember you still feel the same way," she whispers.

"I promise. I will." And that's a promise I'm willing to do anything to keep.

"Let's get out of here. Go explore the island for a while. I saw a place where we could go snorkeling if you'd like to." Jordan slowly exhales as she nods her head yes. Without another word, the tension from moments ago melts away.

Jordan

"Why do you think people hurt the ones they love?" I look up at Chase's face and I can tell he's being serious.

I shrug. "I don't know. I think …I think sometimes you don't know how much you love someone until they're only a memory. Then you're stuck. Stuck wishing and thinking about a time where love was the only thing that mattered. Where memories of a better time are the only thing you have left of a person, and sometimes even that's not enough to make it through the day."

I'm fighting off the urge to cry because what I just said is how I lived my life for a long time. Memories of a time when I was happy, memories of a time I was with the person I thought loved me.

"See that's just it. I woke up without that; without memories and I still knew you were all that mattered." A few tears spill past my eyes and land on Chase's chest. We're lying in bed while I'm draped across him.

"Do you question if your mind is playing tricks on you? That you'll wake up one day and realize that life has more to offer you? More than just me?"

"NO. Never." His answer was quick and firm, and it's the proof I need that his mind isn't completely healed because he did wake up one day and decide that life had more to offer him without me. And until his memory comes back, I can't be positive it won't happen again.

"I know you don't believe me. I can tell by how your muscles tightened when you heard my answer." I don't answer him and after a few minutes, his hand starts rubbing up and down my back. "Have you ever seen on the news when a person turns themselves in decades after committing a crime?"

"Um, sure?" I say, distracted by the feel of his hands.

"That's because they can't handle the guilt of what they did. Their crime is stuck in their brain and their conscience won't allow them to forget." His hand stops moving. "I can't even remember what I did. I can't remember how I hurt you and my conscience still wouldn't let you go. Maybe in the beginning I needed you to forgive me, but I don't think that's it. I think it's just you. I just need you."

I lift my gaze up to his where I see the emotion in his eyes. He truly believes every word he just said. I hope it's possible to forgive someone when they don't know what they did wrong because that's exactly what I want to do.

"Now, before we lay here and allow this mood to drag us down, let's get up and get a move on it. I already have something planned for today."

Chase arranged for the two of us to go hiking through some of the most beautiful cliffs I've ever seen. We stopped and ate a lunch he had packed for us. As the day passed, we talked, we laughed, but we avoided any heavy subjects.

"Are you ready to head back?" I ask.

"Not quite," he answers with a smirk as he laces our hands together. We walk about a quarter of a mile then stop at an opening to a bridge.

"What's going on?" I question as my eyes dart around, taking everything in. That's when I see a sign and understanding comes over me. A panic like no other courses it's way through my body.

"NO. No way! I'm outta here," I holler as I try to turn around. Before I even get a step from him, Chase wraps his arms around my waist and throws me over his shoulder. "Seriously, I can't do this. I'll watch you. Please? Please, please, put me down!" I beg as I pound my hands on his back. Instead of answering me, Chase continues to walk over to the people who are here to help us ...to help us fucking bungee jump.

By the time my feet touch the ground again, my whole body is trembling at the idea of jumping over the side of that damn bridge.

When we were kids, Chase loved a good adrenaline high. He often had to hide whatever crazy idea he had from his dad because God forbid he do something that would have kept him from playing football, but I always knew, and more times than not, I went with him. But while he was riding a dirt bike, or surfing, or even the time he went paragliding, I safely watched from the sidelines.

Now that I'm creeping on thirty, I'm even more deterred by the idea of removing my feet from the ground. A rollercoaster? Okay, maybe, but jumping off the side of a fucking bridge? That's a big no thank you!

"Chase, seriously, is this even safe to do? You just got out of the damn hospital from a severe concussion. I'm sure if Dr. Wallace knew your plans to launch yourself off the side of this bridge he'd say no. Scratch that, he'd say no way in fucking hell!"

I'm shouting while my hands continue to shake and my heart races. I'm having my own form of an adrenaline rush from the fear I feel when Chase smiles and asks me a question that has everything slowing down. "Do you trust me?" I take a deep breath and exhale slowly.

My gut reaction is to say yes, more than anyone I've ever known, but how can that be true? I trusted everything Chase told me ten years ago and the only thing I had to show afterwards was a broken heart. But the man before me today seems different. He makes me think he'd never let anything bad happen to me. And maybe it's not real, but in this moment, it feels more real than anything I can remember.

"Yes," I whisper. Trust or no trust, my nerves are on fire.

"I would rather die than hurt you," he says with another smile.

Crap ...he's trying to convince me to jump, but my heart took his statement to mean so much more. After a long, deep breath, my heart drops to my stomach as I slowly hold out my hand for him to take.

"We're going to jump together," he says, squeezing my hand.

My chest tightens and I'm not sure if it's from fear or from the idea that we're doing this together. "We're doing a couples jump. Come on, everything is all set for us to go. I didn't want to give you too much time to think about it or I knew you wouldn't go with me this morning."

Personally, I don't think I have an unrealistic fear of heights, but Chase has always had an unrealistic ease with them. I'm starting to tremble again when a man walks over with shirts for us that say "*A couple that jumps together, stays together*" and I'm instantly laughing, but not for long.

After we're tied in about a hundred different ways, they walk us out over a strange looking bridge and all too fast the people who work this death trap have us rigged up to each other, then Chase is walking us out onto a ledge. A ledge that I know is going to drop, causing us to fall.

"You still trust me?" I want to point out how I really need to trust the person who wired us to the bridge and the safety equipment they use, but I know what he means. He would never ask me to do this if he wasn't a hundred percent positive that I would be okay.

"Yesssssss." I didn't even finish saying the word then we're falling. I'm almost certain that I'm screaming but everything happened so fast that I didn't really have time to process it.

Life has a funny way of changing. This time last week, I was in my office in New York, moody and pissed off at the world for unknown reasons. But today, I'm hanging off a bridge in Hawaii, wrapped up in the arms of the boy that broke my heart, and I feel the safest I've ever been.

CHASE

I figured it would take an act of God to get Jordan to jump with me, and if I had to push the issue any more than I did, I would have backed off in a heartbeat. A lot can go wrong in a jump. People die every year from jumps that unfortunately don't result in the desired outcome, but as humans, we do things every single day that put ourselves at risk. Sometimes we consider ourselves lucky just to make it somewhere safely in our vehicles, but that doesn't stop us from getting in our car and traveling.

With this particular jump site, I did my homework and

felt the reward outweighed the risk. And the reward was spectacular. My wife, who has always had an irrational fear of heights, overcame that fear today in my arms. I'm not about to fool myself into thinking she's going to become a regular jumper, but I found it inspiring that she trusts me enough to override the fear she was feeling and follow my lead.

Now we're back in our room my appetite for this woman is beyond starving. "You were brilliant today, baby. Made my whole world that you jumped with me."

Jordan gives me one of her shy smiles that only fuels my desire. I walk up to her and seconds later my mouth finds hers. After all these years, the passion we share is still off the charts.

My hands find the end of her shirt, lifting it up and over her head, only breaking our kiss for a second. I reach around and unclasp her bra, pulling it down her arms to reveal her rosy nipples. Next I strip her out of her shorts and panties, then give her a slight shove until she falls back onto the bed.

I set a new record for how fast I can get out of my own clothing then I crawl up the bed between her legs where my mouth stops for a taste of heaven. I start licking and sucking on her clit like an addict until her hips take over and she starts pumping her sex into my face.

"Oh God ...Chase." I continue sucking her deep into my mouth and minutes later Jordan is growling out her release on my tongue.

I lick my lips and moan as I make my way up to her beautiful face. Jordan's eyes are heavy from lust and exhaustion, but I know she's wet and ready for me. I give my cock a few long strokes then I place it at her entrance before slowly pushing inside.

"Oh, yes. You feel so damn perfect." I turn my face back to hers and look directly in her eyes. "Incredible. You always feel incredible." I thrust my hips a few more times, never taking my eyes off of her. "You were made for me." I groan. The affection and love that shines from every part of her makes me feel whole, and this right now, what we're sharing, is the most beautiful part of us. Our connection is more than sex; it's our love, our passion, and our future. Something we'll only share with each other.

My hips take over and I start slamming in and out of her tightness until I feel her clenching around me and moaning in pleasure. Her moans push me to the edge, and I know if I wanted to I could let go and find my release, but I need her to fall with me.

"Baby, I need you to come." I suck one of her delicious tits into my mouth. I keep sucking until I feel her starting to contract on my cock. My thumb finds her clit and I gently rub. Seconds later, I feel her milking me so tight I fall over the edge with her.

"Oh God," I mumble into her neck as I slowly ride out the rest of my orgasm. When we both finally come back down to earth, I look up at her face and again I'm hit with a strong sensation. A sensation that I need to do whatever it takes to keep this woman by my side—and, this time, I need to ensure I keep her for the rest of my life.

chapter 10

Jordan

Our time in Honolulu was unbelievable. Away from everyone else and the stress of the real world, life with Chase was unimaginably perfect. But now it's time to face the music.

Chase opens the door to his gaudy house and waits for me to step in, which I do. I still would like to know if he designed this awful place himself or if he paid someone to go crazy with his checking account because nothing about this place feels like him.

Chase places our bags down before brushing my hair away from my eyes. "Thank you. I really needed that. We needed that. And I can't begin to—"

"Where the hell have you been?" Steve interrupts, anger seeping out of his mouth as he storms into the living room. Chase opens his mouth to say something but quickly closes it.

"I asked you a question, boy. Where have you been?" Nervously, Chase takes a step away from me, which instantly sends a panic throughout me.

"Um, I . . ." he mumbles. Geez, you would think that

Chase was still eighteen and not twenty-eight by the way they're interacting with each other.

Chase takes a deep breath. "We took a little trip, what's the big deal?" Once the words pass his lips, he looks away from his dad. If I thought Steve was angry before, it was nothing compared to how furious he looks now.

"What's the big deal? You fucking leave town without checking in with your team, you disconnect your cell phone number so they can't call you, and you ask me what's the big deal? Plus, your mother's been bitching that you've missed some of your doctors' appointments."

My heart drops. What a horrible excuse for a father. He's more concerned about Chase not talking to his team than worrying about him missing doctors' appointments. And why didn't I know about this? I thought Chase said he got everything cleared so we could go.

"Dad, it's not a big deal. I couldn't play or practice, anyway. I'm done for the year and there's nothing anyone, including you, can do about that." I look over at Chase, wondering where the strong, unrelenting man I spent the last few days with has disappeared to.

"You don't take off like a crazy fucking person, that's for sure. What did she do to convince you to leave with her?" he snarls out, giving me a hateful look.

"No, it wasn't like that." Chase's answer lacks the emotion I would have given if I had spoken. He doesn't even seem upset with the way his dad is speaking to him or about me.

I clear my throat to speak up, however, before I can say anything, three more people walk into the room, adding to the chaos. Donna, Jake, and Lacey.

Shit ...Lacey is here, and judging by the look on her face, she's no more happy with me than Steve is with Chase.

"Why the fuck would you go on a trip with him? Huh? Seriously, I don't get it. The only asshole on this planet that has the power to hurt you and you ...you just walk right back into the lion's den and hand him a whip? Jesus, Jordan, you're smarter than this."

Steve turns towards Lacey. "Don't come into my son's home and call him an asshole, especially when she's the problem," he says, pointing at me.

Lacey might be small but she can pack a verbal punch harder than most people. I'm positive this is why she's a great lawyer.

"Be quiet, old man. No one, including your precious football playing son, asked for your goddamn opinion."

Jake, who took a seat on the couch and is watching everyone like he's at the movie theater, decides to jump in before the situation really gets out of hand. "Okay, okay, everyone, let's just calm down for a second and let them talk."

"I don't need to hear what she has to say to know she's trying to get her claws back in my son again. When she's around, she ruins everything. Isn't that right, Chase? That's why you dumped her ass before you left for college. One quick conversation with me and she was history."

I gasp, not just from the fact that he spilled the information that everyone except Chase knows, but from the demeaning way he said it.

"Steven!" Donna screams as I keep my eyes on Chase. So many emotions cross his face.

Lacey can't take anymore and unleashes on Steve. "God, you're such a bitter old fucker. What? Did someone tell you when you were a kid that you weren't good enough to play football so you decided you'd live out your dreams through your son? And now you think because you've done everything possible for him that he owes you something? You walked your dumb ass in here and started spouting off shit about football this and football that, and not once did you ask about what his doctor said."

The room goes silent but Lacey, unfortunately, isn't finished.

"I hope one day you get screwed by a donkey with a twenty-inch dick because that's exactly what you deserve. Maybe that way you won't be so fucking uptight that everyone in your life allows you to screw them over."

Jake scrunches his eyebrows. "Whoa, I didn't know New York had many donkeys let alone ones with dicks that size. Remind me to double check with you before I visit."

The three of them are looking at Jake but my eyes are still locked on Chase. He looks confused but he also appears to be angry. When he finally looks up at me, he narrows his eyes. "We're not married?" His voice is sad and soft, almost too soft to hear, but somehow everyone in the room does because all the chatter stops and everyone looks at Chase. I'm not sure what I should say, but I can hear Dr. Stein in my head.

Don't lie.

"No," I whisper.

His eyes thin even more. "We've never been married?"

"Of course you're not married to her. You got rid of her ten years ago and everyone except me thought it would be a good idea to let you think otherwise. Chase, you have a life and she's not a part of it for a reason. For a damn good reason."

I open my mouth to yell he's the reason I'm not a part of his life when a beautiful woman who could be a Playboy model steps inside of the open door. She has long blonde hair and exotic eyes. She smiles as she looks around the room, but her eyes stop moving when she spots Chase. She squeals then runs to him.

"Oh, baby. I was so worried," she purrs as she wraps her arms around him and presses her huge tits into his chest as she pulls his head down to her face to plant her lips on his.

Watching this instantly makes me feel sick to my stomach, but it's Lacey that asks the question I want the answer to. "Who the hell are you?"

When she pulls back from kissing him—a kiss that he didn't put much if any effort in to, but one that he didn't pull away from either—she says, "I'm Carrie, Chase's girlfriend."

Jake chuckles under his breath but other than that, no one, including Chase, says a word as I stand here watching her hang on his arm when only moments ago he was telling me he loved me. I guess if I'm being honest, that statement isn't fair. Moments ago, Chase didn't know he had a girlfriend, especially one this beautiful.

I'm seconds away from a major melt down, but like always, Lacey can read me like an open book and saves me from embarrassing myself in front of everyone.

"New York is a huge city filled with tons of assholes, but the ones I've met today in this room are by far the worst." Her eyes turn to Steve. "You think you're someone special and that gives you the right to treat people however you want? Well, you're wrong because, at the end of the day, you're still an asshole. And you"—Lacey turns and points her finger directly at Chase—"never deserved her. If this is the kind of man you are then you did her a favor ten years ago, and I hope that thing attached to your arm bleeds you dry. Let's go."

Lacey grabs my bag and physically turns me then gives my back a push until my legs get the memo and I start walking. I don't look back. I don't need to.

Chase didn't defend me when his father attacked me and he didn't push that woman away from him. That's all the information I need. My breathing becomes labored as my heart speeds up.

God, how in the world did I allow myself to be right back where I started? Crying over a man that doesn't love me the way I deserve?

We walk to a car I've never seen before and Lacey jumps into the driver seat and extends her hand. "Give me your phone."

I wipe away a few tears as I dig my phone out of my purse and hand it to Lacey. She starts driving, heading in the direction of the airport—the place I just came from—when she rolls down her window and chucks my phone out.

"HEY!" I yell.

"No, you need to disconnect from that bastard. Last time you held out hope for way too long that he'd call you, but not this time. This time you're going back to New York and you are getting on with your life. You're going to go out on a date with Caleb and you're going to move forward. Fuck that asshole and his arrogant father." She shakes her head. "Shit, his choice in friends and woman really suck, no offense."

I place my face against the cool glass and remain silent as the last ten minutes remain on repeat in my head.

Why the hell did I ever take Donna Adams's phone call? Maybe if I had listened to my gut in the first place, I would have saved my heart from the agony it's feeling now. I had no business entering Chase's life when he was confused about what role I had in it, especially when I didn't even have one.

In the last month, I've somehow managed to go back to living my life in New York, or pretending to live, anyway. In less than a week, I allowed Chase—for the second time—to break down my firmly built walls.

I should have known better, and if I'm being honest, I did, but I allowed my heart to do the thinking instead of my head.

The first few days I was home, the only reason I even got out of bed was because I feared that Lacey might come unglued if she knew how hard I was truly handling the situation. Therefore, I got up and went to work, pretending life was great, but the second I could, I left and went back home where I locked myself away from the rest of the world.

I couldn't begin to tell you what was going on with Natural Cosmetics because no matter how hard I try, I'm not able to get my head in the game enough to care.

I also haven't taken the time to replace my cell phone. On the bright side, I haven't missed it. I told Silvia that Lacey and my parents were allowed to call me at work, but no one else. And this time, under no circumstances, is she to inform me of personal callers.

This week, however, is different. I'm different. I'm done feeling sorry for myself, and I'm definitely done pining after a man that somehow manages to destroy me every chance he gets. Which is why tonight I'm going out with Caleb.

I still think it's a horrible idea dating a guy that Lacey sees every day, a guy she already considers a friend, but the alternative isn't much better. Caleb sounds like an all-around great guy, and if he does somehow screw me over, he'll have to deal with Lacey's aftermath firsthand, which is why I caved and agreed.

I left work early today because I've been neglecting certain areas of my body, parts that may or may not be noticed tonight, but I'm not willing to risk it. After a few hours at the salon, I feel worlds better, which has me acting bolder. For my date, I choose a tight skirt that is shorter than anything I would wear to work paired with an off the shoulder sweater. Add in the fact that I have on my favorite pair of five-inch Christian Louboutin, and I feel fantastic.

I hear a loud knock on my door. Well ...this is it. I'm going out with Caleb Ramsey. I open the door and I'm almost blown away because he looks worlds better than I remember. He's tall with light blond hair that's almost on the shaggy side paired with dark eyes that are currently undressing me. Caleb is tall, probably over six feet, but thanks to my shoes, he's not standing much taller than me at the moment.

"These are for you." After he spoke, I forced my eyes away from the beautiful man in front of me to see that he's holding a bouquet of flowers. *The man brought me flowers.* I can't recall the last time a man gave me flowers and didn't have a secretary send them to me.

"Thank you." Taking them into the kitchen, I grab a vase, fill it with water, and arrange my flowers in it. Turning back, I see Caleb is watching my every move.

"I hope I'm not being too forward but damn you

look stunning." Inwardly, I'm screaming like a girl at his comment, a comment that came from a man who could make any woman under fifty want to toss her panties in the trash.

"Thank you." Geez, is that all I can say? Thank you?

"Are you ready to go? I made reservations at a place downtown."

"Yes, I'm ready."

Caleb reaches for my hand and laces it with his. "Then let's go."

chapter 11

CHASE

"Do you think it's going to be fair to her? Chase, between school and football, you're going to be too busy for anything else and eventually the two of you will break up, anyway. If you do it now, you'll both be able to go off to school with a clear head and focus on what's really important."

From the second I accepted a full ride to Ohio State on a football scholarship, my dad has been on my ass about having a girlfriend. "I don't need one. Girls will only distract me from what's really important. She's trying to trap me." *And the one that he really likes to drive home ...* "I'm too young to know what real love is."

I know what I feel for Jordan is love, real love, but I also know we have a rocky four years ahead of us and it has me worried. Am I being selfish by not allowing her to live her life? I'm going to be busy and I'm not sure I'll even have time to call or text her often. I'm afraid she will eventually start to hate me and that's not a reality I can live with.

I look over at my mom, who clearly doesn't share the same opinion as my father about my relationship. From the day

I announced I was taking Jordan Taylor out on a date, my mother has been thrilled, and the more she got to know Jordan, the more she liked her. But for the most part, when my dad's around, she stays neutral, too neutral, like she's doing right now.

"Chase, if you and Jordan are meant to be, then you'll find your way back to each other." That is not what I was hoping my mom would say and she can see the disappointment in my eyes.

"What happens if she falls in love with somebody else?" I voice my second biggest concern, the one that follows right behind her hating me.

With a sad, almost apologetic smile, she adds, "Then it wasn't meant to be."

But we are meant to be and living in a world without her doesn't seem possible.

"Chase, have you ever heard the saying 'If you love someone, let them go. If they come back to you, they're yours forever. If they don't, then it was never meant to be?' You're young, both of you have your whole life in front of you. If Jordan is your destiny, then it will happen. One day, she'll come back to you."

"Chase, did you hear the question I asked you?"

It's been weeks since Jordan walked out my door and my memory still isn't completely clear, but it's coming back. Flashes here and there are shining a light on the things I somehow blocked out.

"No, what did you say?" I ask before sighing loudly.

Right now, I'm at my bi-weekly appointment with Dr. Stein, who seems to piss me off more than anyone I know.

Probably because he's the only person that is brave enough to ask me anything about her.

"I asked you the same question I ask you every time you're here. Why are you angry?"

I roll my eyes. "And I'll tell you the same thing I always say. I'm pissed because everyone lied to me!" I growl. I hate this man and his stupid questions.

"Who lied to you and about what?" This is exactly why I hate him. He knows what happened but he's hell bent on getting me to repeat everything verbatim.

"She said she was my wife," I rush out.

I never know what this man is thinking because outwardly, his appearance never changes and that pisses me off.

"Did she call herself your wife? Did she introduce herself as your wife to anyone? Did she ever call you her husband? The question I'm asking, Chase, is did she really lie to you?"

My blood pressure spikes at his question. "Yes, she lied. Lying by omission is still lying." I rub my hands over my face. I can't stand this room or talking about her.

"I agree. She allowed you to believe something that wasn't true. Have you ever wondered why?"

Yes ...only every minute of every day. I wonder if it was some sick game or maybe it was payback for breaking up with her.

"Chase, you tend to shut down when we talk about Jordan, but I think it's important for you to properly move forward that you talk about what happened. Here in this room, with me, you're safe."

I inwardly groan while he waits for me to say something, but like normal, I keep my mouth shut.

"Let me ask you this, what emotion do you feel most

when you think about Jordan?"

I'm never going to be released to play football until Dr. Wallace signs off saying I'm ready, and Wallace is waiting on Stein's approval. If I want to get on with my life, I need to tell him whatever he wants to hear.

"I'm angry. That's what I feel when I think about Jordan. I'm pissed as hell that she allowed me to look like a fool in front of her. I'm pissed at my parents and Jake, too, for that matter." My little outburst surprises both of us.

Dr. Stein nods his head. "Again, have you thought about why everyone allowed you to believe something that wasn't true?" Instead of answering him, I look away because I have no intentions of saying anything more. That's a question I don't have an answer to and I'm not willing to listen to any of their excuses.

"I looked at your medical file and, personally, Chase, I find it questionable if you should have been playing football in the first place. When you hit your head, you didn't just suffer from a normal concussion, you had severe swelling in the cerebellum of your brain. It's uncommon but not unheard of that patients wake with thoughts that aren't real, but convincing a patient otherwise sometimes does more harm than good. Typically, in cases like yours, once the swelling is completely gone, their memory returns. Your CT scans show your swelling is virtually gone, which leads me to believe your memory will return in full if it hasn't already. Some things may never be completely clear, but otherwise, I believe you'll be fine."

I desperately want to leave this room. I don't want to hear how playing football, something I've done all of my life, is the reason I'm messed up, even though I know that's not completely true. But football is all I have and right now

I don't even have that.

"Chase, the first time you woke up, you asked for Jordan, and then you proceeded to call her your wife. When your father corrected you, you got beyond upset and had to be sedated. Do you remember any of that?"

My stomach drops. "No." I don't have any memory of any of them telling me I was wrong, that Jordan and I weren't together anymore.

"Dr. Wallace asked my opinion on how to handle the situation if you woke up again believing Jordan was your wife. I reviewed your file and I saw the monitor reports from when you had to be sedated. Your blood pressure skyrocketed. My advice was not to upset you again, to allow your memory to return on its own when you were ready to process reality. I was the one who told them to go along with you and the reality you believed you lived in."

Is he expecting me to be grateful? If anything, he makes me sound even crazier, and I didn't think that was possible.

"When you kept insisting that Jordan was your wife, I asked your mother if there was any way this woman could come and see you. I had hoped it would spark your memory. From what I was told, you hadn't seen her in ten years; therefore, she had to look different."

She did look different. She's an alluring version of the girl I once knew, but she's not mine, and she let me think otherwise. Instead, I'm dating a groupie who will do anything to be with someone that has money and fame.

After the day Jordan left, Carrie—whoever she is—tried to act like we were in a committed relationship, but no one other than Jake knew who the hell she was. I hadn't introduced her to my parents because Jake said '*She's not that kind of girl*,' therefore, she wasn't allowed to see me when I was in the hospital.

After I kicked everyone out, she kept coming back, trying to entice me back in to our *relationship*, but I wasn't interested. Everything about Carrie seems fake and after the last few weeks, I need real in my life in the worse possible way.

"Chase, do you have any idea why you thought Jordan was a part of your life? After ten years of not once seeing her why she's the person you wanted when you woke up?"

I'm still not looking at him and I have no plans to answer his question. "Let me ask you this, Chase. Outside of your family, have you ever loved someone? Have you ever been in love?"

My eyes snap to his. "I didn't have time for love. I had football, and now I might not even have that." I close my eyes in pain. Shit, this asshole is good. I didn't mean to say any of that out loud.

"You sacrificed love for sport?" he asks with one eyebrow cocked.

"Football isn't a sport, it's my career ...it's my life"

"Chase, who told you it had to be one or the other?" My father. My coach. Anyone who ever wanted to ensure I was on my A-game. Women are for satisfying a need but other than that, I should steer clear of them. After I gave up Jordan, it was easy to do, because I never met a girl that I even considered dating.

"There are plenty of happily married athletes. Why should you be any different?"

Again, I ignore him. "Chase, I don't expect you to answer me, but I'm going to ask you, anyway. I want you to think about your answer and when you come back for your next appointment, I want you to answer me."

Slowly, I move my eyes back to his. "When you found out that you weren't actually married to Jordan, that you'd never been married to her, were you relieved or were you upset? You claim to be mad at Jordan but do you think you're actually mad that you gave her up? That you gave up a life that you clearly wanted with her?" Dr. Stein pauses again, waiting for me to say something, but I cast my eyes down to the floor, wishing I was anywhere but stuck in this room.

"Maybe you aren't mad that she fooled you—lied to you, as you like to say—I think it's possible that your anger stems from the fact that she doesn't actually belong to you. Think about that, Chase, and when you get here on Thursday we're going to start where we just left off."

I get up and leave before he can say anything else. I'm pissed, plain and simple. Why does everyone have to know every single detail of my life?

When I arrive home, Jake's car is in the driveway but I don't see him. I find him on my couch, eating my food and watching my TV. I'm pissed at him, too, but he's the only one that doesn't seem to give a damn.

"What are you doing here?" I ask as I toss my keys on the table.

"Watching TV. Where have you been?"

"Doctor."

"Ah, I see. How is Dr. Feels doing? Did he have you spilling your guts?" He chuckles.

Shit, it's hard to stay pissed at a guy that tries so fucking hard to make everyone laugh. "No, at least not how he's been hoping."

Minutes pass as we both watch some crap television then Jake makes another attempt to get me to talk. "Have you put your mother out of her misery and started talking to her again?" he asks without taking his eyes off the TV.

"I'm not really talking to anyone but you don't seem to take the hint."

Jake turns towards me and gives me an amused smile before looking back at the TV. I feel like I know Jake really well. At least, I don't think that I've blocked anything out regarding him, and right now, I'm not sure what he finds entertaining.

"What?" I snap.

His eyebrows go up as he gives me another shit-eating grin. "Nothing. At least, nothing you want to hear, and if you're not going to listen, then I'm not going to waste my time talking."

Jake is pushing my buttons and we both know it. I could give him the cold shoulder but the bastard wouldn't care, which would only piss me off further.

"Okay, wise guy, what do I need to hear?"

He laughs while shaking his head at me. "Okay, let's do this," he says, rubbing his hands together. "From the day I met you, I've always liked you. You're down to earth, you never brag about how amazing you are, even though you have every right to, but instead you're humble. You treat everyone that crosses your path with respect but lately that hasn't been the case. Lately, you're narcissistic and your perspective and attitude is downright shitty."

I'm taken aback by his comment, and while I'm sitting here processing what he just said, he turns back and starts watching TV again like he didn't just verbally attack me.

"Oh, by the way, Carrie was banging on your door when I got here. She said she came by because you're not answering her calls. I told her she should clue in. That you don't want to talk to her. But, frankly, I don't think she's smart enough to understand what I meant. Well, I should get going." Jake hops to his feet and starts heading to the door.

I quickly stand up and start following him. "Did you really mean what you said?"

Jake laughs. "Absolutely. Carrie has to be one of the dumbest chicks I've ever met. You only kept her around for one reason. I heard from a few guys on the team that she does deliver a good time, though ...so there's that."

I don't think it's possible for Jake to be serious for more than a few seconds at a time, but I don't like what he said, and if he really feels that way, I want to know.

"No, about me. Did you really mean what you said?"

Jake's demeanor changes and it seems he's back to being serious. "Chase, have you stopped and thought about how unfair you're being to everyone else? You're the one that woke up with your memory out of whack and everyone was told to go along with it. If I were you, I would be asking myself why I woke up thinking I was married to a woman I hadn't seen in over ten years but couldn't remember the girl I was fucking on and off for the last six months." My stomach drops hearing his statement.

"I'm not sure if you remember this or not, but one night a few years ago when you were drunk off your ass, you mentioned how you messed up the best thing that's ever happened to you. You never told me her name, but I'm assuming you were talking about Jordan, and if you keep this shit up, then one day very soon you're going to be telling the same story. That girl dropped everything in her life to be here for you and I saw firsthand the welcome wagon she was greeted with. I just hope when you stop throwing yourself this pity party it's not too late."

Fuck, why did I ask him? I knew Jake wasn't going to tip toe around about what he thinks. And I guess a part of me feels like shit that I haven't stopped to consider what I would have done if I was in their shoes. They didn't set out to be dishonest; I accidentally set them up to take a fall and now I'm punishing them for it.

The truth is I'm ashamed of a lot of things. I'm ashamed that I listened to my dad and broke up with Jordan. I'm ashamed of how I've lived my life for the last ten years, and I'm ashamed of how little I have to show for myself. Other than a lot of money, I have nothing that really matters in life. Jake and my parents are the only people that aren't around me for what I provide for them. Well, I don't think I can say the same about my dad. He might not want money, but he's never wanted me to do anything except play ball.

"I think it's already too late. I listened to my parents and I ruined us."

Jake slowly shakes his head like he's baffled by me. "Dude, I know you're having problems with your memory but are you honestly telling me the woman you spent a week with acted like anything was ruined?" I breathe out a frustrated sigh.

"Chase, if you ruined anything, it's because you let her walk out your door while Carrie was attached to your arm. I may not be a pro at relationships but even I know that wasn't a smart move."

Everything was blurred when Jordan walked out of my house. That fog that had settled in my brain was trying to clear and all I heard was dad's voice, of course. *"You're not married to her."* I suddenly felt like a fool.

All of the things I had said to her, believing I had cheated on her, none of it was real, and I was a cross between being embarrassed and pissed thinking I was just a big joke to the people I care the most about.

"I'm not with Carrie!" I holler to Jake, who is half way out my door.

"Yeah, asshole, I know this but there's a person that doesn't and that's what counts."

I want to call her, I want to hear her voice, but I'm so fucking afraid that Jordan will reject me, and she has every reason in the world to. I may have only been eighteen but I knew what she meant to me, and I didn't fight for her, for us.

"I've gotta go, but give me a call when you pull your head out of your ass. I'm sure it's been up there long enough that even you have to smell it by now."

I don't know what I should do, but I know I'm sick of feeling this way. It's the same way I felt ten years ago, the same feeling that started me on a path that almost ended my life.

chapter 12

Jordan

"Do you think we should get married before we start college or wait until after?" When Chase talks about us getting married, he always says when, not if.

"I don't think your dad will be okay with us getting married, especially not any time soon," I say in a weak voice.

"Well, it's not up to him. We love each other and I know I'll never love anyone else the way I love you, so why should we wait?"

The closer we get to graduation, the more Chase has been talking about getting married. I would love to follow him to Ohio State but I've already been accepted into NYU's business program and have everything set up for my fall semester.

"Chase, you don't have to marry me to keep me. But, if you let me, I'll love you forever."

"I'll always want you and I plan to make you the happiest woman alive."

"You already have," I whisper as he wraps me up tight in his arms.

I've tried everything under the sun to keep myself busy today but nothing has worked. My mind keeps wandering to him. Today is November 21st, Chase's twenty-ninth birthday. He's probably out celebrating with his girlfriend. Argh, I can't believe I was dumb enough to allow myself to be hurt by him again.

After almost six weeks without a cell phone, I broke down and bought a new one, which is currently buzzing with a text.

Lacey: Drinks tonight at Club Zen. Next weekend I'll be in hell so I need tonight to last me awhile.

Lacey has amazing parents but her relationship with her three older sisters is less than desirable. When it comes to the Davis sisters, they're always out to one up the other one, which makes for entertaining holidays. Well, entertaining to everyone that doesn't have the last name Davis, that is.

Two years ago, when my parents went on a cruise over Thanksgiving, I went home with Lacey and had one of the most memorable holidays I'll ever have. Lori, the oldest Davis sister, told her three younger siblings that none of them are capable of holding their alcohol as good as she can. Three bottles of vodka later, Jena was declared the winner because she was the only one that was able to recite the alphabet without messing up. For me, Thanksgiving morning was almost as hilarious as the night before when Mrs. Davis's four daughters were taking turns in the bathroom getting sick, thanks to the delicious smelling turkey.

Lacey acts like she can't stand her sisters, but deep down, no matter how crazy they behave, I know she loves them. Being an only child myself, I would love to have someone to bicker with at family holidays, and I remind Lacey of that every time she complains.

Me: Okay. I'll be there by ten.

I was hoping earlier this week that Caleb would ask me to do something tonight to keep my mind on more satisfying things, but he's working on a case that Lacey wasn't assigned, and from the sounds of it, it's turning out to be bigger than they originally thought. Being the low man in the group, Caleb had no idea how late he was going to work and didn't want to disappoint me by canceling at the last minute.

During the last couple of weeks, Caleb and I have gone out on three official dates, but a day hasn't passed since I purchased my phone that he hasn't called or text me, and I'm discovering how much I really like him. There's just one small problem ...I don't feel any magic when we're together. Don't get me wrong, he's a great guy, and he's extremely attractive. I think if I would have met him before I went to Arizona then I would be head over heels in lust with the idea of him already, but sadly, that's not the case.

I do like him, and I wish I liked him more, which is why I'm not throwing the towel in yet. If I've learned anything from Chase, it's that love can hurt, and it's not always equal. For now, I'm okay with how much Caleb seems to like me. Hopefully, with time, my feelings for him will grow into something more.

CHASE

I come awake when I hear someone pounding on my door. I roll over and have to force my stomach to calm before I get sick.

Bang bang bang!

"Hold the fuck up. I'm coming," I shout loud enough that whoever is at my door can hear me. My driveway is guarded by a gate that requires a passcode to open, which means whoever is here is someone I know.

I rub my hands over my face and slowly make my way to the door. Without looking through the glass, I yank the door open only to groan in frustration. "What the hell do you want?"

"Baby, what's wrong?" Carrie purrs in a childlike voice.

"What's wrong is you're banging on my fucking door uninvited." Carrie sticks her bottom lip out, thinking she looks cute.

"You used to love it when I stopped by to see you." She smiles, trying to look sexy. "Let me come in and I'll make all of your problems go away." She takes a step forward as I put my hand up to stop her.

"Look, I'm trying to be nice here. Clearly we had fun, but whatever we shared is over. You need to move on and leave me the hell alone." My voice is firm and I've lost what little patience I had with this chick. Outside of her smokin' body and huge rack, I can't for the life of me figure out why

I would have entertained the idea of more than one night with her. She has greed written all over her.

"What are you talking about? We're dating; you can't just kick me out of your life?" Her words feel like a punch to the stomach.

"Yes, I can. Apparently, I'm a pro at kicking people out of my life." Her eyes widen as panic sets in. "We're over. I don't want to see you again. Now get the fuck off my property," I tell her as her mouth drops open as I slam the door shut.

I turn and head back to my bedroom with hopes of dying in peace. I no sooner crawl back in my bed when I hear my doorbell ring again.

"Fuck you," I shout as my brain continues to pulse in my head. Carrie must be really fucking determined because she's alternating between banging on my door and ringing the bell. With as much effort as I can muster, I push myself off the bed and head to the front door.

"Open this damn door right now!" Fuck me, it's not Carrie ...it's my mother. I've been avoiding her and most of the world for almost two weeks now, but she's obviously here to check up on me, and I know she won't leave until she's seen me.

I open my front door to a very small but very angry woman. Donna Adams is a gentle woman that wouldn't hurt a fly, but at the moment, I'm not sure that's true, especially after she looks me over from head to toe.

"Hey, Ma! What are you out doing today?" I ask with a smirk on my face. I'm thankful it's my mother and not Carrie this time, but truth be told, I'm not in the mood for either of them.

"Have you been drinking?" she asks with a shaky voice.

Of course I've been drinking, but I'm not about to admit to anything. "I'm a grown man, Mother. I'm allowed a drink when I want. But please, by all means, come in and bust my balls about it why don't you."

My mother gasps after my rather rude and definitely uncalled for comment, but the kicker is her glassy eyes. *Shit. Shit. Shit.* I did not mean to make her fucking cry. Without saying another word, she turns, ready to walk away.

"WAIT. Please don't go. I didn't mean what I just said. I'm pissed off and, unfortunately, I'm willing to take that out on anyone, including you."

She hesitates, but after debating for a few seconds, she walks back up and comes inside. What a fucktastic way to start my day. First Carrie, then my mother. No, I haven't been drinking today, but I'm hungover from drinking way too much last night—something I'm positive I shouldn't have done.

"I've been worried about you. You haven't returned a call or even a text in over a week. Jake told me he's seen you a few times so I thought I would give you some breathing room, but I wanted to see for myself that you're okay. But that doesn't seem to be the case, especially after seeing that woman leaving."

"She wasn't here like that. She showed up and I refused to let her in." Ma sighs with relief but I'm not okay; I'm barely hanging on. Last week, after reviewing my medical files, the NFL Commissioner deemed me not eligible to play the rest of the current season with next year already questionable. I might as well kiss my football career goodbye.

When the news was announced, my father practically went postal, blaming everyone, including me, for ruining my life. At that point, I made a stop at the liquor store where I'm positive the guy behind the counter thought I was throwing a massive party. I went home and started drinking my worries away.

That was last week. However, nothing has changed this week other than I haven't left my house, even for my appointments with Wallace and Stein. I was only going in hopes of seeing the field again and that's no longer the case.

"I'm fine. Pissed at the world, but otherwise fine." I know my mother can see right through the show I'm putting on for her. Either way, she appears shaky and insecure about how to handle me. "Ma, I'm serious. I'll be fine. I'm sorry I was a dick to you earlier."

After my comment, she straightens her shoulders and gives me a confident smile then proceeds to rock my world. "I'm divorcing your father."

"Whaaaaat?" I mumble out, not sure if I actually heard her correctly.

My father hasn't been by to see me after his meltdown and I haven't seen Ma in over two weeks. I have no idea if something has happened while I've been checked out on life.

"I've thought about this for a while now, but I've somehow always convinced myself I need to do what's right. For him, for you, but now I'm going to do what's best for me."

My dad's an ass, and I'm sure as fuck glad I'm not the one married to him, but I never imagined that my mom would leave him. "This is really what you want?" I question in concern.

Her eyes water to the point I'm shocked she's not fully crying yet. "Chase, I'm not sorry for leaving your father, but I'm sorry for the horrible example we set."

"What are you talking about? You've been the best mother a kid could ask for," I say as I take a step closer to her.

"Mother, yes, but your father and I weren't the best example as to how a married couple should act. I grew up believing that true love conquers all, then I met your father and he swept me off my feet, but it wasn't the kind of love my mother convinced me existed. I was ready to break up with your father when I found out I was pregnant with you, so I stayed. For the most part, your father was a good man and he was able to provide for us in ways I wouldn't have been able to do by myself, so I gave up the fairytale and decided to live in reality." She sniffles and looks up into my eyes.

"The first time I ever witnessed the kind of love my mother told me about was when I saw how you looked at Jordan."

I'm still a little drunk from the night before but hearing my mother's last comment feels like another punch to my already sensitive stomach.

"I knew your father was dead set that the two of you should part ways before you left for school, and he somehow convinced me to go along with it. But I kept thinking they'll be okay because I know true love conquers all." Mom pauses to wipe a tear from her face.

"Do you remember what I told you the night before you broke up with Jordan? 'If you love someone, let them go. If they come back to you, they're yours forever. If they don't, then it was never meant to be.'" My eyes remain locked with my mom's as she continues to fight back more tears.

"Chase, Jordan came back to you and you just let her go. You let her walk out your door without even a word from you. Why? Why on earth would you do that?" That's not a question I want to answer because I'm not ready to admit what a coward I am.

"I'll admit, it was harder than hell to get her on the phone, but once I did, she was by your side less than twenty-four hours later."

Where Jordan is concerned, my anger has been replaced by guilt, and right now my mom is pouring salt on an open wound.

"From the second your father saw her, he acted like she was there to personally ruin your life, but she held her own. I knew then she wasn't the same little girl I remembered. Instead, she's a grown woman who's as magnificent on the inside as she is on the outside."

I slowly close my eyes in pain because every word my mother spoke is the God's honest truth. Jordan is worlds better than me and as the fog finally lifted from my head, I remembered all the reasons I never contacted her. Every horrible thing I did to not only her but to other people came flooding back, and the bottom line is ...I don't deserve her.

"Ma, with everything I've been through, it would be completely unfair of me to drag her down."

Ma's eyes flash. "Chase, don't lose the woman God meant for you over some foolish pride. Football was never your dream. It was your father's. Yes, you enjoyed playing it, but if you were truly given a choice, you would have picked Jordan a million times before football. And it's clear, whether she wants to admit it or not, that she's chosen you, too. She put her life on hold for you even after you broke her heart; she did that because true love really does conquer all. Don't let that go, don't sacrifice any more than you already have, and don't worry about the things you can't change. If I know Jordan like I think I do, then everything that happened while you were in school will be long forgiven because, honestly, it's only you that hasn't forgiven yourself."

I'm positive I don't deserve forgiveness, especially from Jordan. I take a deep breath and hesitantly say, "I'm not the same person she fell in love with." My voice is weak as the emotional ride I've been on the last couple of months takes over.

"Of course you're not. You've grown up; you're worldly now. Not every decision you've made has been the right one but you've grown up and you can't allow yourself to live in the shadows of your past. Forgive yourself for what happened and finally move on."

To the outside world, college appeared to be an amazing time in my life, but truthfully, it was a struggle, a struggle I lost for a period of time.

"Chase, it's time to let it go. Find that passion you once had and start living life. Your football career might have been shorter than you like, but you held a position that millions of men would die to have a shot at. You're financially secure and you have a college degree. Now go get your girl and make yourself happy."

I exhale loudly. "Are you going to be okay? I mean, without Dad?" I don't want her to be unhappy but I still can't come to terms with the idea that she's actually going to divorce him.

"Of course. This is something I've thought about doing for years, and recently I was reminded of why I need to. You don't walk over the people you love, you walk with them, remember that, Chase."

Jordan

"Let's do another shot!" Loud clubs, dancing, and drinking is how Lacey likes to unwind, but I would love to be home with a glass of wine and a little peace and quiet.

"Oh, look at that man over there. He's so freaking hot. You should go get his number!" I narrow my eyes at her. I thought since I've been out on a few dates with Caleb she wouldn't be pushing me off on every guy she spots, but that hasn't been the case.

"I'm kind of seeing Caleb. I shouldn't be out scoring other guys' phone numbers."

A strange look passes over her face when she adds, "You're not exclusive yet, right?" My eyes thin even more after her question.

"Well, no, but I think it's wrong to be going out with more than one guy at a time, don't you?" Lacey and I don't share the same views on men. She's never been in love before and isn't sure she'll ever find love. In the meantime, she's happy with Mr. Right Now. Me, on the other hand, while I enjoy sex, I've been looking for something—anything— close to the type of relationship I had with Chase.

"What's going on? Do you know something I don't?" Lacey gives me a sour look before spilling information I can't believe she hadn't already told me.

"Caleb went out on a date last night with some girl he met a while back. I thought he told you, but after talking to you, I could tell he hadn't."

I hinted around about going out last night but all Caleb said was he had plans that he made a while back and couldn't get out of them, which meant I wouldn't get to see him at all this weekend. Yet he had time for someone else.

"Oh," I say, looking out at the dance floor. I hate feeling vulnerable and exposed. With Caleb, I was already missing that spark I wanted to find again but was willing to keep trying. All the while, he's still playing the field. How stupid am I?

"Jordan, I don't think it was anything serious, so I wouldn't worry about it." Lacey reaches across the table and squeezes my hand.

"I'm not worried, believe me. However, this is exactly why I said I shouldn't date a friend of yours. Maybe next time you'll listen to me." My voice was slightly harsher than I intended.

"Wait, just because he went out with someone else doesn't mean the two of you can't date."

Yes, it does and it's all Chase's fault. I want to meet a man who after one look at me knows ...I'm all he wants. I already knew I wasn't feeling that way about Caleb and I'm going to take this as a sign to move on.

"Let's do another shot and then I'm going over there to get that guy's number!" I say with more confidence than I feel.

"Whoo hoo! Let's do this!" Lacey screeches over the music seconds before I throw back probably one shot too many.

I'm hungover or, hell, maybe I'm still drunk. My doorman has rung my apartment three times already. If he rings it one more time, I might find my ice pick and go stab his eyes out.

As I climb back into my bed after using the bathroom, I hear an incoming text on my cell, which I grab off my nightstand. I groan when I see it's from Caleb. I also have four more missed texts from him. Shit. When I open up my message app, I see why. Holy crap, I sent him a text last night ...I don't remember doing that.

> Me: I hope your date last night rocked your world because I won't be rocking it from now on.

> Caleb: Please let me explain.

> Caleb: I made plans with her before I went out with you and I didn't want to be rude and cancel.

> Caleb: Lace told me you're drunk. Please call me so I know you're okay.

> Caleb: I'm downstairs. I want to talk to you. Please let me up.

> Caleb: Who's the other guy waiting to see you?

Other guy? I slowly get up, walk over to the monitor, and hit the call button.

"Hello, Ms. Taylor. I'm sorry to have rung you so many times today but it seems you're popular this morning." Don nervously laughs.

Lacey and my parents are my only approved visitors so I know I can rule out any of them being down there.

"I have a Mr. Caleb Ramsey and a Mr. Chase Adams here to see you."

An overwhelming need to be sick comes over me when I hear Chase's name. What in the hell is he doing here? "Don, I'm not feeling well. Could you please inform both men that I'm not in the mood for visitors?"

"Very well, ma'am."

"Thank you, Don."

Seconds later, my phone goes off with another text from Caleb.

> **Caleb:** Seriously WTH? Let me up and I'll take care of you.

I don't need him to *take care of me*. Maybe I'm being unfair seeing as we weren't exclusive, but casual or not, I don't want the man I'm seeing out with other women while he's dating me.

> **Caleb:** Who the hell is this guy? Are you seeing him and giving me hell for a date that meant nothing?

My head is pounding and I just want both of them to go away. Ten minutes later, I get half of my wish.

Caleb: I can't sit here all day like this jackass can. I'm expected back at the office soon. Text or call me later. Please.

Thank God. One of them is gone and I'm sure Chase will give up soon.

I'm compelled to go down there with my ice pick, but instead of stabbing Don, it would be Chase. I'm not sure what he's doing here, but I have no intention of finding out.

CHASE

When I finally pulled my head out of my ass and went to my appointment with Dr. Stein, he agreed it was time to put my past behind me and focus on my future, whatever that might be. Medically speaking, if I want to keep football a part of my life, I can. My scans show that my brain is healing, and it's definitely possible that I can play again next year, but at what risk? The last time I suffered a concussion, I woke up distorted and living in a made up world. Next time might be worse. Before I saw Jordan again, that was a risk I was willing to take, but not anymore.

My talk with my mother inspired me to want more for myself, but after spending the week before in a drunken haze, I needed a little help to get my life under control, especially if I was going to call Jordan.

I made an appointment every day for almost two weeks with Dr. Stein, and every time I was there, I talked his ear off. At first, I felt extremely awkward admitting to everything I've ever done, but the most enlightening moment came when I finally admitted out loud that Dr.

Stein was right, that my anger towards Jordan always stemmed from learning that she didn't actually belong to me anymore, which was completely my doing.

After I took responsibility for my actions and owned up to shit I've avoided for years, I was ready to call Jordan and beg her, if necessary, to talk to me, only I ran in to a roadblock. Jordan's phone had been disconnected and she doesn't take personal calls on her work number—for any reason. I even told the lady that answered the phone that it was a matter of life and death. That got me nowhere. She said I should call her personal cell if it was that important. And, of course, if I knew Jordan Taylor personally, I would have her private number.

Another thing I discovered about Jordan is she doesn't just work for a cosmetic company. She's the CEO of a company that's known worldwide. During the week we spent together, she never hinted around that she has a job as powerful as the one she holds, which again only spotlights how little I know about her these days.

I'm guessing it's due to her title that she stays off social media sites, or at least if she has any, she's not using her real name, which is something I understand all too well. I hired a man in New York to look around to find out any information he could about her, and within a day he had her home address, but nothing more.

When my concern, or rather my fear, started rearing its ugly head again, my mother assumed I would drag my feet long enough to ruin any shot I might have. As a birthday present, she purchased me a one-way ticket to New York.

Between the time change and a delay at the Phoenix airport, I arrived in New York too late to show up at Jordan's apartment. I checked into a hotel not far from where she lives and decided to wait until morning to pay her a long overdue visit. Only once I arrived, her doorman said she wasn't answering and my fear of where she might be this early in the morning ate away at me. My panic increased when another man stopped in and asked the doorman to ring Jordan's apartment. The only peace I received came when she finally answered the call and she wasn't any more eager to see this other guy then she was me.

As of now, I've awkwardly sat in her lobby for almost five hours while the doorman has pretended I don't exist. On the inside, I'm going out of my mind waiting, but on the outside, I've tried to ensure I don't look like a crazy person. Only someone seriously desperate or insane would wait over five hours for a woman to leave her apartment. Maybe I am a little bit of both. I wouldn't be surprised if the police are called before much longer.

My eyes start to shut as my body slowly gives up the battle to stay awake. That's when I hear the elevator doors open. Not expecting it to be her, I crack one eye open and I'm treated to the best gift my mother could have given me for my birthday, even if it came a day late.

At first, she appears to be on a mission to get the hell out of her building, but she slows once she spots me.

"You're still here?"

Her tone and demeanor are clear signs that she's not thrilled to see me, and after sitting here for five hours, I shouldn't find this surprising.

"I wanted to talk to you," I say, jumping to my feet. "I'm sorry for how things went that day at my house, I should have . . ." Fuck, I should have done a million things differently, and I'm not sure where I should start.

"That's okay. I'm over it. I've moved on," she casually says as she bites her lip and sighs. "Happy birthday, by the way," she softly adds.

Her words send a twist of emotions through me. For starters, it's not okay, and there's no way I'm okay with her moving on, at least not without hearing me out. But she remembered yesterday was my birthday. After ten years, she not only remembers the day but she knew it was yesterday, which means she's been thinking about me.

"Thank you. Could we please talk? Maybe go get a coffee or something?"

She seems suspicious and the idea that she's hesitant to even have a cup of coffee with me absolutely kills me. Barely two months ago, we were making love multiple times a day and now she's completely distrusting where I'm concerned, but I have no one to blame but myself.

"Actually, I was heading out to get a cup of coffee. You can tag along if you want." Before she even finishes her sentence, I'm nodding my head.

As we're walking out the door, the doorman looks at the two of us with a confused expression. He apparently didn't think after Jordan left me down here for hours that I would get a shot at talking to her. I give him a shit-eating grin as I follow her out the door like a dog on a leash.

After we walk a few blocks, we arrive at a hole in the wall coffee shop where every worker seems to know Jordan on a first name basis. "This is arguably the best coffee you'll ever have and the owners are wonderful people."

I've always found Jordan's take on life fascinating. No matter where she's at or who she talks to, she always does it with such gratitude, a way I haven't seen a person act in front of me in years.

Jordan walks to a small table in the back of the café

where she sits down, looking at me but not saying a word. I'm desperate for this woman. I'm desperate to officially have a place in her world. Right now, that has me beyond worried that I'm going to mess up and say the wrong thing; that I'll ruin my chance before I even have one.

"After waiting for hours, I expected you to have a lot to say," she tells me with a firm voice. I take a deep breath and nod my head.

"Yeah, I came to apologize. I don't think it's possible for you to understand what was going through my head at the time because I didn't even completely understand myself until a few weeks ago."

She slowly nods her head like she agrees with me, but all too soon I realize I don't want her to.

"I should apologize, too. I never should have come into your life the way I did, and I definitely shouldn't have gone anywhere with you while your memory was unclear. I mean, for crying out loud, you had a girlfriend and I caused you to—"

"No, I didn't. You didn't cause anything." My heart skyrockets from the comment she was about to make. "Carrie is just a girl I used to mess around with. She was trying to convince me and everyone else that we had something more than we actually did." My heart continues to rapidly beat in my chest while I wait to see if she believes me.

"Oh," she finally says. Just '*Oh*' is all I get from her. I guess she probably wants to talk about Carrie as much as I want to hear about the douchebag that came to her apartment earlier.

"I've done things in my past that I'm not exactly proud of and you deserve to be with a man who's worlds better than me. But then ...then Ma told me that true love conquers all and that we were meant to be. Otherwise, I wouldn't have woken up thinking I was married to you and you wouldn't have dropped everything to come help me.

"Jordan, I'm here to apologize and I'm hoping one day— hopefully soon—you'll want me back in your life." She chews on her lip while she watches me carefully.

"Would you still want to be a part of my life if you're only a friend? Because I'm not sure I can offer you anything more than that."

A friend? A fucking friend ...I can feel my chest tightening at just the thought of being only a friend to her. Hearing about her with other men, possibly having to see her with another guy. No ...absofuckinglutely no, but, for now, I'll promise her anything if it means I can open the door to our future.

"I'm willing to take anything you have to offer."

Jordan

I'm willing to take anything you have to offer. Can I really handle being friends with Chase? After everything we've shared together? I'm not sure, and to be honest, I only offered because I wasn't expecting him to say yes. Now I don't know how to reply.

"When is your flight home?" I ask with a fake smile.

Chase's eyes are penetrating me like he's picturing me naked, and while the idea of getting naked with him sounds amazing, I know nothing good can come from it.

"Hello, Chase?" I wave my hand in front of his face.

"Oh, yeah, sorry. I don't have any plans to return to Arizona right now."

I was taking a sip of my coffee when he answered, causing me to choke. "Whoa ...Ugh, excuse me. What did you say?" I question with wide eyes.

Chase takes a deep breath and locks his eyes with mine. "Jordan, while most guys will tell you love at first sight doesn't exist, I know differently. Maybe I didn't love you the second I saw you but I knew something was different from the moment my eyes collided with yours. During the last ten years, no one has ever come close to making me feel the way you do.

"I fucked up the day I let you walk out of my life, and I continued to fuck up every day afterwards by not doing everything in my power to make you mine again, but not anymore. I want you ...and I want you forever."

My eyes instantly water up as I watch his chest rise and fall with every breath he takes, waiting for me to say something. "But you just said we could be friends," I whisper.

"I lied. I can't be *just friends* with you, but I promise that will be the last time I ever lie to you. Please, at least give me the chance to explain ...explain why it's you, only you that owns my heart."

A tear escapes and I'm pissed. I never freaking cry this much but around Chase it's all I seem to do. "Why? Why do you think you deserve another chance?" Where Chase is concerned, I'm petrified to even consider opening another door for him. I'm not even sure I have it in me to try.

"I don't deserve another chance, but I promise if you give

me one, I'll spend the rest of my life making sure you don't regret it." His voice is strong and his eyes are pleading with me to believe him.

I'm compelled to get up and run back to my apartment but I get the impression that Chase would follow me and wait however long it takes to see me again.

"I don't know, Chase. I'm not the same girl you once knew. I tried to be as palatable as possible when I thought I was helping you but that's not who I am anymore. I'm moody, disagreeable, and even obnoxious at times. I'm not going to sacrifice who I am to please you or anyone else in my life."

"Good." His reply was quick and unwavering. Sitting here staring at his gorgeous face isn't helping my desire to stay away from him.

"I need to get back, but if you're going to be here for a while then I'll see you around."

"Do you still have my cell phone number?" he asks as he reaches out for my hand.

"Um. No. My cell phone didn't make it back to New York."

A knowing smile crosses Chase's face after my remark. "Here, give me your phone and I'll program myself in." Without even thinking, I hand my phone over and the second he punches in his number he hits call.

"Now I have your new number. Your secretary isn't too keen on allowing anyone to talk to you. Apparently, all of your friends have your cell number, which, thankfully, I now have as well."

What a sneaky bastard. I can't believe I fell for that. I'm going to blame the fact that I'm still hungover for my stupidity.

I grab my phone out of his hand and give him what I hope is a nasty look as I get up and head out of the coffee shop, but the second I make it out the door, Chase is already walking next to me.

"I would say I'm sorry for taking your number without asking for it, but then I would be lying and I promised you that I wouldn't do that."

"Yeah, well, it wouldn't be the first time you've broken a promise to me." I regret my words the second they slip out of my mouth, especially when I see the pain that crosses his face. "See, moody ...and I guess I forgot to mention bitchy."

He exhales slowly. "No, it's okay. I deserved that. I did break my promise to you and I almost allowed that to ruin my life."

The way Chase talks about ruining his life makes me wonder about something. "Chase, does Dr. Stein know you're here in New York?"

"Yes. Dr. Stein actually encouraged me to come here and make my play for you. After a good push from Ma, I decided to tell him everything that I could remember. He helped me sort shit out in my head. He helped me realize that I might not feel I deserve you but you're worth fighting for. And if I have to spend the rest of my life alone then I want to know I did everything in my power to win you back first."

I'm standing in the middle of a busy sidewalk with my mouth hanging open. I know it's ridiculous to consider even for a moment that I should give Chase another chance but when he says crap like that, my heart and brain seem to be on different planets.

Without another word, I turn and quickly march back

to my building. "I have some work I need to get done," I say over my shoulder as I start to walk through the main entrance of my building.

Chase gives me a mischievous smile before he adds, "Okay, I'll call you soon."

Ugh, this man already acts shameless in his attempt to win me back but he has another thing coming if he thinks I'm about to roll over and forgive him for breaking my heart, especially when I'm not convinced he won't do it again.

Jordan

"That's it. I'm canceling my trip to Connecticut," Lacey says with her hands on her hips as she shakes her head back and forth.

Lacey called me a couple of hours after I saw Chase, and while I was in the middle of reviewing a new product line for Natural Cosmetics, something I've neglected the past two months. Therefore, I ignored her first call, which didn't go over well.

Caleb called her and told her about the text I sent him and how I refused to see him. Then he made sure to add how there was another guy waiting for me in the lobby of my apartment. Add all of that together and she was at my apartment an hour later.

"Don't be ridiculous, Lace. Your parents are expecting you home for Thanksgiving and you're not about to use me as an excuse not to go," I firmly say, because I know even though she's worried about me she's also eager to have a reason not to go.

"Fine, you're coming with me, then."

I'm not able to stop rolling my eyes at her. "Lace, I'm not

staying here. I'll be in Asbury Park with my parents."

When it was clear that I wasn't leaving New York, my parents wanted to move close enough that they could see me regularly but they had no desire to move into the city. They chose a fairly small town on the New Jersey shore and that's where I'll be spending Thanksgiving.

"There is no way I can go home and relax with that jackass trying to weasel his way back into your life."

I burst out laughing. "You weren't going to relax when you went home so stop looking for reasons to ditch your family on Thanksgiving."

"Well, where is the asshole going to be while you're with your parents?" she huffs out while tapping her foot on the floor, waiting for an answer.

"I don't know, Lace, because until a few hours ago, I had no idea I would ever see him again. For all I know, he's going back to Arizona to spend Thanksgiving with his mom."

"If he's smart he will," she growls out.

God, I love Lacey but if I want to for even one second consider something with Chase, she's going to have to back off, and I'm not sure that's possible.

"What about Caleb?" she asks.

Ugh ...really? "I know you aren't going to believe me, but I felt like something was missing. I wanted to like him and I was trying my hardest to give it a real effort, but the second you told me he went out with someone else I was a mix of relieved and pissed. Pissed enough that I don't have the desire to fake it anymore with him. I don't think it's too much to ask when you're dating a guy, no matter how casually, that he not go out with you one night then another woman the next. Personally, that tells me he wasn't feeling a spark with me either and we should throw in the towel before we waste anymore of each other's time."

"You are one picky bitch!" she snaps back with her eyes narrowed.

"I'm not picky. I just know what I want out of a relationship and being anyone's second choice isn't it."

Lacey rolls her eyes at my comment, which also proves why I shouldn't be dating a guy she considers a friend in the first place.

"Did you even hear him out? He agreed to go out with this woman before the two of you even went out on a date!" She bites her lip, a clear sign that she's trying her best not to yell at me.

"Exactly! If I was someone he wanted a relationship with, he would have canceled with this other woman. Instead, he kept his options open!" I holler.

She's really starting to annoy me and I'm doing nothing to hide my frustration. Lacey curses under her breath before her eyes come back to mine and she turns serious.

"Whatever you do, promise me that you aren't going to run back to him. I remember what you were like when he crushed you ten years ago, and I remember what happened two months ago when he let you walk out his door with Whore Barbie attached to his arm." This is why I love this girl. She might be the most aggravating person I know but her love for me is truly unconditional.

"I don't know what the future holds. All I know is that Chase appears to be my kryptonite and he claims he's here to stay." Lacey looks disappointed by my answer but it's the truth and there's no sense in hiding it.

"I hope for your sake that he's changed but even if he hasn't, I know you're strong enough that you'll be able to recover when he does the only thing he's known for, which is breaking your heart."

Her voice was gentle but her words were firm. No matter what has happened in the past, Lacey is convinced that Chase will always end up hurting me. Now I need to decide if she's right because if she is, I don't share the same confidence in my ability to recover a third time.

"When will you get to town?" My mother is always excited when she knows I'm taking off work and visiting for a few days. With Thanksgiving two days away, her excitement level is off the charts. "The company is closed tomorrow but I'm coming into the office to get a few things done then I'll get on the road."

"Um ...okay, sweetheart, just make sure you send me a text as you're leaving the office so I'll know when to expect you."

"I will, Mom. Tell Dad I said hi and I'll see you both tomorrow."

"Love you." With that, we both hang up. I've gone two days without seeing Chase, but he's called and text me a few times and Don, the daytime doorman at my apartment, said he stopped by yesterday afternoon, but he was gone by the time I got home, but Chase never said anything to me about it.

Where Chase is concerned, I feel like I'm dealing with two separate people. The guy who makes my heart beat faster than anyone I've ever met, and the guy who's able to break my heart at a moment's notice. And while I've only seen the second guy two times in my life, he's the one that's had a lasting impression.

When I arrived at my apartment building later that evening, I find Chase sitting in a chair in the lobby, messing around on his phone. When he looks up and spots me, he instantly hops up with a charming smile on his face.

"Hey. I wasn't sure when you'd be home so I thought I would wait around for a bit hoping to see you."

He made it sound like he might have plans. "Did you have somewhere else to be?" I question in a voice weaker than I intended.

"Yes, in the morning, but I need to get a good night's rest."

His announcement catches me off guard and I want to ask more but I stop myself. "How long have you been waiting?"

His eyes go soft as he answers, "Not that long but for you I'd be willing to wait forever." I start shaking my head in annoyance because he knows exactly what he's doing when he says crap like that.

"Chase, seriously?" Even with my harsh tone, his beautiful smile never wavers.

"Are you going to invite me up to see your place?"

My whole body freezes at his request as an irrational fear of what could happen if I allow Chase into my home takes over. I'm not ready for us to do or be anything other than two people who occasionally talk and exchange texts.

"I don't think that's a good idea," I weakly say.

He looks confused by my comment, like he has no idea how easily my body could betray me if I was alone with him again. "Okay. I won't push. What are your plans for Thanksgiving?"

I clear my throat. "I'm visiting my parents, how about

you?"

He shrugs. "I don't have any. Where did you say your parents live now?"

I stop myself from laughing. He's fishing for information. His comment still strikes me as odd because I can't believe his mother doesn't have a huge holiday planned with his extended family since he doesn't have to plan it around his NFL schedule.

"Your mom doesn't have plans?"

He's already shaking his head no as he starts to answer, "Nope. Her plans consist of filing for divorce, which leaves me on my own." My eyes go wide from shock. Donna Adams wants a divorce?

"What?" I breathe out.

"Yeah, I guess my dad has finally pushed her too far. I was just as shocked as you but then when I stopped and thought about it, I don't think my parents have ever really been happy. They stayed together because it was easier than being apart, but after how my dad's been acting, she's finally had enough." He watches me closely for a second. "I have, too," he adds.

The majority of our problems have stemmed from Steve Adams and the control he has over his family. I've always known this, but I am surprised that Chase and Donna have finally realized this for themselves.

"He's your dad, Chase. I'm sure you'll still see him."

"No, I'm done." His answer was quick and sharp as if he's already come to terms with what this means for him.

"I'm sorry." I don't particularly like Steve but I love my father and I couldn't imagine not having him in my life.

"That right there is why I'm fighting for you. My dad's actions have cost you a lot—cost us a lot—still you feel sorry about me cutting him out of my life."

"Um . . ." I mumble, not sure what I should say to his unexpected remark about fighting for me. "I don't have to like your dad to feel bad for you. You've always respected him, looked up to him, and now . . ." I trail off with a shrug because I have a hard time believing he's really done with him.

"I did respect him. I did look up to him, and by doing that, he cost me everything other than my mother that's ever mattered to me, including my football career that he so desperately thinks he's been protecting."

"You're done with football?" I softly ask. He looks sad but with a hint of pleasure as he answers me, "I'm done playing it, but it will always be a huge part of my life." His answer feels cryptic, like there's something more he's not telling me.

"When did you say you're leaving for your parents?" And he's back to fishing. The sudden change in our topic has me smiling.

"I didn't. I'm going to get some work done in my office in the morning then I'll probably get on the road by mid-afternoon."

He suddenly looks sad and I know I shouldn't care but I'm a sucker, especially where he's concerned. "Are you going to be spending Thanksgiving alone?"

He smiles. "Nah, don't worry about me." And I shouldn't worry about him, but for whatever reason I do, and I think I always will.

"Oh, well, I was going to say if you're going to be alone then maybe you could come to my parents' house and have dinner with us."

Chase perks up at my invitation. "Oh, I didn't realize

your parents lived that close to the city." He gives me another beautiful smile that sends flutters to my stomach.

"They live about an hour and a half south of the city. I don't know if you're renting a car or—"

"I can. I will, I mean, if you're sure it's okay that I come."

Honestly, I have no idea how my parents will react to seeing Chase, but the idea of leaving him all alone even in a city with millions on Thanksgiving will eat me up inside.

"Okay, I'll text you their address." Chase stares at me for a few seconds before giving me a sexy grin.

"I'm looking forward to it, beautiful."

Oh good Lord, what did I just get myself into?

CHASE

I couldn't care less if I spend Thanksgiving alone or not. All that matters is that Ma and Jordan are happy. My mother I'm not too sure about, but I know I need to give her time to move forward with her life now that she's leaving my dad. Jordan made me one happy man when she unexpectedly invited me to join her at her parents' house. Since I joined the NFL, Thanksgiving and Christmas are two holidays I don't typically get to participate in, but I'm looking forward to today and spending Thanksgiving with Jordan and her family. The address Jordan gave me is to a nice two-story house right on the water in a coastal town in Jersey. The size of the town reminds me a lot of Oak Cove, small but not too small.

I park my rental and walk up to the wraparound porch. Before I have the chance to knock on the door, Jordan's father, Doug Taylor, steps outside with a stern look on his face. "Chase."

I remember Doug and Janette Taylor being amazing parents. They supported and loved their daughter exactly the way I plan to do with my own children one day. After I left Oak Cove, I often wondered what they thought of me. By the looks of it, it isn't good.

"Hello, sir," I say, extending my hand for him to shake.

Doug gives it a long, hard look before he finally takes it and gives me a firm shake. Doug clears his throat. "I don't know what your intentions are regarding my daughter, but if you ever hurt her again, I will hunt you down and show you how skilled I am with a gun." I let go of his hand as my heart speeds up.

As I watch him closely, I realize he's not joking. Doug is a retired military officer, which means he probably has more experience with a gun than anyone I know. And right now, by the way he's looking at me, I know he meant every word.

"Next to my wife, my daughter is the strongest woman I've ever had the pleasure of knowing, and I'm not about to stand by and watch you break her again." His words send a pain through my body. All I ever wanted to do was help build Jordan up, but no matter my intentions, I seem to do the opposite.

"Mr. Taylor, I wish I had the power to change the past but I don't. If I did, there are a lot of things I would do differently, starting with the night I broke up with Jordan. I don't know if I have a shot in hell with her, but I promise you that if I do, I'll be willing to stand in front of your gun without a fight if I hurt her again."

I'm nervous to the point that my hands are trembling. I respect this man and I lost any respect he had for me when I single-handedly broke his daughter's heart.

Doug sighs and his shoulders start to relax. I'm not positive but I think by admitting my failures and not trying to make excuses for them, I may have redeemed myself a little in Doug's eyes.

"Come on in, my girls are in the kitchen." *His girls*.

I love the pride Doug has when he talks about his family. That was something that stood out to me the first time I had dinner at their house. The four of us sat down, talked about our day, and I remember clearly wondering if all families were like that because mine certainly wasn't.

When I walk inside, I look around and then I instantly freeze. This is why Jordan hated my house in Scottsdale. The Taylor's don't live in a house; they've made their house into a home. I have no idea how long they've lived here but it's more of a home than my parents' house in Oak Cove. Pictures are on the wall in no particular order, the furniture looks comfortable but doesn't necessarily match, and there's a blanket thrown over the side of a chair. This room is inviting and it definitely seems like someone uses it regularly.

I'm brought out of my trance when I hear the magical sound of Jordan's laughter. When I look over at Doug again, waiting for him to take the lead, I see that his eyes are searching mine for something but I'm not sure what.

"This way."

The two of us walk towards the back of the living room that's connected to the dining room then we enter the kitchen where Jordan and her mother are still laughing. Jordan's body goes solid and her laughter stops when she spots me.

"Oh, hey. I didn't know you had made it to town yet."

After her comment, her eyes wander to her father's, and I can tell she's questioning what he might have said or done already.

"Your dad spotted me pulling in. Thank you for allowing me to tag along today, Mrs. Taylor."

Jordan's mother greets me with soft, gentle eyes. "You're more than welcome, Chase. Dinner will be ready soon. Can I fix you a drink?"

"No thank you."

"Chase, Jordan informed us you might not be playing in the NFL anymore." Jordan starts biting her lip as she looks over at her dad like she wasn't expecting him to repeat what she told him.

"Yes. Unfortunately, it doesn't appear my career playing football will be as long as most players, but I'm still fortunate enough to have years of playing under my belt." I'm nervous and I'm positive they can tell.

"If you're not playing football then what do you have planned for your future?" Doug fires back.

To an outsider, I'm sure it looks like the second my career is over I went running back to Jordan, but it's actually the opposite. It's because of Jordan I'm tossing in the towel before I fuck myself up past the point of having a future.

"I wasn't released to play the rest of this year, but it appears that I could play next year, withstanding a full medical check. However, the risk of playing no longer outweighs the future I'd like to have, which is why I officially retired and accepted a job in New York."

At my announcement, Jordan gasps and places her hand over her chest. "Doing what?" she asks without taking her eyes off of me.

"I've lived and breathed football every second of my life, and even though I have a degree in marketing, I feel like football is all I know. Yesterday I became the newest Human Resource Coordinator for the NFL. My office is at their headquarters in New York City."

The room is eerily silent until Mrs. Taylor speaks up. "Well, that's wonderful news, especially if that's what you want to do." This right here is what I missed out on in life. *If that's what you want to do.* Outside of Jordan, no one, including my mother, has ever cared about what I wanted.

"Jordan, why don't you go set the table," Janette says, breaking the tension in the room.

"I'll help you," I quickly add. Jordan gives me a smile that makes my heart race. Maybe knowing I'm going to stick around will help break down the walls I've caused her to build.

chapter 15

Jordan

Thanksgiving consisted of my parents, two aunts, an uncle from my father's side of the family, Chase, and me. Being an only child that's not married and has no children, our family is fairly small. My dad has an older sister and a younger brother, who came along with his wife, but none of my cousins are close enough to attend.

Being a small, tight-knit family, there wasn't a person at the table that wasn't aware of the history between me and Chase, but everyone treated him with kindness, which I don't think Chase was expecting.

After dinner was over, the older adults headed to the family room to visit while Chase and I went for a walk down the beach.

"Your family is wonderful." They are and I'm lucky enough to appreciate every moment I have with them.

"Thanks. How's your mom doing?"

He takes a deep breath then sighs. "Ma says she's okay, but I'm not sure I believe her. I was willing to go to Arizona or Florida today and spend time with her but she kept insisting she's fine and wants to be alone."

When Donna called and begged me to come see Chase, I wasn't surprised at the lengths she'd go to make him happy. She loves her son and would do almost anything for him, except go against Steve. That's why I'm still shocked that she's asked him for a divorce.

"Your mother is a strong woman. I'm sure she'll be fine."

"Yeah, I'm sure you're right." Chase is acting awkward all of a sudden and I don't understand why. "Do you want to go out on a date this weekend when you get back to the city?"

I chew on my lip for a moment. I knew he'd eventually ask me this, but that doesn't mean I'm prepared to answer him. "I don't know." I breathe out a sigh. "Where you're concerned, Chase, I don't always use common sense. Have you ever heard of the saying, 'Past behavior predicts future behavior'? If that's the case, then I need to run far away from you." I try to laugh off my remark, but we both know my words were anything but funny.

I see the pain in his face. "God, I hope I'm the exception to that rule." His jaw tenses. "But ...maybe I'm not." He gives me a sad smile.

"I still—God, Jordan, there's so much I need to tell you. So much happened after ...after I left Oak Grove." He swallows loudly. Chase's body is coiled tight with tension as his mind drifts to his past; a past I wasn't a part of. "I went off the deep end after we broke up, and I almost screwed up my life worse than I already had, but that's a story for another day."

"Did you get married? Do you have a child?" I nervously ask.

"God, no," he rushes out, which instantly settles my nerves.

"You've made remarks about going off the deep end but I'm not sure you actually did as bad as you think you did."

His eyes widen with alarm. "I didn't get married and I don't have a child, but I did fuck up big time, and if you're willing to go out with me, then I'll share my past with you. But make no bones about it, I'll be hoping and praying you still want anything to do with me afterward."

I'm not a nosey person, but I'd be lying if I didn't admit I desperately want to know about Chase and the past that seems to haunt him.

While I'm trying to decide what to say, Chase takes my silence to mean something else. "Does your hesitation have anything to do with the guy that was at your apartment Sunday morning? Is he your boyfriend or something?" he asks, his nose scrunched up in what I think is disgust.

"He's not my boyfriend but we have gone on a few dates," I say with a shrug. Chase sighs but keeps his eyes locked with mine.

"He pissed me off, and I wasn't kidding when I said I could be moody. I sent him a text after one too many drinks Saturday night and he showed up Sunday to apologize. However, as you already know, I wasn't in the mood to listen to him." I groan. I didn't mean to tell him about Caleb, but the truth slipped right out of my mouth.

"I'm glad he's not your boyfriend, but even if he was, I'd still fight like hell to win you back." Kryptonite. Fucking kryptonite, that's what this man is to me and this is exactly why.

"Chase, I'm not sure I'm equipped to handle the kind of heartbreak you dish out, and if you want me to be honest—right or wrong—I'm not sure I've forgiven you for hurting me."

His eyes are gentle. "Good thing for you I'm better equipped than I once was. I won't be dishing out any more heartbreak. I'm ready to serve up a happily ever after but only to one person, and I'm willing to wait however long that takes."

I push back the tears that threaten to fall. I've waited a long time to hear those words, but now it's time to decide if I believe him. "Okay, this weekend we'll talk, but at this point, that's all I'm promising."

His shoulders relax and a grin forms on his face. "I'll take it."

I wet my lips and Chase's eyes follow the path of my tongue. I clear my throat, causing his eyes to shoot straight to mine.

"Well, it's starting to get late, so I better get back to the city," he hesitantly says.

My heart drops to my stomach and I'm alarmed at how quickly my emotions flip because I'm already sad that he's leaving when minutes ago I thought I was ready for him to go.

"Would you walk me in so I can say thank you to your parents?"

I nod my head yes. The walk to the house is made in silence. I glance over my shoulder as I open the door, only to find him staring at my ass, which causes me to burst out laughing.

"What's funny, dear?" my aunt asks, but I shake my head and mutter a quick "Nothing." I turn to look at Chase, finding humor in his eyes.

"Thank you, Mr. and Mrs. Taylor, for having me. I hope I get the chance to see you again."

"You're welcome here anytime, Chase," my mother says.

A full round of goodbyes happens then I walk him back out to his rental.

"Drive safe and I'll talk to you soon," I tell him.

"Goodnight." His voice is soft, and I swear I can see lust and desire in his eyes. With another smile, he gets in his car and drives away, leaving my fragile heart a few beats away from cracking open.

CHASE

A lesson I learned early in life is that money can buy you a lot of things, including information. For a steep price, I found out what floor and apartment Jordan lives on, and for an even steeper price, her neighbors were willing to move. Of course Jordan is unaware of this and hopefully, after I unburden my past on her, she'll still want to see me, especially once she learns I'm her new neighbor.

Originally, I thought I would wait until I was positive I have a future with Jordan, but once she admitted the guy from the other day is someone she's dating, I knew I needed to make sure I had an in. And what better way in could I have than living across the hall from her?

Hopefully, she's not having sex with the guy because if she is and I have to listen to it, then I'll head back to Asbury Park and borrow her dad's gun to kill the asshole with it.

By the time Jordan returned late Saturday night, I had her old neighbors moved out, but I didn't have enough time to move anything into my new place. I was inside the apartment when she returned, so I immediately sent her a text.

Me: I hope you made it back safely.

Seconds later, my phone signals a message.

Jordan: Actually, I just got home.

Me: Good. Want to get together tonight?

She replied the first time in a matter of seconds, but this time it's taking her awhile. Knowing Jordan, she's thinking about her response.

Jordan: Depending on where your hotel is, it could take you a while to make it here with the weekend traffic.

Instead of replying, I get up and walk out my door then knock on hers. A few seconds later, she opens her door with a startled expression. "The traffic wasn't bad." I can't help the shit-eating grin that takes over while she stands there staring at me. "Can I come in?"

"Um ...sure," she says, still confused. I turn and walk past her, leaving her to guess how I arrived so quickly. When I look around, I see a different version of her parents' house. Everything is nice, neat, and clean, but her place also looks very relaxed.

"I can tell why you hated my house in Scottsdale so much. This place is incredible. I bet you decorated it yourself."

I hear her draw in a breath before she finds her voice. "I live by myself, so of course I decorated my apartment." I stop and take a long look at her. She can't begin to understand how different she acts compared to a lot of people that have money. I lived alone and I paid a professional to come in and decorate my house. I ended up living in a museum.

I point with my eyes towards her sofa. "May I?"

"Of course. Sit down. Sorry, I'm still trying to figure out how you got here so fast and upstairs without the doorman ringing me." There's no sense in keeping anything from her. It will only do more harm later.

"I'm your new neighbor," I proudly state.

Her eyes scrunch in confusion. "My new neighbor? What are you talking about?"

"I moved in across the hall."

This time her eyes widen in shock. "The Kublers? You moved into the Kublers' apartment? But ...where—?"

"They moved out, I moved in." If I didn't think it would piss her off, I would start laughing at the shocked expression she's wearing.

"They moved out and you moved in?" she repeats like she's testing out what I said.

"Yep." Jordan slowly drags her hands through her hair in frustration and suddenly I'm regretting my decision to tell her about my new living arrangements.

"Do you think that was a smart idea? We haven't even gone out on one date and you've already moved in next door?"

I knew she wasn't going to be thrilled, but where this woman is concerned, I can't seem to control myself. "I've lived in a lot of different places in the last ten years, but I never lived where I felt like I belonged. That changed today when I moved in next to you."

I wait a moment, giving her a chance to process what I said. "I've been searching for a place where I could belong, and deep down I think I always knew that place could be anywhere in the world, as long as I'm near you."

The room is silent except for the sounds of the bustling city below. Jordan is staring at me, appearing stuck between shock and annoyance by my invasion into her life.

"Why don't you tell me whatever it is that's been bothering you. Whatever has happened that you think will affect the two of us from having a future together."

Her comment causes my stomach to turn. My past is about to collide with the future I've always dreamed of having and the thought scares me beyond belief.

I let out a long sigh and do my best to tamp down my nerves. I glance up and lock my eyes with hers, preparing myself for the moment that could ruin my chances with Jordan. As hard as this will be, it's inevitable. I will do anything necessary to ensure we have a chance at the future I've imagined, even if that means sharing my darkest secret and deepest shame.

"When I woke up in the hospital, I didn't just allow myself to think we were married. I also blocked out most of the details from my time at college."

My chest rises as I gather my courage to continue. "After you left my house and returned home, details about my life started coming back. I disappointed myself. It's no wonder I made up a life I could be proud of." She's watching me closely, but remains silent.

"The summer before I left ...I never had any intentions of breaking up with you. Then a week before I was scheduled to leave, my dad decided to try a new tactic—one that worked. He told me how selfish I was being by keeping you tied to me, that you deserved to go off to college and experience life without being strapped to a guy you'd hardly see."

I roughly run my hands through my hair. "I wasn't stupid. I knew he had a mission to separate us, but he got me thinking and with the kinds of demands I knew were set for me, I started questioning if keeping you tied to me was a selfish thing to do. I wanted to do the right thing for both of us and I caved under the pressure."

Jordan sniffles as her eyes water. "That night when I got home, all I could hear were your words.

"The man I'm going to spend the rest of my life with won't need a break from me. He'll know from the second I enter his life that I'm worth keeping."

I jump to my feet. "I knew that. God, I knew you were worth keeping and I knew I just fucked up the best thing that had or ever will happen to me." I pause, allowing her to mentally catch up, but I have to look away when I see her start to cry.

"I packed my things and left for school, but when I got there, I couldn't focus for shit. As a freshman, I wasn't going to see any playing time, but I was still expected to practice and show everyone what I had to bring to the team. Instead, I looked like a huge joke." I breathe through the pain and force myself to continue. "My dad, who was in Ohio more than he was in Florida, caught wind of my behavior. Between him and my coach, I was constantly being yelled at. I needed to know you were okay, that you didn't hate me. No matter how hard I tried, I couldn't get past the sinking sensation that we should be together and because of that, I couldn't concentrate for shit.

"My coach paired me up with a junior linebacker as my mentor. At first he was cool and let me whine about my problems, but then he started dragging me out to parties. His idea of helping me get over you was to surround myself with women." I can see the hurt in her eyes, which kills me. I knew this was going to be hard for her to hear, and I haven't even gotten to the worst of it.

"At first, I didn't want to be around anyone, but then I met a guy named Drake that had dropped out of school a few years prior. For some reason, the two of us hit it off." I take a deep, calming breath before turning my face away from Jordan.

"During my free time, I started going to Drake's house, where sometimes he'd have parties. Mostly we'd just hang out. He understood the pressure I was under and at the time he seemed like the only person that actually cared about what I was going through. That's when he first offered me something I could use to relax." I pause and look back to see her eyes narrow but she stays silent.

"The first time I tried any kind of drug, it was just a few drags off a joint. Then it was a pill here and there. Next thing I knew, I was doing lines of coke every other day just to make it through the day. Hiding it was easy, drug tests for players that aren't suiting up aren't as common, and I somehow managed to go to enough classes to keep my grades up. But any chance I had, I was at Drake's house." There are many turning points in my life and this is definitely a major one. If only I could somehow go back to this point in my life and pull my head out of my ass, my life might be worlds better.

"Give or take a month after I started using hardcore drugs, I had spells where I would blackout for days, or the opposite would happen and I wouldn't sleep for days on end. I..." I nervously swallow. "I would wake up in random places with women I didn't remember meeting after doing God only knows what. Still, I somehow managed to keep that part of my life hidden from those who weren't doing it with me. Until ...until I woke up in a hospital bed with my father yelling at me for being such a fuck up.

"I don't remember much from that night, but I guess Drake and I were going to a party about an hour from campus. I was driving and already messed up on something, and I crashed the car into a tree. Drake was killed instantly and I somehow managed to only hit my head." Since my memory returned to normal, Drake and what little I do remember from the night of the accident has remained on repeat.

"Karma's a real bitch because Dr. Wallace thinks that initial blow to my head is what has caused me to get concussions easier than other players." I pause, giving her another moment to process all the shit I just laid out for her.

"Other than Drake's friends, no one really knew we hung out and somehow my dad paid the right person—or people—to make it look like Drake was the one driving, which wasn't hard to sell because we were in his car." I start shaking my head with disgust. "I'm not sure if the hospital ran any blood work but nothing appeared in my file. I wouldn't be surprised if my dad paid to have that disappear as well.

"As far as the school was concerned, I was just a student that happened to get in an accident, but in reality, I killed the only person that really cared about me." I have no fucking clue what she's thinking right now, but if I had to guess, she's feeling sorry for me. I'm not looking for anyone's pity, especially when that's the last thing I deserve.

"I returned to school and everyone I knew was feeling bad for me, that I had somehow managed to get into a car that Drake Jones, a well-known druggie, was driving. I was told I was lucky he didn't kill me. The worst comment came from a teammate of mine that told me the world was a better place without a guy like him." I wanted to beat the shit out of Mark, and I probably would have if my dad hadn't been in the next room talking to our coach, ensuring I didn't lose my spot on the team.

"I was dying on the inside because it was me ...*I* killed him. *I* did that, but instead everyone was acting like I was some stupid hero. At that point, all I wanted was a hit of something or a fucking pill. I didn't even care what. I would have taken anything from anyone." I shake my head, still fighting back the pain.

"Even without Drake, I was desperate enough that I found the right people to hook me up, and a few months later, my dad found a bag of coke inside one of my jackets. He went completely insane, screaming at me that I was wasting my future. That he raised me to be better than some fucked up druggie. That was the first and only time he ever hit me. I was shocked. I was pissed, but looking back on it, I deserved it. I deserved a lot more than a punch in the face but in that moment it really hit home what a huge disappointment I was." I glance out the window, looking for the courage to continue.

"My mom convinced my dad I had a real problem. That I was addicted and screaming and hitting me wasn't the cure I needed. That summer, I left and went to a private rehab."

I rub my hands down my face. I'm back to hating myself for the type of person I turned out to be. Jordan is looking at me, but I can't tell what she's thinking. I don't know if I should be scared or relieved that she hasn't interrupted my confession. Either way, I've started and I have to finish. There's no going back ...only forward. My last and only hope is that she hears me out until the end and isn't so disgusted by the person I used to be that she can't see past it to the man I've become.

"That was the last time I ever did any drugs, but when life gets stressful, I tend to grab some alcohol and drink. So far, for whatever reason, I can drink myself stupid, but I've yet to become addicted to the point of alcoholism. Even with that being said, I know I should steer clear of it. I'm an addict in the truest sense of the word and it's not worth the gamble. Usually, I don't have more than a beer here and there, but a few months ago—shortly after you left—I drank myself beyond anything I've ever done before. That's one of the main reasons it took me so long to get my act together and come for you. I didn't want to be fighting any urges while begging you to want me ...a killer and an addict."

Pain laces her voice when she finally speaks. "Chase, what happened to your friend was very unfortunate but you can't wear that on your conscience for the rest of your life. You both did drugs, you both got into that car, and you both made choices that put each other at risk. I can't speak for certain, but if I had to guess, I'm sure Drake wouldn't want you to live the rest of your life with this kind of guilt."

I shake my head because I know I shouldn't be allowed off the hook that easy. "If I wasn't driving the car that night then—"

"Then it probably would have happened another night. The two of you using drugs like that all the time ...it was only a matter of time before something happened." Her voice is soft and kind—nicer than I deserve.

"But people think he died because he was a druggie loser when I was just as bad, but . . ."

Jordan moves closer to me and places her hand on my back. The strength I draw from her amazes me. "I'm sorry your friend died, and I'm sorry other people spoke ill of him once he had passed, but speaking up wouldn't have changed anything, at least not for Drake." Jordan places her other hand over mine and gives me a weak smile.

"The charge of aggravated vehicular homicide in the state of Ohio is two to eight years. I could have confessed to what happened and turned myself in. Instead, I went on with my life like it never happened and made it to the NFL."

Jordan chews on her lip before speaking again. "Chase, would Drake have wanted you to turn yourself in? To spend two to eight years in jail for what happened to him?"

I step away from her and holler louder than necessary, "What Drake wants doesn't matter! He's dead!"

Her eyes search mine, waiting for me to calm down. When I do, she tries again. "I understand that Drake doesn't have a say, but if he did, what would it be? And before you answer that, ask yourself: Would you want Drake in jail if the roles had been reversed?"

No. Of course I wouldn't want Drake in jail. He was my friend, but I won't say that out loud because it excuses my behavior. Instead, I stare down at the floor and remain silent.

"After I started at NYU, I was struggling, too. I met my

friend Lacey during freshman orientation and somehow she could tell I needed a friend. I ended up latching on to her. My first semester, I didn't do a lot but after winter break, I came back and started over."

She exhales loudly. "Lacey and I ...we did things I'm not proud of, things I would rather not talk about, but we were young. We were a team and I know without a doubt that if something happened to us like it did you, I wouldn't want her to spend even one night in jail because she loves me. Sometimes ...people make crappy decisions.

"If your car had hit another vehicle, if someone completely innocent from the situation you and Drake put yourself in was hurt, then this would be an altogether different story, but that's not what happened." I hate the fact that she's giving me an out, but knowing the unbelievable person Jordan is, I shouldn't be shocked.

"Chase, I can't tell you what you should do because I don't have to live with the consequences, but turning yourself in isn't going to bring your friend back." After a long pause and sigh, Jordan steps closer and grabs my hand again, only this time she gives it a tight squeeze. "Have you thought about turning your experience in to something positive? I don't know, maybe an affordable rehab for people that don't have the money to pay for it or a program that offers players or, hell, even college freshman the additional support they need? Ugh, I don't know. I'm thinking out loud here but I think the world would be better served if you gave something back rather than sit in a jail cell for years."

When I returned to school after my stint in rehab, my family never uttered a single word about what happened my freshman year. My dad wanted to live in a world where his child wasn't a fuck up and talking about it only served as a reminder. Because of that, I've never given any thought to what Jordan has suggested. The guilt I feel at times eats me alive but she's right. Sitting in jail isn't going to bring Drake back, but doing something, hell, anything that might keep a situation like that from happening again is something I can do. Something I should do.

"Thank you for listening to me, for not thinking I'm a horrible person, and for the suggestion. It's something I definitely want to think more on." Jordan's face goes soft and I wonder, not for the first time since I woke up in a daze, if I am capable of keeping her.

"Would you like to go for coffee tomorrow?" I ask.

She gives me an amused smile. "I can't. When I moved in here, I made a strict rule about not dating any of my neighbors. I guess you blew that to hell by moving in next door. Even though it makes the walk of shame a little easier, I've found being stuck in an elevator with a one night stand makes for awkward times." She laughs off her comment but I'm secretly dying on the inside.

Only a fool would think a woman as gorgeous as Jordan would go ten years without sex, and knowing I definitely indulged with the opposite sex, it makes me a hypocrite to be pissed at her for doing the same thing, but I can't help it. My blood boils at the idea of another man touching her.

Out of the two of us, if we do move forward with a relationship, I'm the one that's more than likely going to meet men she's slept with since I'm now on her turf. The idea is about as pleasant as smashing my head with a hammer.

"Well, you've already slept with me so I'm excused from your rule," I tell her.

God, this woman does something to me that I've never experienced without her. She makes me want to be a better person, to start living a life that I can actually be proud of.

"I guess you're right. Maybe I should try to avoid the elevator when I see you." Her voice was soft and joking, which has me leaning in and tucking her hair behind her ear. When she doesn't pull away, I tilt her head back and brush my lips softly across hers. Thankfully, she seems receptive and within seconds, my tongue seeks out hers, but all too soon she pulls back, leaving me desperate for more.

"If, and I do mean if, I'm willing to try something with you, then we need to move forward slowly. I understand what you were up against with your father, but still, you didn't fight for me. You didn't ask me what I wanted. You left and from the sounds of it, we both suffered majorly because of your decision."

She pauses to take a deep breath before exhaling slowly. "Then two months ago, right or wrong, you allowed me to walk out of your life without even so much as a word, and that's scares the shit out of me because I'm not positive you won't do it again. Your dad not being around is *the only* reason I'm even considering seeing you. Chase, I'm not asking you to get down on your hands and knees and beg for my forgiveness, but I do need time. I need to see that you're serious, that trusting you is the right decision because I'm not sure that it is."

I'm already nodding my head in agreement. I understand where she's coming from and if she needs baby steps then that's exactly what I'll give her.

"What you just said sounds perfect. We need to discover each other all over again, and if you give me that chance, then I'll spend the rest of my life giving you a reason to keep me around."

The shy smile on her face causes my chest to tighten and only proves what I've known for twelve years: this is the woman I'm meant to spend my life with.

chapter 16

Jordan

I'm attempting to unlock my door when I hear Chase behind me. "How was your day?" I jump and drop my keys on the floor, which he quickly picks up.

"My day was fine. Were you waiting for me to come home?" I ask. Instead of answering, he gives me a sexy smile as he hands me my keys. When it's clear he isn't going to give me an answer, I turn around and unlock my door then step inside with Chase right behind me.

"What did you do all day?" I ask while I strip off my coat then promptly ditch my heels.

"Nothing, really. I answered a few emails and texts, watched some mindless TV, but other than that my day was uneventful."

The Chase I once knew was always a busy person. Between his dad, school, football, and work, he had a high demand on him at all times. Right now, he seems a little lost talking about how boring his day was.

"I'm sure you'll find your groove soon. When do you start your job?" Chase is staring at my chest, but once I clear my throat he looks up, not caring in the slightest that

I caught him ogling me.

"Your job? When do you start?" I repeat.

"Hopefully soon. I've officially retired but nothing has been made public yet, and I can't start until it has."

I motion for him to sit down on the couch. "Is this your normal time to get home from work?" Today is the Monday after Thanksgiving and my first workday since Chase became my neighbor.

"Nothing about my work or hours falls in the normal category. Some days I get home before the sun sets and other days I barely get home before it's time to go to bed."

Chase's eyes thin, like he didn't like my answer. "But your job ...you like it?" I can't tell what he's thinking but he seems confused.

"I love my job. Shortly after I arrived in New York, my grandfather told me the company would be mine if I wanted it. I was only eighteen and I couldn't imagine running a company. As my college years passed and I started to settle into life here in the city, I decided this was where I was meant to be."

Chase is staring at me with an odd expression, probably because during the two years we were a couple I never talked about my grandparents' empire. "I was given my position as CEO versus actually earning it and that has proven to be a challenge, but I think in the last few years I've finally proven myself to my employees. It's the rest of the city that still seems to judge me." Chase turns his head, giving me a confused look.

"It's been hell on my dating life," I say with a laugh, but the second my comment slips out, I regret it. Chase's shoulders tense and his head drops.

We were separated for ten years. We both have pasts,

relationships that have involved other people, and while discussing it in detail might not be a great idea, we can't ignore the last ten years, either.

"Have you dated a lot?" he softly asks. I watch him closely for any indication that I'm opening a door that I shouldn't.

I shrug my shoulders. "I'm not sure I would say a lot, but yes. I've dated my fair share of men. What about you?" I really don't want to know the answer to this question. I'm acting like what he's about to say is no big deal, but my heart is racing and it feels like it could shatter at any moment.

"No. I've never dated anyone." My eyes naturally narrow. "I said dated," he quickly adds then sighs. "Jordan, I fucked up the day I told you we needed to take a break. I knew within seconds I had given up the best thing that had or probably ever would happen to me." He breathes out a sigh.

"After being with you, women in general didn't hold the same appeal. I lived ten years going through the motions of life, but I wasn't really living."

After my first semester of school, I stopped trying to picture the life he was living and, truthfully, there was a time when I hoped he was suffering, but I cared about him too much to want him to live ten years with this amount of regret.

"Things happen for a reason, Chase. We don't always know or understand the reason. Right now, that's the best thing we can hold on to."

"When I heard you say we'd never been married, my memory didn't just suddenly come back. I was confused, and to be honest, I was pissed that everyone allowed me to look like a fool." He cast his eyes to the floor again after admitting how everything has affected him.

"I'm sorry. God, I'm so sorry," I whisper.

"No. You have nothing to be sorry about. After I decided to get off my ass and really start talking to Dr. Stein, my memory—at least, most of it—started to come back. I know why I woke up thinking you were my wife because that's what I've been wishing was the truth for years." He clears his throat. "I'm surrounded by people every day but I was lonely. Those four years of college probably would have been hard on us but I'm sure we would have come out the other end a stronger couple. And in my head, we would have been married by now, probably with a couple of kids. That thought wasn't just in my head the day I played my last game ...I've been picturing what my life would have been with you for the last couple of years."

My heart drops. He's been thinking about me for years? I'm not sure what to say because the same doesn't hold true for me. By the time I graduated college, Chase was a distant memory. He was the boy that broke my heart and nothing more. I *had* to think that way because I was still set on the idea that the perfect man was out there waiting on me ...I just never imagined that man being the same person that broke me ...that broke us.

"Life definitely turned out different for me. Different then how I imagined when we were together," I tell him.

"How do you imagine it turning out now?" His question was quick and his eyes are penetrating mine. He's asking if I'm picturing him in my life and I'm not sure I should.

"I learned it's best not to expect life to turn out a certain way. That way, when it doesn't happen, the fall doesn't hurt nearly as bad." His eyes are still locked with mine as I give him another blow, one I could keep to myself but to move forward he needs to truly understand the level of hurt he inflicted. "Chase, the day you broke up with me, the day you asked me to meet you in the park, I thought ...I thought you asked me there to propose. I walked into that park thinking I was going to become Mrs. Chase Adams, and I walked out with a broken heart, one that even ten years later hasn't completely healed."

Chase's body is locked tight with tension while his eyes are blazing with fire. "You had every reason to believe I'd ask you to marry me, and while it doesn't change a damn thing right now, I want you to know that's exactly what I wanted. That's exactly what I should have done."

I sigh and shake my head. "You're right. It doesn't change a thing." His eyes painfully close. I hate how deep our conversation has turned and I'm ready to lighten the mood.

"Are you hungry? I was planning to fix dinner."

A gentle smile crosses his face. "I'd love to eat dinner with you." And just like that, the tension from our conversation melts away.

CHASE

I might have a slight addiction—one that's worse than any drugs I've taken—and that's my obsession with Jordan Taylor. She goes to work and I start a countdown in my head until I think she'll be home.

I know I'm bored, which is a new concept to me, but never in my life has a clock moved so damn slow as it has since I've moved in next to Jordan. I've gone out, bought new shit for my place, and I've found a few restaurants nearby I like. I even purchased a membership at a gym a few blocks from our apartment building, but I can only work out for so long. To help kill time, I've even gone out Christmas shopping for my mom, and I'm seriously embarrassed to tell anyone how much TV I've watched in the last few days. But as soon as the evening rolls around, I jump and run to my door the second I think I hear her return. Which is exactly why I know she just arrived home.

I gave her roughly ten minutes before I knock on her door. I'm hoping that's enough time to avoid looking like a stalker, which I almost am.

I knock a second time and she opens her door with a smile on her face. She's already in casual clothing, meaning she either ditched her work attire the second she arrived home or she didn't come from work.

"Hey, come in," she says as she steps back, allowing me to come inside. The moment I'm in her apartment, I spot a vase filled with flowers—expensive flowers, if I had to make a guess.

"What are those?" I ask, pointing towards the vase as Jordan's eyes follow my hand.

"Flowers?" I can't tell if that was a question or an answer.

"From your parents?"

Jordan nervously bites her lip. "No."

Fuck. My eyes search for a card but I don't see one. I wonder if it's the same douchebag that was waiting on her last week or if I have more than one guy I'm competing against.

"What are your plans for the holidays?" Jordan obviously doesn't want to discuss her flowers or the person that sent them any more than I want her to have them.

"I don't have any. What about you?"

Her eyes scrunch. "What do you mean? Your mother hasn't made plans to be with you?" Ma has checked out on life, at least where I'm concerned. But I'm not mad. She needs this time to figure out who she is and I have no desire to leave New York or Jordan to fly across the country—at least not until I know where I stand with Jordan.

"No, she's not ready to have a family thing yet. She'll get there," I add.

Jordan walks around her sofa then takes a seat, waiting for me to do the same. Every night this week I've come over to her apartment. We usually end up eating dinner and watching TV but that's where we stop. Neither of us has tried to take it a step further, and with those damn flowers sitting behind us, I have to wonder how quickly I need to make my move.

"I usually go to my parents' house for Christmas. Even though it's freezing, I love sitting out on the beach on Christmas day. I'm sure if you don't have plans my parents will be okay with you joining us." She gives me a beautiful smile.

"I would love nothing more than to spend the day with you and your family," I say.

My mood lifts instantly. Someone sent her flowers— flowers that are screaming "*Pick me!*"— but she just made plans with me for Christmas day. I might not know what I'm up against, but I know I'm not about to go down without a fight.

chapter 17

CHASE

I see Don as I make my way inside my apartment building. I'm about to greet him with a smile when I spot my father sitting in the same chair I used the day I waited forever on Jordan.

"What are you doing here?" I question as my nerves fray. My father has always been firm and demanding, which in turn means everything is his way or else.

"I thought you would come to your senses by now, but I guess your head is more screwed up than I thought." My breathing picks up as his comment consumes my good mood from earlier.

"How dare you," I say. Out of the corner of my eye, I spot Don's eyes go wide with shock.

"How dare I? You have a lot of nerve, kid. After everything I've done for you, you just up and fucking quit? You don't even wait to see how next year might play out?" he growls, trying but failing to keep his voice quiet.

I shake my head in disgust. I can't believe it took me twenty-nine years to see my father for what he truly is.

On some level, I've always known he was working his own agenda, but I never thought he'd continue to push if my health was at risk.

"You don't seem to understand this, but this is my career. This is my life, and I'm the one that has to live with the consequences." My voice was soft but firm.

"Just like that? You can walk away from the only thing that matters?"

I narrow my eyes and growl, "No, not just like that. Finally, I'm able to *walk towards* the only thing that matters."

My dad looks at me with pure disappointment. A few months ago, it would have bothered me, but not anymore.

"What kid in their right mind doesn't dream of being a professional player? But at some point in my life, it stopped being my dream and became yours. You've spent years trying to convince everyone—including me—that this is what I wanted but that was crap. I wanted Jordan and you wouldn't listen to me, but I'm done with that. I let her walk out of my life to please you and I've spent the last ten years miserable." He flinches slightly but otherwise remains quiet. "I could be married, still happily playing ball, and probably would have a few kids by now if I hadn't listened to you. I still want that life. One that includes people I love and family that will have my back no matter what, but unfortunately, right now, that doesn't include you."

His irritation is clear as day. "You'll regret this. One day you'll regret giving up your career for a girl." My eyes drift painfully shut. When I open them, I draw in a deep breath.

"Instead of fighting for Ma, you're here fighting for my career—something I've already given up. Maybe if you had given Ma even an ounce of the effort you've put towards my career you'd have a good marriage. Instead, yours is heading towards a divorce."

His eyes flash with anger. "That's none of your business," he says, barely above a whisper.

"None of my business? You're my parents, of course this is my business." I lean in closer. "My life in the NFL was none of your business, but how you treat my mother sure as fuck is."

He scowls, baffled as to how to handle me. I've never stood up to him before and I can't for the life of me understand why I waited until now to finally say what I feel. "I don't think there's anything you can do to fix your relationship with Ma, and at this point, I'm not sure if there's anything you can do to fix things between us, either." To my surprise, a look of pain and maybe even sorrow crosses his face. "Go home, wherever that is, and live your damn life for a change. Maybe one day I'll forgive you, but that isn't going to be today—or anytime soon, for that matter."

My dad swallows and slowly shakes his head as I spot Jordan standing next to the main entrance. I have no idea how long she's been there or how much she's overheard, but I smile and hold my hand out for her, which she gladly walks over and takes.

"Mr. Adams," she mumbles as she stands next to me. My father's eyes latch on to our connected hands before looking me in the face and sighing. I'm not naïve. I know my father isn't going to magically change his opinion about my relationship with Jordan, but I think he might be admitting defeat.

"It's nice to see you again," Jordan says, trying her best to be polite. Instead of answering her, he stands in front of us for a few seconds before turning and walking out of our building.

I knew at some point I would have to face my father, but I wasn't expecting it to happen today.

Jordan squeezes my hand. "Are you okay?" she questions with concern.

I shrug. "I don't know." Still holding her hand, I turn us towards the elevator and push the button.

After the doors open and we step inside, Jordan steps in front of me and wraps her arms around my waist. "I'm sorry." She breathes into my chest.

"Me, too," I say as I wrap my arms around her. "I wish he'd see how great life could have been with my mother if he even tried for a second to focus on his own life instead of mine." Everything good in my life has happened thanks to my father, but the same can be said for everything bad that's happened.

Jordan pulls back and studies my features for a moment. "I think deep down your father's motives came from a good place. He's just not capable of seeing past what he thinks is right." My father has never been nice to Jordan, and I didn't stand up for her when I should have. Instead of hating both of us, she shows me compassion, something I'm positive I don't deserve.

"Thank you."

Her eyebrows scrunch. "For what?"

"For being you and for allowing me a place in your life."

Jordan gives me a beautiful, almost shy smile as the elevator doors open. "You hungry?"

Normally, anytime I have had to listen to my father rip into me, all I want to do is be left alone, but tonight I want to be with Jordan. "Starving," I add with a smirk, causing her to laugh.

"Good, because I have dinner all planned out," she tells me as I follow her inside her apartment, feeling happier than I have in a very long time.

Jordan

Chase has lived in New York for close to three weeks now and two of those weeks he's been my neighbor. Every night when I get home from work, he finds a reason to wander over. We usually end up spending an hour or two catching up on the last ten years. When our conversations wind down, he heads back to his apartment. The thing that surprises me the most is he hasn't once tried to make a move on me. Not even a kiss. Our hug in the elevator the day his father showed up was the last time we shared a real moment—a moment I thought was a step closer to starting a relationship. A part of me is disappointed that nothing has happened since, and the other part of me is relieved because I don't want to mess up this unique friendship we've formed.

Not that long ago, Chase told me he could never be just my friend, but maybe that's changed. Either way, I'm in a dilemma. I need a date—or it's highly suggested that I go with a date—to an annual Christmas gala in which Natural Cosmetics is a major contributor, and as the CEO, I'm expected to attend. Last year I went with Derek Brooks, the same man that tends to call me anytime he wants a date without a hassle—the same man that keeps sending me flowers—but I haven't actually spoken to Derek in months, and I'm not sure I want to open that door again.

Asking Caleb would be wrong. He texted and called me off and on for a few days after the morning he showed up at my place, but I told him nothing was going to happen between us. I haven't seen or spoken to him since before Thanksgiving and the last thing I want to do is lead him on by asking him out.

This leaves me wondering if I should ask Chase. Asking him seems like the practical thing to do, but what if it ruins the friendship we're building? I've seen Chase looking at me—in ways that aren't always friendly—but he's never acted in a way that's anything but friendly.

I continue to stew over my own thoughts as I hear the nightly knock on my door. However, tonight when I open it, Chase looks like he's ready to head out on the town, and I quickly find out that's because he is.

"Hey." I close my mouth so he won't see me drooling over how tempting he looks. Chase has on black pants paired with a dark blue shirt, no tie, and has the collar unbuttoned, looking professional but relaxed at the same time.

His dark wavy hair is brushed back in a way that's totally Chase. He hasn't shaved in almost two weeks and the beard that he's growing only adds to his impeccable look. Everything in my body goes haywire when he licks his lips.

"Hey, yourself. I have to go out tonight with a group of people I'll be working with. We're going over my retirement announcement and exactly what and when things will be released, but I wanted to stop by and tell you personally that I wouldn't be home."

After the way he's been acting, I was under the impression

he was going to do everything in his power to win me back, but right now I'm not sure what to think. If he were only casually meeting his new work friends—on a Friday night, no less—I'd expect him to ask me to go with him. Unless he's meeting a woman and this is more of a date than a business dinner. Oh God ...my stomach turns and I become light headed at the thought.

No matter what his real plans are, he's heading out into the city looking like sex on a stick on a Friday night. I, of course, didn't make plans because I was banking on him coming over and the two of us talking all evening.

"Oh, okay. Well, have fun," I mumble as I start to close my door, but Chase puts his hand up, stopping me from closing it.

"Is everything okay?" His eyes narrow as he watches me closely.

I'm being emotional for no real reason. I asked for slow and that's exactly what he's delivered. I can't punish him for doing what I asked.

"Yep. Everything is fine. Maybe I'll see you tomorrow?" I add in a tone I hope sounds chipper.

"Maybe?" he questions, sounding confused. I know he can tell something is bothering me, but luckily for me my cell starts ringing loud enough that Chase is able to hear it from the hallway.

"I better get that. See you later." This time I put on a huge smile, and thanks to either my smile or the fact that he needs to leave, he drops his hand and steps back.

"Yeah, I'll see you tomorrow." After another baffled look, he turns and walks towards the elevator. I grab my phone and see that it's Lace, someone I've really neglected lately.

"Hey, what's up?"

"I'm at Zen, hurry your ass up and get down here! Fucking hot guys everywhere!" Before Chase knocked on my door, Zen was the last place I wanted to go, but knowing he's out on the town, I don't want to sit at home like some loser, especially on a Friday night.

"Give me an hour."

Club Zen is packed like normal. When I arrived, I couldn't find Lacey anywhere but when I finally spot her I stop dead in my tracks. That's because Caleb is sitting at her table. He isn't the only person in the group she's with, but still a little heads up would have been nice.

"Jordan!" Everyone standing within ten feet of her turns and looks at me. "Holy shit! You out did yourself, bitch." My entire body goes tense at her extremely loud comment.

When I was picking out something to wear, all I could picture in my head was Chase and some model like Carrie having drinks then going back to her place, which had me choosing a very sexy, very low cut black dress. Paired, of course, with five-inch heels that make my legs look amazing. And if the way Caleb is staring at me is any indication, then I must look good.

"Thanks, and not that you care, but you're not talking you're screaming," I tell her.

Lacey completely ignores my remark. "Our firm won a huge case today. I didn't work on it, but Caleb did and he invited me to tag along. Since arriving here, I've enjoyed several adult drinks." The music changes and Lacey lets out a scream before taking off towards the dance floor.

"She's right, you know. You look fantastic." I take a deep

breath and turn towards Caleb, who is standing behind me, talking softly into my ear.

"Thank you and congratulations on the win," I add with a smile.

"Thanks. I can't take too much credit. I was the fourth chair, which was more of a glorified errand boy." This must have been the case he was working on when he was too busy to go out with me but not too busy to go out with that other woman. Geez, apparently I'm still a little bitter because thinking about that still pisses me off. "Can I buy you a drink?"

I tilt my head towards the drink in my hand, the one I purchased while I was looking for Lacey. "Thanks, but I'm good."

"I'm glad you came tonight. I've wanted to explain about that other woman—"

I interrupt before he has the opportunity to piss me off. "I know the rules. We weren't exclusive. Hell, we hadn't even had sex yet so I have no right to be upset with you, but you told me you were going to be tied up with the case you were working on all weekend when in fact you went out with another woman."

Caleb looks disappointed but he also sounds like he's coming to terms with the fact that I'm not backing down. "You're right. I owed a buddy from law school a favor and he set me up with his cousin that had just moved into town. I went, acted nice, and then called it an evening. I chose not to share that with you because to me it wasn't a big deal. But I should have told you and that's on me."

My stomach twists. "Maybe it was a sign. Did you at least like this woman you went out with?" I smile again, hoping I can turn this around and at least be friends. After all, we share a friend that seems to be important to both of us.

"No, not at all. She moved here from Philly with five cats. *Five*. I called my friend Jason up and told him I hated him and if the day ever comes that I need something, he's going to owe me big. That was before I found out you were scraping me off because of it."

"Um . . ." I mumble my words because I feel like shit, but at the same time, I wasn't feeling a connection towards him in the first place. "I'm sorry. I didn't know it at the time, but things for me would have turned awkward, anyway. My ex just moved into the city and is renting the apartment directly next to mine."

His eyes narrow. "The guy that was waiting on you?" I bite my lip and nod my head yes. "Is he hoping to rekindle something with you?"

I take a sip of my drink before replying to give myself a second to decide how to answer. "I don't know. I thought he was but then ...I'm not sure." I shrug.

Caleb looks me directly in the eyes as he adds, "He's a fucking tool if he doesn't and he didn't strike me as one. And let me add that if he moved in next to you, knowing where you lived, then he wants more. I can barely stand living in the same city, even one as big as New York, with a few of my exes. I would never in a million years rent a place next to any of them if I wasn't trying my hardest to win her back."

I smile at his comment. "I thought that, too, but he's being friendly, just friendly," I add.

Caleb sighs. "Friendly is the way any guy wants to start. Especially if he's afraid he might scare the woman off. I'm going to go out on a limb here and guess that he's probably the one who fucked up the first time to make him your ex. If so, he's more than likely trying to ensure his place in your world before he officially claims you."

I swear my heart speeds up at his words. If tonight has proven anything to me, it's that I want more from Chase. Baby steps might still be required but I know I want to be more than just his friend.

"Thanks, Caleb. I'm sorry things didn't work out between us but I don't think they were meant to in the first place. And since we're both friends with Lacey, this is probably for the best."

We turn at the same time to see Lacey practically having sex with a man on the dance floor. "Yeah, we might need to team up when she goes out on the town. She's more than one person can handle these days."

Shit, that's no joke. I thought when Lacey graduated and landed a job she would start settling in more as an adult but the opposite seems to be happening—at least the last few months have felt that way. Maybe it's time I force her to sit down and talk to me about what's really going on.

"I think you're right. I'm glad I saw you tonight."

Caleb slowly nods his head. "Yeah, me too."

CHASE

Last night I had dinner with four executives that I'll be working with once my title is official. Everyone was nice and easy to get along with, but the whole time I couldn't stop thinking about Jordan and how different she acted once I told her I had plans.

I've been struggling to keep things simple and friendly between us, but I've been trying to make her realize I'm not the same punk ass kid that broke her heart.

I wasn't sure what last night was going to entail and I didn't think bringing a friend would be deemed acceptable. A girlfriend maybe, but I couldn't take Jordan and then introduce her as my friend.

Dinner lasted about two hours and I was home less than three hours from the time I left, which was around ten o'clock. I decided it wasn't too late so I stopped at Jordan's door and knocked. She didn't answer. It was possible she went to bed but I wasn't sure, so I called her and I got her voicemail.

I knocked again on Jordan's door today around eight in the morning. I figured if she went to bed early the night before then it wasn't rude to ring her that early in the morning, but again she didn't answer her door. Now her phone isn't even ringing. It's going straight to her voicemail.

Every time I hear the elevator door open, I run to the peephole to see if it's her, and this time it finally pays off. Only when I open my door, I feel like I'm going to be sick.

I find Jordan unlocking her door and she's wearing a skimpy, tight black dress that does very little to cover her body paired with some wild bed head. The kicker is, it's ten in the morning and she's just now returning from whatever or whoever she did last night. *Fuck*. Why did I think it was a good idea to move in next to her? Oh, that's right. It was because I was positive I could win her back.

"Hey. How did last night go?" she asks before she

nervously starts chewing on her lip.

My eyes take her in from top to bottom, but I can't form words to reply to her. "I went out last night," she adds while fidgeting with her dress and trying to tame her wild hair. "Did your dinner go as planned?"

I nod my head yes. When it becomes clear that I'm not going to talk to her about the particulars of my evening, she finishes turning her key and opens the door. "Okay—"

Before she can finish her statement, I've backed her into her apartment and kicked the door shut with my foot. "Who did you get dressed up for?" I ask in a firm, almost angry tone.

She gives me a bewildered look before looking down at her dress. "No one," she quietly says.

I wet my lips and take a deep breath in an attempt to keep my cool. "Lacey called me after you left for your dinner. I met her and ended up back at her place."

Fuck, I hope that's the truth. I know I don't have any reason to believe she would lie to me, but right now seeing her in that dress, knowing guys were probably imagining what she looked like naked, has my blood boiling.

"So, this is how you normally dress when you go out with your friends?" I ask, gritting my teeth, trying my hardest to keep the growl out of my voice.

"What is it to you, Chase? I went out, had fun, and crashed at Lacey's. It was either that or take a cab by myself at three in the morning."

I painfully close my eyes at the thought of her dressed like this and wandering the city at that time of night, or any time of night for that matter.

"I would have come and got you. If you ...I will . . ." I'm stumbling around with what I should say. I want to scream and yell and demand she never walk out her door dressed like a fucking sex goddess without me again but I don't want her to send me packing, which is exactly what I fear will happen if I do.

"I tried calling you. Did you turn your phone off?" I ask.

"Oh." Jordan flips open her tiny purse and grabs her phone then walks over to a charger to plug it in. "My phone died. Since I wasn't expecting to go out last night, I hadn't charged it since before I went to work. I was going to charge it at Lacey's but I forgot all about it."

Phoenix and New York are nothing alike, but even I know it's dangerous to be out in this city without a phone, add that to how she's dressed and I'm wondering how Jordan has survived here this long without being seriously harmed.

"Last night, it went okay?" she asks again, trying to change the subject.

I crack my neck and start rubbing my temples. "Yeah. Last night was fine." I did nothing to keep the irritation out of my voice.

"Well, seeing how you're being surly, I think I'm going to take a bath. I'll talk to you later, Chase." Jordan turns, ready to walk away from me.

"I'm sorry, it's just ...I'm having a hard time here," I painfully admit.

Her annoyed expression hasn't wavered. "What exactly are you having a hard time with?"

I try my best to keep my voice neutral when I say, "I wanted to ask you to go with me last night but it was a business dinner. That's not something you take a friend to, and I wasn't sure if I asked you to go and someone asked if you were my girlfriend how you'd handle that, so I thought I could go do what I had to and then make it back home in time to see you again.

"Instead, I come home three hours later only to find you were gone. Then you don't come home until today, wearing a dress that probably gave a hard on to every man you walked past." Her eyes go wide with shock as I take a deep, calming breath.

"In my head, you're mine and other men shouldn't get to look at you the way I do. So, forgive me but ...I'm having a hard time dealing with this." I wave my hand between us.

Jordan's face relaxes and she slowly walks over towards me. "Last night when you told me you were going to dinner, all I could think about was how you were probably out with a *Carrie* and then afterwards you'd go back to her place. When Lacey asked me to join her, I put on a dress I bought but never had the guts to wear then headed out to meet her." I'm both pleased and confused by her comment.

"I'm very fucking thankful that you don't make a habit of dressing like this when you go out drinking with your friends. But what in the hell do you mean I was out with a Carrie?"

She shrugs. "Carrie, you know, the girl that called herself your girlfriend."

Carrie is a part of my memory that has never completely cleared. Dr. Stein said it's possible she played such a small role in my life that my brain might never remember her.

Stein said it's the same principle when you meet someone casually then later on not remember where or how you know them, which follows in line with what Jake has told me: Carrie was nothing more than a woman I occasionally had sex with, and she was definitely not my girlfriend.

However, Carrie walked into my house and attached herself to me during a time I wasn't mentally functioning properly. That's all Jordan remembers. What I need her to understand is Carrie, or any other woman, doesn't hold a candle to her.

"Jordan, I'm trying to ensure that I don't push you too fast too soon, but that doesn't mean I want anyone else. You are it for me. Fuck, I woke up imagining you were my damn wife when in reality you're a woman I hadn't even seen in ten years. Even my subconscious wants to be with you. Not Carrie or any other woman that might try to throw themselves at me." I exhale loudly, "I haven't been with a woman since we were together in Honolulu, and I don't want to be with anyone except you."

Jordan's hands reach the bottom of her dress and she slowly pulls it up and over her head, leaving her standing in only a pair of black sheer panties. She tosses her dress somewhere but my eyes are locked on her fantastic tits that are out on display.

Arguing with Jordan wasn't making me horny but the second her dress disappeared my dick became painfully hard. My mouth starts to water as I close the distance between us. "Jesus, baby. This right here is why I would never want another woman," I say with a groan as my eyes haze over with desire.

Jordan reaches up to my neck and pulls my head down to hers. Our mouths start moving together in a kiss so hot I'm hoping it's a sign of what's to come.

When Jordan pulls back, the lust and desire I see in her eyes has me wrapping my hands around her waist and lifting her up. She wraps her legs around my waist and I walk us in the direction of her bedroom.

I toss her on the bed then start to unbuckle my pants. "Baby, are you sure you're okay with what I'm about to do to your magnificent little body?" I ask, hoping like hell she doesn't shoot me down.

"I guess that depends on what you plan to do to me." Her smile tells me everything I need to know. She wants me, she wants this.

"I'm going to make you come as many times as possible."

Her eyes shine after hearing my promise. "Well, then by all means, do whatever you want to me," she says with a laugh in her voice.

I crawl up the bed then start kissing her lips. I explore her hot mouth before I pull away to work my way down her exquisite body. I kiss her neck, then her collarbone, and then I find myself sucking one of her rosy nipples into my mouth.

"Um . . ." she mumbles. Her nipples harden and stay at peeks as I work my way down her flat stomach. When I reach her pubic bone, I smile. This is exactly where I've wanted my face for weeks. I push open her folds and allow my tongue to enjoy a taste of heaven, which rewards me a delicious sounding moan from Jordan.

I lick her from top to bottom until I suck her clit into my mouth. Her hips start to lift off the bed and her moans become one long, never-ending noise. Her heels start digging into the bed as I add a finger. I pump it in and out as she starts to succumb to the pleasure I'm giving her. She's close, I can tell by how tight she feels on my finger. Her mouth opens but no more sounds come out as I add my thumb to her clit, causing her whole body to tremble with pleasure.

"Oh. My. God." Jordan is out of breath while she's coming down from her climax, while I'm smiling like the happy bastard that I am.

"Sheesh, Chase. That was ...you need ...to do that again sometime in the very near future." My body manages to relax even more knowing she doesn't plan for this to be a one-time deal.

"Baby, I would be more than happy to go down on you every day if you allowed me to."

She smiles with her eyes half-closed. "Well, I guess it's a good thing you're my neighbor, then." And just like that, my body coils with tension. I want to be more—a lot more than a fucking neighbor to Jordan.

Her eyes fully open as she takes in my sudden change. "Hey, what's wrong? Why did you check out on me?" Jordan asks as she searches my eyes for an answer. If she wants an answer ...then I'll give her one.

"I don't want to be your neighbor anymore; I want us to be more than that."

Jordan's eyes go wide with shock but I don't know why, not after everything I've laid out for her today.

"I want to be with you, too, but I don't think we're ready to live together." I scrunch my eyes, taking my own turn to look confused.

"You said you didn't want to be my neighbor anymore, and while I'm good with us exploring where this might go, I'm not sure I'm ready to live with a man quite yet."

Phew. "I didn't mean it like that," I rush out. "I meant I want my title in your life to be more than your neighbor. I want a real place in your life. One where I don't have to share you with other men, where I don't have to wake up every day wondering if I might do or say something that could ruin everything," I add.

A comical expression comes over Jordan. "I'll tell everyone you're my lover. How does that sound?" She smirks.

This woman is batty. "Yeah, baby, you can introduce me to everyone you know with the exception of your parents as your lover. However, I think I need to start fucking you so I can probably earn my title." I quickly hop off the bed and strip the rest of my clothing off before climbing back up her body.

I'm sure if I was listening to someone else tell me how they fell in love at sixteen after one glance at the girl they wanted to spend the rest of their life with I would think they were ludicrous, but it happened, and it happened to me. I'm positive not a day has gone by in twelve years that I haven't loved this woman with all of my heart, and as I spread her legs open and slowly sink inside of her, I know I'll never find another person I'll love more.

"Oh God." she moans out. I absolutely love how vocal Jordan is during sex. She doesn't appear to hold back anything. "Don't stop," she breathes out. I grab one of her legs and wrap it behind my back then start ramming into her.

"You feel so fucking good. Jesus, Jordan," I growl out.

Jordan's glossy eyes ignite my desire even more. "Faster. I need it faster," she says, arching her back and pushing her hips up to meet my thrusts.

"I love fucking your hungry little body," I tell her with a smirk. I can feel her quiver against my cock. She moans again as her body starts to shudder then seconds later she's squeezes me tighter than I can ever remember.

"You said you wanted a bath, but how about a shower?" I reach my arms around her back and pick her up. I walk the two of us to her bathroom, keeping my dick buried deep inside of her the entire time. Once we're inside the shower with the water on, my need to move takes over. I thrust then groan from how hot and tight she feels, but I can't hold off any longer. Gripping her hips, I start slamming in and out of her as hard as I can.

Her arms are wrapped around my neck as we stare into each other's eyes. Jordan was the first girl I ever had sex with, therefore my first experience involved emotions. Emotions have not played a part in any physical relationship I've had with a woman in the last ten years, which left me feeling like my sex life was always lacking. And it was. It was lacking the right person.

What we're doing, what we're sharing, is much more than just sex, and there's no way I can go back to anything stupid or meaningless again.

I moan out her name as I continue to thrust in and out of her. She feels too damn good paired with how long it's been since we've had sex, and I know I'm not going to last much longer.

After two orgasms, Jordan's body doesn't seem nearly as close as I'd like her to be. I move a hand between us and I start rubbing her clit in circles. "I can't. Chase, I can't," she says while shaking her head.

"Yes you can." Her heavy eyes lock with mine. I keep my finger on her clit as my dick continues pounding into her.

"Oh shit," she mumbles as I feel her starting to twitch against me.

"That's it, baby. Come on my dick," I say. My cock is ready to explode any second but thankfully Jordan appears to be close.

"Oh. Fuck. Oh God," she screams as she arches her back with her head resting against the shower wall. Her mouth drops open but again nothing comes out as I feel her come on my dick. When her body shakes with the last of her release, I finally let go and follow her. "Fuck …Goddamn, Jordan." I tilt my head down and I look at her face to find a range of emotions, but satisfaction seems to be the one that's most clear.

"This right here is ours. No one else gets this." I take a deep breath and watch her closely. She agreed to more but I want to make sure she knows exactly where I stand with other men being in her life.

When she speaks, her voice is soft and gentle. "I spent ten years looking for someone that could make me feel the way you do, but it's you. Only you my heart wants." My body finally relaxes, probably for the first time in years.

"God, Jordan. Somewhere along the way, I lost the person I really am, but I was able to find him again, thanks to you." A beautiful and happy smile crosses her face.

"Good, now let's really take a shower, then I need a long nap because I was up all night taking care of Lacey."

"Okay, baby. Shower then sleep."

chapter 18

Jordan

Sunday morning, my eyes drift open as the sun shines brightly into my bedroom. When I start to move, I feel an arm tighten around me, pulling me even closer to his very warm and very naked body.

"Where do you think you're going?" Hearing Chase's voice first thing in the morning might be my new favorite thing.

"I need to use the bathroom."

Chase leans forward and tucks my hair behind my ear then he starts kissing his way down the curve of my neck.

"Hurry back. The bed will be too cold and lonely without you," he says with his face nuzzled into my neck.

I giggle then hop out of the bed. Before I head to the bathroom, I turn and stand next to the bed, completely naked.

"You could always put on some clothing ...to warm up your cold body." He grins but he's not looking at me, he's staring at my boobs.

"If we put clothes on, we'll be taking them right back off. Now hurry up or I'll start without you." He chuckles.

"Start without me, what . . ." I stop talking when I see his hand go under the covers and he starts stroking himself while his eyes are still glued to my chest. "Hey, none of that. Give me a second and I'll be right back to make sure you're taken care of."

I quickly use the bathroom and I'm washing my hands when I hear a knock at my front door. Other than another neighbor, there are only three people who can get up to my room without my doorman notifying me: my mom, dad, and Lacey. My parents would never come into the city without giving me advance warning; therefore, I'm putting my money on it being Lacey.

I slip into my robe as I walk back into my bedroom. "Hey, I think Lacey is here." A strangled moan that sounds on the verge of pain comes from Chase.

"You're fucking kidding me, right?" Before I can answer, I can hear another knock much louder than the first one.

"Okay, this is a special exception. Feel free to carry on without me." I smirk before walking to my bedroom door.

Chase immediately pulls his hand out from the covers. "Fuck no I'm not using my hand. Go talk to your friend and we'll continue this together after she's gone," he says with a pout.

I move my finger across my lips like I'm trying to decide what to do when Lacey starts banging and shouting for me to open the door. "Hold on, I'm coming." I yell, hopefully loud enough for her to hear.

As I'm walking out of my room, I hear Chase mumble something like "Unfortunately you're not."

I have no idea why Lacey would be at my apartment this early on a Sunday morning, but after the way she drank herself stupid Friday night, I'm a little worried about her. I open the door and Lacey is standing there with an annoyed look on her face.

"Seriously? What took you so long to answer the fucking door?" Lacey comes off rude and abrasive to a lot of people, but happy, mad, or anything in between, this is how she always speaks, unless, of course she's in a courtroom.

"Good morning to you to, sunshine. What has you out and about this early on a Sunday?" I ask.

Lacey's eyes are burning a hole in me when she blurts out, "Did you fucking get laid? You're never this happy unless you got yourself a piece of ass."

Before I can tell her shut the hell up and be quiet, Chase is clearing his throat, probably bothered from overhearing Lacey's remark.

"Oh. I didn't know you had company. That explains why you left me outside forever."

I roll my eyes and shake my head rather than argue about how long she waited on me. "What about your rule that guys don't sleep over?" she rudely questions.

"Lacey!" I shout. "Don't come over here and act like a bitch." I glance over at Chase and he's gone from bothered to fuming, and I don't know if it's because how Lacey is acting or from what she said.

Lacey sighs and softens her voice before she speaks up again. "I came over here to see if you wanted to go grab lunch. I owe you for taking care of me Friday night, but I should have called first, sorry."

Lacey rarely apologizes using words. Usually when she's done something to piss me off, she butters me up to make sure I'm no longer mad at her. This only confirms what I was already thinking: something's wrong.

"What's going on with you?" I softly ask. My best friend

appears lost and lonely, and I know in my heart she's keeping something from me.

"Nothing." She exhales loudly. "Seriously. I'm just stressed about my workload. We seem to go out less and less these days so when I do get the chance to cut loose and have fun I try to soak up as much as I can. And before you say anything, I agree Friday night I drank beyond my limit, and if it wasn't for you and Caleb, God only knows what might have happened to me." She gives me a half-smile. "That's my reason for coming over today. I wanted to thank you for taking care of me."

The second Caleb's name slips out, Chase goes rock solid and his pissy mood from moments ago is back, only now he appears to be furious.

"Caleb? Isn't that the guy you dated a few weeks back? And you were out with him Friday night?" he questions in a harsh tone.

"No."

"Yes."

Lacey and I both answered at the exact same time. "Lacey, be quiet for a second." I turn my back on her and walk until I'm standing directly in front of Chase. "I went to meet Lacey at Club Zen. I didn't know Caleb was going to be there until after I got there. I promise it was no big deal. If anything, we cleared the air and things between us don't feel awkward anymore."

Chase's bad temper hasn't settled in the least bit.

"Chill out. They were being friends. If it hadn't been for them, I don't know how I would have made it home."

His face reddens more. "He went back to her place with the two of you?" He growls out his question as his eyes narrow to slits.

I'm not sure what he thinks happened between Caleb and me but his comment is dripping with accusations, which catches me off balance. We spent the last twenty-four hours naked and in bed together and he's debating whether the night before we slept together—actually, only hours before—if I was screwing another man.

"Yes, Caleb helped me get Lacey to her apartment. He wanted to make sure we both made it home safely. After Lacey was done getting sick and in bed for the night, Caleb left and went home." The entire time I was talking I made sure my tone was cool and distant, hoping he'd understand how distasteful his comment was. And it worked. His face softens and his shoulders sag.

"I'm sorry. I didn't mean to be an ass, but thoughts of you, him, and that dress went through my mind and I couldn't stop myself." His voice is calm and relaxed, but I can tell he's still trying hard to keep cool.

"That dress was fucking hot. I didn't know you had it in you to wear something like that without already being smashed," Lacey adds.

My patience for this conversation is officially over. "Okay. I get it. The dress was sexy, and I won't be wearing it again. And, Lacey, please watch how much you drink. I don't care if you only go out once a month, Friday night was excessive and you had me worried."

I can tell I made my point when Lacey's expression softens. "I'm sorry. If I get like that again, you have my permission to kick my ass. Promise."

Chase's arms slide around my waist from behind as he pulls my body tight against his chest, causing Lacey's brows to scrunch. "When did this happen? I thought you two were just friends?" she questions.

I can't help the enormous grin that comes over my face. "I found her coming home in that dress yesterday morning and I couldn't help myself. Needless to say, I haven't left her apartment since," Chase adds.

Lacey looks back and forth between us, and I can tell she's unsure of what to say. I told Lacey how much I want Chase and how scared I've been to open that door again, and the whole time Lacey didn't have much to say, which is shocking.

Lacey takes a deep breath and locks her eyes with Chase. "In the year and half that I've been practicing law, I've worked on five murder cases. Despicable, horrible things you couldn't even begin to imagine, I read about in detail. I've also read how some of these murderers got off free and clear. I'll take that knowledge and use it to kill you and get rid of your body without anyone ever knowing who wacked you if you ever hurt my girl again." Lacey clears her throat, "Are we clear, Mr. Adams?" she adds in a sweet voice that doesn't match her words.

I've only had the pleasure of watching Lacey in court a handful of times and I never doubted her ability. This right here proves what a hardass she can be when push comes to shove; a world of difference from the woman you'd meet out at a bar after a few drinks.

Chase blinks hard a few times. "Um ...I understand where you're coming from. That's an extreme way of getting your point across, but I hear you loud and clear. Believe me, no one wants to see Jordan hurt again, least of all me."

"As long as we're clear. I take it he's going with you Saturday, then?"

Oh shit, my stomach drops. I forgot all about that stupid gala. "What's going on Saturday?" Chase asks, looking directly at me.

I pipe in before Lacey can once again make matters worse. "I have to go to this formal charity function for work. It's no big deal. I was going to talk to you about it later." I shrug.

"She needs a date and—" Lacey turns her attention to me "—I think that dumbass Brooks finally got the hint that you wouldn't be going with him again this year. How many dozens of flowers did he have to send before he got the message?"

"Brooks?" That comment comes from Chase, but he's looking at Lacey while he waits for an answer.

"Oh, he's a loser ex of Jordan's. He's fucking gorgeous to look at, but he sucks in the relationship department. And he's been sending Jordan flowers every other day for weeks now, but it doesn't do anything to change what a rich loser he is. This one time—"

"Okay ...enough!" I shout. "The last thing I need is for you two to start swapping stories," I add in an annoyed voice.

My little outburst seems to have saved me from a pissed off Chase.

"Seeing as you have better things to do then have lunch with me, I'm going to head home."

"No, we can go have lunch," I quickly add as Lacey is already heading towards the door.

"Nah, I wasn't really hungry, anyway. I needed to know you weren't mad at me."

Chase lets go of my waist and I follow her to the door. "Of course I'm not mad, but seriously, let's talk soon about whatever is bothering you." Lacey tries to hide the pained look that quickly crossed her face, but I still caught it.

"Yeah, we'll get together soon without the drinks," she says.

After a quick kiss on my cheek, she's gone. I shut the door then turn and I see Chase standing with his arms crossed over his chest. He's watching me like he's waiting for me to say something, but I remain silent.

He starts tapping his foot as his patience slips. Lacey said several inappropriate comments that I'm sure upset him. Like it or not, I have a past and so does Chase. We both did things we'd rather not talk about—things we'd rather forget—and I'm not about to be punished for my past. Instead of saying anything, I walk right past him but he tags me around the waist and pulls me into his chest.

His face nuzzles into my neck. "I want ...no that's not it. I need to fuck you so you'll remember who you belong to. Listening to your friend ...Shit. I want to tie you to my bed and do filthy twisted things to your sweet, fuckable little body. The next time either of us thinks about sex, it will be this moment, my fingers, my hand, my cock that you remember making you come."

I swallow loudly. Holy. Shit. Goodbye to the sweet boy I remember and hello to the shameless man that just promised me dirty pleasure.

"Yes, please," I say with a smile.

CHASE

I'm standing in a pretentious ballroom surrounded by rich assholes in a suit and tie and I hate it. I fucking hate it, but the alternative was Jordan coming with someone else, and I wasn't about to let that happen.

Jordan told me her friend Lacey's firm was invited but not Lacey personally. I think that was a good call because I have an overwhelming feeling to walk up to one of these rich assholes and say something beyond inappropriate just to see how they'd react, something I'm sure Lacey would actually do.

After I first moved in next to Jordan and we were rekindling our relationship, she had mentioned that Lacey wasn't my biggest fan, and I'm not surprised. Actually, it's because of that loyalty I find myself respecting her even more. She has my girl's back no matter what and that's the way a true friend acts.

What I don't care for is listening to the obnoxious tales of Jordan with other men. I'm hoping for my fucking sake that some of the shit she's said in the last week has been exaggerated, otherwise I might go crazy.

After the visit from Lacey that Sunday morning, Jordan patiently waited for me to ask if anything, or all of what she said, was true, but instead of asking, I allowed my depraved mind to have its way with her. After a nice, long, hard fuck, my mind seemed to relax knowing the only person she was thinking about was me and how I make her feel.

While she's over talking to a group of uptight assholes, I head to the bar for a drink. My mother hates that I have a drink even occasionally, but alcohol was never my vice.

Other than a couple months ago when Jordan left, I've treated alcohol like any other fool. I may have a drink here or there, and if I do get smashed, I wake up feeling like shit and drinking again in the near future is out of the question.

"A football player, huh? Jordan seems to be dipping into all sorts of society these days."

I set my drink down and look over at the smug bastard who undoubtedly thinks he has something over me. "Yes, I'm Chase Adams, and you are?" I hold my hand out, playing the game that everyone here is expected to play, which is to put on nice clothes and pretend to like everyone, all the while making sure everyone knows you're better than them.

This man, who obviously has money, is looking at my hand like he'd rather me knee him in the balls than actually greet me with respect.

He looks down his nose as he finally shakes my hand and confirms my suspicions. "Derek Brooks." Brooks. That was all I had to hear to know that this man was once with my girl.

Something I never want to admit to Jordan is I probably wouldn't recognize a majority of the women I've screwed in the last ten years. I went from being too messed up to remember them to fucking groupies. Most of the women that hang around players are looking for one of two things: a good story to tell or they're hoping to land a husband. I always looked for the first option. Of course, that doesn't explain how Carrie got her hooks in me. But other than Carrie, everyone else is a nameless, faceless woman that never mattered to me.

The same doesn't apply to Jordan. Even living in a city as large as New York, it appears she dated men from the same circle she lives in. That means I need to learn to control my urge to kill every man that's ever known her in a way my own stupidity allowed.

Brooks gives me an arrogant smile before throwing out another insult. "Jordan always struck me as someone with too much class to subject herself to an athlete." His eyes narrow as he gives me a shitty grin.

I hold my smile, never once letting on that his comment actually stung. "I was thinking the same thing about you. I've known Jordan since we were teenagers and I never would have guessed her to date a pretentious prick, but evidently she has," I add, acting smug myself.

"Hello, gentlemen." We both turn at the same time to see Jordan staring at us with questioning eyes. I hold out my hand to her, and like the incredible woman I know she is, she walks straight into my arms. I look over, keeping the smug smile on my face, to see that Brooks doesn't look the least bit phased by my claim on her.

"Jordan, I was just telling your friend here that I was surprised you'd have to stoop so low as to ask a man that plays a game for a living to be your date."

I'm ready to punch this fucker in the face and show him the type of game I play when I look at Jordan, who has an evil smile on her face, which has me holding back.

Jordan points her finger at me while she keeps her eyes locked on this prick. "I almost told Chase's secretary when she called that I wasn't available, but then she informed me that my date included an endless amount of orgasms if I were to agree, so I thought what the hell. A girl can't pass up an offer like that." Jordan shrugs then gives me a beautiful smile.

Brooks's whole body goes tense at her comment. I'm

not sure exactly what point she was trying to make, but I know almost certainly that she was complimenting me and not him. Without another word, he turns and walks away, causing Jordan to laugh. Her smile and carefree attitude is downright sexy.

"I guess I officially owe you endless amounts of orgasms, Ms. Taylor. Remind me if I ever get a secretary to thank her." I chuckle.

"Oh, you're so funny, big guy. Let me go mingle for a few more minutes then we can get out of here."

I grab ahold of her hand. "Not so fast. Endless orgasms can be a lot of pressure on a guy. We need to go somewhere so I can give you one now. I assure you mingling afterwards will be much easier."

Jordan's eyes go wide and she starts to protest, but I've already turned her, walking us out into the hall to find somewhere to be alone. This insane need to mark her as mine every time I'm reminded of her past could easily backfire, but for now she's tolerating it.

I jerk us into a corner at the end of the hallway that leads away from the ballroom, and within seconds my mouth is attacking hers. My hands move from her arms to her tits, stroking each nipple to a hard point. I move the top of her dress to the side and pull an exquisite breast into my mouth.

"Geez, Chase, someone could see us," she pants out.

I reluctantly pull away from her chest to look her in the eyes. "I won't allow anyone to see you, believe me, baby. All of this is only for my eyes." With my comment, her face changes. Lust and desire for what I'm promising takes over, encouraging me to go on.

I look over my shoulder to confirm no one is around

then I lean down and slip her panties down and off her legs, tucking them in my pocket. On my way back up, I catch the end of her dress and bring it up with me as my other hand is unzipping my pants.

Seconds later my dick is sliding into her wet pussy while my fingers are digging into her ass, keeping her in the exact place we both desperately need. Our breathing becomes fast, almost labored, but that doesn't stop me from sucking a nipple into my mouth, causing her to moan my name rather loud.

"Shhh, baby, this is for us. We don't need an audience."

Jordan doesn't say another word as she arches her back against the wall, causing me to go even deeper. "Fuck, baby." I moan out, probably louder than Jordan did moments ago.

"Faster. I need you to go faster," she says through a pant.

I can feel her tightening on me as I'm rocking into her with as much speed as I can manage since I'm the one holding both her and her damn dress up. Thankfully, a few thrusts later I feel her start to clench down on me. I continue to slam inside of her, and moments later she starts to come on my dick. She shudders her release, causing me to fall with her.

As we start to come back down from our sexual high, I take a good long look at this woman and I realize I'm not just crazy about her; I'm totally in love with her.

I thought I loved her before when my memory was still hazy, and afterwards, I was left confused about what my real feelings were, but there's nothing to be confused about now. I absolutely love this woman and somehow life has offered me another chance. A chance, I without a doubt don't deserve, but one that I would have been a fucking fool not to take.

"Wow." She sighs with a smile on her face. "When I thought about coming here tonight, getting fucked against the wall never crossed my mind. You sure have a way of delivering a memorable time, Mr. Adams." She's relaxed and joking, just the way I want her.

"I'm glad to hear that, baby. Now go back and mingle so we can get the fuck out of here and away from these rich, snobby assholes."

I pull out of her then she slides down the wall until her feet reach the floor. After she fixes her dress, she starts to walk away. She stops a few steps from me and looks over her shoulder. "I've never mingled without panties on before," she whispers with a smirk on her face.

Before I have the chance to offer them back, she's gone. I just claimed her, marked her as mine in every way a man can, and still I'm going half-berserk at the idea of her walking around those assholes smelling like sex and without any panties on.

God, I need to get a ring on that woman's finger, but she's not ready. I know that much. In the meantime, I guess I'll reap the rewards of my own irrational thoughts.

chapter 19

Jordan

Christmas and New Year's came and went, and Chase spent every moment of the holidays with me. The two of us made the trip together to my parents' house. We stopped a few times on the drive down at places I knew he'd love.

We invited his mother to come and stay with us, but she's hell bent on the idea of establishing a life that doesn't have her depending on her son or soon to be ex-husband.

I somehow convinced Chase we shouldn't exchange gifts. Even though it's been three months since I first saw him again, we spent most of that time apart, and I knew what would happen if we bought each other presents. It would be something impersonal like a gift card or something over the top like a piece of jewelry. When we do start exchanging gifts, I want them to be gifts from the heart. Items only a person that really knows you would think to buy, and as much as I care and probably love Chase, we're not to that point yet.

Chase and I are doing what we do best on a Friday night. We're staying in and watching a movie. Ten minutes into the movie, my intercom buzzes. Chase, who's practically moved in with me, climbs out from behind me on the couch and walks over to answer it without even questioning if he should.

"Yes?"

"Oh, Mr. Adams, you're the person I was looking for. You told me if I thought you were home and not answering at your apartment to try Ms. Taylor's." Chase turns and smiles at me. He seems quite proud of himself that he's informed Don of his usual whereabouts. "You have a visitor here, a Mr. Jake Girard. He'd like approval to come up."

"Oh. Sure, send him up." Chase's brows bunch and he sighs, acting displeased that his friend is here.

"Would you also tell Ms. Taylor that Ms. Davis is on her way up as well?"

"Certainly. Thanks, Don," he replies in a flat tone.

I stand up and walk over to him, keeping my eyes glued to his. "I take it you didn't know that Jake was in town?" I ask as I wrap my arms around his waist.

His jaw ticks. "No. We didn't make the playoffs so he's officially done for the year, but I would have expected him to call before coming all the way here."

I look around. "Where's your cell phone? Maybe he tried calling you."

Chase nervously laughs. "Fuck, I don't know. Ma rarely calls and when I'm with you I usually don't pay any attention to where I've left it."

I walk to the door and open it so Jake will know which apartment we're in. When I turn around, I run straight into Chase's chest. His arms wrap around me as he nuzzles his face into my neck. "You mean the world to me, you know that right?"

Everything in me stills. I thought his friend was here

to visit him, but something's not right. Before I have the chance to say anything, Lacey and Caleb step off the elevator and start marching down the hall towards our apartments.

Lacey walks up to Chase, acting like she's ready to kill him. "You stupid son-of-a-bitch!" she hollers, pointing her finger at his chest.

"Whoa, what's going on, Lace?" I'm definitely missing something.

Before Lacey can get another word out, Caleb speaks up. "Chill the fuck out, Lace. If you get arrested, I'm not bailing your ass out, especially for assault charges."

As Lacey starts ranting about killing Chase—and the many places she'll dump his body—the elevator opens again with Jake's arrival. He walks down the hallway with a smile on his face that fades away when Lacey turns to me.

"Did the asshole tell you that she's pregnant?" My heart drops to my stomach because Lacey is still pointing at Chase. My eyes thin to slits. *Chase got someone pregnant?* "Whore Barbie made a very public announcement earlier today that she's expecting this jackass's kid."

I immediately step away from Chase as his eyes are searching mine for something. "I don't understand . . ." I whisper.

"He fucked her and now she's knocked up. Unfortunately, there's nothing else to understand," Lacey snaps back.

"Seriously? What's wrong with you? Lacey, you need to learn a little tact when you're dealing with someone else's emotions," Caleb tells Lacey, who turns her glare towards him.

I shake my head. "Oh my God." I walk back into my apartment, not caring if anyone follows me. I reach the back of the couch, the same place we were laying peacefully just moments ago, when Jake speaks up.

"Looks like I arrived just in time for the party," he adds in his normal, arrogant voice.

"Yeah, blockhead, you arrived just in time to take your jerk of a friend home with you," Lacey tells him.

I sit down and place my head in my hands, trying like hell not to cry. "Chase, dude, when was the last time you tapped that nitwit Carrie?"

Oh, shit. I'm going to be sick if I have to sit here and listen to this. "And you said I didn't have any tact? What about this asshole?"

At the moment, I agree with Lacey.

"I only asked because I know for a fact that Carrie has been fucking just about any guy with a few zeros in his checking account, and unless Chase here fucked her after he woke up, after you came and went, then the kid she's having—if she's even pregnant—isn't his."

Before I can even process everything he just said, Chase jumps to his feet in excitement. "Yesssss!" he says, punching the air.

"Hold the fuck up, how does that prove he's not the father? He's admitted to having sex with her," Lacey says while narrowing her eyes at Chase.

My hands are trembling in fear; fear that the life I started to picture isn't going to happen—again. "Because Carrie is dumber than a box of rocks. She told the tabloid that bought her story that she is eight weeks pregnant. Chase's concussion was almost fifteen weeks ago, so unless he had sex with her after his memory went haywire, then due to her own words, it's not his kid." Jake crosses his arms over his chest and waits for Chase to say something.

My eyes find Chase's, looking for him to tell me again

there's no way this could be his kid. "I didn't. I swear. I'm sure there was a time in my life when I had sex with her, but I don't even remember it," he tells me as his eyes closely watch my every move.

"Jordan, his head is messed up. Without a DNA test, you can't be positive." I look at Lacey then back to Chase, who's getting pissed.

"I had a hard time remembering shit that happened *before* I hit my head not afterwards. I know for a fact I didn't fuck Carrie after I woke up in that goddamn hospital!" he growls at Lacey.

Caleb tugs on Lacey's arm and thankfully she relents on whatever she planned to say next.

"You have to believe me, Jordan. I know when you walked out of my door she had herself attached to my arm, but that is the one and only time I remember being in the same room with her. She came over to my house several times after you left, but I refused to even let her step foot in my house." He pauses and I can hear the desperation in his voice.

"The two months we were apart, I spent it either alone, with Ma, or with my doctors, and the entire time I was obsessing over losing you. I wanted to be with you, to be good enough to be a part of your world, but I also knew I had fucked up twice. I couldn't come back to you until I had my shit together, but not a second of that time did I spend with Carrie or any other female other than my mother."

He's waiting for me to respond. I know Chase is panicked and desperate enough to do anything to keep me, but I don't believe he'd lie—not about this.

I take a calming breath. "You knew something was

wrong earlier. Why? Why didn't you come to me with this if you knew?" My voice cracks and I sniffle, still holding in my tears.

Chase drops to his knees in front of me and takes my face in his hands. "Remember when I purchased a new phone?" I nod. "That was because Carrie kept calling and texting my old one. I never gave her my new number but somehow she got it and shortly before Christmas, Carrie started calling and texting me nonstop, telling me she needed to see me. I never responded to a single one and eventually I blocked her number, but then she started calling me from her friend's phone, but I ignored them, too. I knew in my gut the second Don said Jake was here it had something to do with Carrie's calls. We've been in a great place for a while now. I didn't want to ruin it. That's the same reason I didn't get a new number. You would've ask me why and I promised I wouldn't lie, remember?"

I remember. Of course I remember. "But why would Carrie say that ...?"

Jake speaks up before Chase has a chance. "Happens all the time. Carrie either doesn't know who the father is or Chase here makes more money than the other fool. After all, he hasn't publically announced his retirement yet so she could be looking long-term. Keep in mind, Carrie may not even be pregnant. Women sleep with professional players all the time hoping to get something other than just sex out of it." Jake shrugs. "Personally, I never dipped my stick in Carrie because she had *money hungry bitch* written all over her," he adds.

Everyone was watching Jake until Lacey pipes up. "Are you fucking serious? Tact? I don't have any tact but this asshole does? I need to seriously reevaluate my friends."

Chase's eyes come back to me, looking for me to tell him everything is okay. "I love you." I rush out.

I told Chase I loved him when we were teenagers, I told him again when we were living in a magic bubble in Honolulu, but this is the first time I've said these words to him since he arrived to New York.

"Thank fuck. God, I love you, too. I never stopped and I never will."

Chase wraps me up tight, breathing me in at my neck while everyone else in the room slowly leaves.

"I'll spend the rest of my life being the man you deserve. I promise."

That's all I needed to hear. My heart has belonged to this man since I was only sixteen years old. I tried my hardest during the ten years we were apart to find what we have with someone else and I never came close. Now I'm starting to understand that's because he's the only person my heart will ever want.

CHASE

Jake Girard became a good friend the day we started playing ball together, but he became my best friend when he got on a plane and flew across the country to ensure Carrie didn't ruin my relationship with Jordan.

I'm sure long before Carrie has her baby, I would have done the math and figured out for myself that I couldn't have been the father. But who knows the damage that could have caused in the meantime.

Seeing as our team didn't make the playoffs, Jake's season is officially over and yesterday I announced my retirement as an NFL player. I also publically spoke about my pending job here in New York. With everything going on, Jake has decided to stay and spend a few days with me.

Announcing my retirement at the age of twenty-nine has proven to be harder than I originally thought. There are only two things keeping me sane at the moment: Jordan and my new job. Outside of being an actual coach, this is the second best job a retired player could have. As a communications rep, I'm the middleman working to ensure both the players and the commissioners are satisfied. Seeing how the other side works, I know it's unlikely I'll ever coach someday. In my file it shows *pre-existing memory complications.*

Looking at that on paper was hard. I had a unique form of retrograde amnesia that was a direct result of the blow to my head, and it's unlikely that it will ever happen again. On paper, however, I look like a liability, which sucks and will more than likely keep me from my dream of coaching.

Jake is sleeping off a crazy night in my guest room. A room I only set up in hopes that my Ma would come and visit, but she hasn't. My concern for my mother is worsening each day. I understood her reasoning for skipping Thanksgiving with me, but not Christmas and New Year's. She told me she's spent the last thirty years of her life being a wife and mother and she needs to figure out who she is again. Now I'm giving her the only thing she's asked for: time.

As I get out of the shower, I can hear my phone ringing, but I didn't grab it in time. The damn thing started ringing again seconds later with an unknown caller.

I ignore it and see that I have several missed calls from unknown numbers when the damn thing rings again. I have no idea what's going on, which has me answering the fucking thing. "Hello?"

"Hello, is this Mr. Chase Adams from the Arizona Cardinals?"

"Uh..." I mumbled because I already know I shouldn't say a word to whoever this caller is.

"This is Dennis Murphy from Beyond The Ball. I was hoping to get your statement regarding your drug addiction and your stints in rehab."

My mouth opens but nothing comes out as I quickly end the call. However, my phone immediately starts ringing. Holy fuck. How in the world did anyone find out that I went to rehab?

I can feel my chest tightening because there are only three people in my life that know about my drug use and if any of them had a part in the media finding out about this I'll lose my fucking head.

How in the hell did that jackass even get my goddamn number in the first place, or any of these fuckers who keep calling? Unless, of course, Carrie sold my number, which wouldn't surprise me.

My phone hasn't stopped ringing since I hung up on the bastard. When it rings again, I pick it up and slam it against the wall, shattering the screen. Thankfully, the damn thing stops ringing. My chest is heaving with rage as I take deep breaths, attempting to calm myself.

This is just fucking spectacular. The day I walked out of rehab my dad made it clear that we were never to talk about my problem again. I went years pretending like I wasn't an addict. I avoided going anywhere I thought someone could be using because in the back of my mind, I wasn't sure I fully trusted myself.

Once I graduated and was drafted by the NFL, I felt like I was truly past my problem or, at least, my daily struggle to stay clean. Drug use of any kind is forbidden at the college and professional level, but once I was away from the college lifestyle—the constant parties—I found I could better control my environment, mainly because I was surrounded by people who wouldn't dare touch the stuff.

I find it convenient that whoever leaked this story waited until after I announced my retirement, which has me wondering if it is, in fact, my dad. But after how strict he was about never speaking about it again, I find it hard that he would want to hurt me this way.

"What the fuck did you throw against the wall?" I look over my shoulder at Jake, whose hair is going every which direction while he's wearing only a pair of boxer briefs.

"Don't worry about it," I growl out.

Jake starts rubbing his eyes. "Fuck, dude. I'm too hungover to deal with a pissy attitude this damn early."

I've thought long and hard about what Jordan said to me in regards to what happen with Drake. I want to do something. I don't want his death to be in vain. However, I wasn't exactly ready for the world to know about my problem, definitely not when my new job hasn't officially started.

"Sorry. Some fucker from a gossip site somehow got my number and asked me shit I didn't want to talk about, so I threw my phone across the room," I say with a shrug.

"Fucking Carrie. The dumb bitch is trying to make sure she makes your life hell. Probably hoping you'll at least pay her to shut up and go away."

I'm compelled to laugh off his statement and go lock myself in my room, but it's only a matter of time before Jake hears the real story floating around. As a friend, he deserves to hear the truth from me.

"No, it's not Carrie this time."

Jake drops to my couch, waiting for me to say something. "After I broke up with Jordan and left for school, I didn't handle my freshman year very well. I got hooked on some serious fucking drugs. Ruined a friend's life and almost my own. I ended up in rehab, got out, and I've never touched a drug since. I'm not sure how but someone leaked that story to the press."

My unexpected announcement catches him off guard. I can tell by the shocked expression he's still wearing. "Wow, dude. I had no idea. Does Jordan know about all of this?"

This is exactly why I like Jake. I tell him something awful about me and instead of making a huge deal he's worried about how this information could affect me personally.

"Yes, thank God. I told her when I first got to town. I know I probably sound like a pussy when I say this, but I knew from the second I laid my eyes on Jordan she was going to change my life. She inspired me to want a future that had nothing to do with football or college, and letting her go was the dumbest thing I've ever done. I have to take ownership for my actions but I go back to that moment and I wonder if I had only followed my heart, where would I be today?"

"You can agonize the rest of your life over the ifs or you can start living the life you have. I would have a hard fucking time if I couldn't play ball anymore, but I also don't have a woman like Jordan waiting at home for me every night. Take the life that's in front of you and start living it. Own up to the shit in your past and then move forward."

When I look up at him, he has a know-it-all smile plastered on his face.

"Okay, Dr. Phil," I reply.

"Whatever, asshole. I'm going back to sleep." Talking to Jake settles my nerves. I wish I had the chance to tell my story—definitely would've liked to do it on my terms—but ready or not, now is the opportunity to truly put everything behind me.

chapter
20

Jordan

"You need to make a statement that you attended last month's gala with Mr. Adams as a friend. He's your neighbor but you two are nothing more than friends."

I start shaking my head in disgust. "No, I won't," I grumble out. "I love Chase and this is an unfortunate incident that will blow over," I firmly state.

I can hear the sighs throughout the table. "Ms. Taylor, you're the CEO of Natural Cosmetics. Our profits have been up quite a bit in the last year and a half, and we can't afford to take a hit, even a small one because you're only looking out for your own personal interest."

Today when I woke up in the same bed as Chase, life was great. I went to work and started my day out like any other, then Silvia came in. Apparently, my business phone was ringing off the hook from reporters hoping to get my comment about the fact that I'm dating a drug addict.

I had a hard time processing what was happening. Chase's addiction is a secret, or at least I thought so. I know Chase would have told me if he had plans to make such an announcement, which leaves me to believe the story was leaked, but the who and why part is still a mystery—at least to me. I would love to ask Chase what's going on, but he's not answering his phone.

"Chase Adams's story is not mine to tell, but I will say this much. What the media is running with is something that happened almost nine years ago. I'm not the CEO of a pharmaceutical company, and Mr. Adams has held a position for years in the NFL where players are regularly drug tested. He was never found with a trace of anything illegal in his system."

I stop and look around the boardroom. About half of the members are missing, seeing as this was a last minute meeting to discuss my personal life.

"Jordan, hun, personally, I understand where you're coming from and I agree with you. But as the CEO, you're the face of this company. When a woman goes to buy our products, we don't want her wondering if the money she's spending is going to profit a drug deal. Announce that the two of you aren't actually a couple and later if this blows over and he's able to prove your claims of innocence, then go back to however you're living your life," one of the nicer board members says.

My stomach sinks at the idea of denying Chase for even a second. He's without a doubt the love of my life. I like my job, before Chase I actually loved it, but if I'm forced to choose, it won't be Natural Cosmetics.

"If you are asking me to make a decision right now, then it won't be the one you're looking for. The media hasn't even heard what Chase has to say and everyone in this room has already condemned him. My grandfather left me in charge of this company before he passed away, but it doesn't have to stay that way."

Another board member named John, who has remained silent, speaks up. "Jordan's right. We need to sit back and see which direction this blows with the media before we force her to make a decision that could impact this company in ways that are just as unhealthy. Like Francis said earlier, the last year and a half has been very good for the company, and Jordan played a huge part in making that happen."

My heart starts to settle for the first time since I walked into this room. I mouth a small thank you to John for being the only voice of reason.

"One week, Jordan. Get this messed cleared up and do it in the best way possible for Natural." Francis is older than dirt and worked with my grandfather for thirty plus years. He's also of the mindset that any negative news will cause the company to go under. If I had to wager a guess, it would be that ninety percent of the people who purchase our products never pay any attention to what's going on in the CEO's life.

I'm more worried about how this will affect Chase and his new job.

I stand up after everyone else starts to clear out of the room and switch my phone that I've had in my hand the whole time, off of silent. I was hoping that Chase would finally call me, but no such luck. As I'm walking back into my office, my phone starts ringing.

"Hello," I rush out.

"Jordan, sweetheart, are you doing okay?" I breathe out a sigh. It's my dad. "I saw online that people are claiming that Chase is a drug addict."

I close my eyes. This is the last thing I need. At Thanksgiving, my parents were cordial to Chase because they aren't the type of people to act rude to someone that's treating them with respect, unlike Steve Adams. However, they weren't pleased that he was back in my life. Like Lacey, they personally had to deal with the aftermath of our breakup and they immediately worried about Chase's intentions towards me.

Christmas was a different story. My parents saw how happy Chase was making me and because they are truly amazing and forgiving people, they let go of any anger they once had. My mother actually told me, *'If you are able to forgive him, then so am I.'* When Carrie's announcement came a few days ago, my mom called and I could hear the concern in her voice. Once I explained everything, her concern switched from me to how Chase was handling the situation.

"Dad, everything is fine. After Chase left for college, he struggled for a while with the pressure he felt he was under, but he got help and hasn't touched a drug since."

"Well, I didn't figure he would have been in the NFL for that many years without failing a drug test if he had a real addiction, but Jordan—" he clears his throat "—someone who even dapples in drugs is asking for problems."

I take in a deep breath, one I'm positive my dad heard. "He doesn't. He hasn't touched a drug in almost nine years. The media is just looking for crap to talk about and a former football player who is also a recovering addict is sparking interest during playoffs."

"I'm relieved to hear this, but if it's all the same, I think I might come up and stay with you tonight. Your mom is visiting Aunt Becky and she's the reason we don't go into the city more often as it is."

I had pictured my night a little different: going home and talking with Chase, finding out when he's going to tell the media what really happened, then I planned to take his mind off everything that's going on in a different way; a way that isn't going to happen with my dad in the apartment.

"Yeah, Dad, that sounds great. I'm actually leaving Natural now so I can head home and check on Chase."

"Okay, sweetheart. I haven't even packed a bag yet and with the drive, it will be a close to three hours before I get there."

I smile knowing my father won't rest until he's assured that I'm really okay. "I'll see you soon, Dad."

"Goodbye, sweetheart."

Before my meeting, I had Silvia cancel the rest of my day so I could head home early. This is the first time that my anxiety with Chase isn't over us. I'm worried about how he's handling the news, and since I haven't been able to talk to him, my worry is slowly turning into panic.

CHASE

I spoke with Jackie, the human resource specialist that hired me at headquarters, and quickly explained what happened. I felt the dread seep in as I told another person in my life that I'm a drug addict. With Jackie, however, I left Drake out of the story. As of now, his name hasn't come up in any of the online articles, and no matter how badly I want to redeem his death, now is not the time.

Without a comment from me, the media is spinning

a story that makes it sound like I'm a regular drug user that somehow never got caught while playing professional football, and my drug problem is the real reason I retired. This story on the heels of Carrie trying to pin her pregnancy on me, and my announcement to retire, are not painting me in a very good light. I felt the urge to be sick set in when I saw a report wondering if the CEO of Natural Cosmetics is also an addict.

Last weekend was the first weekend of playoffs and Jackie said after a full investigation, and if my story checks out, then my job should be safe, but right now, everyone is more worried about ensuring the playoffs happen without any scandals.

The only statement the NFL plans to make at the moment where I'm concerned is to announce that I was regularly tested and every test came back clean. The NFL does not tolerate drug use of any kind and they believe that any or all drugs taken by me didn't happen while I was a professional player.

All of this sounds promising long-term. I just need to keep to myself until this blows over.

I'm brought out of my thoughts when I hear a knock on my door. Thank God for a doorman, otherwise I would be worried about it being a pap looking for their next big break.

When I look through the peephole, I see Jordan turning away and walking towards her own door, which has me opening mine.

"Hey."

She continues to unlock her door then she sits her purse inside and turns back to me with a worried look on her face. "Are you okay? I tried calling you but you wouldn't answer and I heard what they are . . ."

She's rambling and I feel like an ass that I couldn't remember her number by heart so I could have called her from Jake's phone. "Yes, I was pissed off earlier and my phone took the brunt of the anger."

"Oh. Um, do you want to come in and talk?" I want to go in and make her feel better but I dread talking about my day, but it needs to happen. Jordan has a right to know what's going on.

"Sure."

The second I pass through Jordan's door, I feel at home. Her apartment isn't any nicer than mine, but this is where my heart belongs.

"Well?" she says, waiting on me to tell her something.

I swallow loudly. "With Carrie trying to pin her pregnancy on me and my retirement, I've been in the news a lot. A reporter thought he would dig a little deeper to see if he could find any skeletons to add to the gossip rags. Somehow, he found a transaction for the payment my father made to River Side that listed me as the patient. The reporter ran with it. He didn't have any idea why I was there but he knew enough and ran the article implying I'm an addict. Since then, every fucking reporter wants an interview."

Worry takes over her expression. "I thought patient information was supposed to be protected." I can see the pain in her eyes, pain for me, and pain for what I'm going through.

"River Side announced a few hours ago that someone breached their security. They will not comment whether I was or was not a patient of theirs, but they're looking to prosecute anyone that was involved with hacking into their system."

"Oh, good. No one knows about the other thing, about your . . ."

She's asking about the fact that I killed my best friend almost four months before I went to rehab. Seeing as my medical records didn't include the drugs that I know I had in my system at the time, my accident wouldn't look like a real story unless I admit to what really happened that day. "No. Nothing about the accident has been brought up, and I doubt it will."

The relief in her eyes is instant. "Thank goodness. That's the last thing you need. When do you plan to make an announcement about what really happened?"

"I don't." The relief I saw in her eyes starts to melt away.

"You don't? Why on earth not? The press is making it sound like you *have* a problem. That you've been using drugs for years and somehow managed to hide it."

"I don't care what other people think about me. I know that I played my ass off every time I stepped out on a field. The NFL doesn't want me to comment right now because they want to keep people's focus on the playoffs, where it should be, and not on a retired player. The people that mean the most to me know what actually happened so fuck everyone else."

Jordan's hands come up and she starts rubbing her temples. "Shit."

Now it's my turn to look confused. "What's wrong?"

"They called a board meeting today at Natural Cosmetics. The members are older than dirt and most of them want me to release a statement that I'm not in a relationship of any kind with you. That we went to the gala last month as friends. Apparently, it looks bad when a twenty-nine year old CEO is dating a known drug addict." She practically laughs off her statement as I feel my world go dark.

They called a board meeting at her company today because of me. Because. Of. Me. I would gladly run to any reporter and start spilling my story regardless of how that would affect my new job, but there will always be people that won't believe me. Once news—especially bad news—surfaces, it's always there, floating in the back of people's minds, even if it isn't true. But in my case, it is. If we stay together, she'll always have people in her life judging her. Judging her for my actions. Holy shit. My heart painfully drops to my stomach.

I take a deep breath when I realize Jordan is talking to me and I haven't heard a word she's said. " ...not going to worry about it."

How the fuck can I let this blow back on her? Jordan is such an incredible person. I can't ...I won't let this affect her job or her life. When people see us together, they'll wonder about her. They'll make assumptions about her based on the shit I've done and I can't let that happen. As she continues to talk, I'm not able to hear a word because all I can hear is my own heartbeat. I can feel the acid turning in my stomach at what I know I have to do, for her.

"I think they're right." I clear my throat. "If we're together, people will always think poorly of you thanks to my reckless behavior. If you aren't with me, then you'll be fine. You're a good person, everyone knows that."

Her eyes thin as her nose scrunches up. "But—"

"No," I quickly cut her off as my heart continues to pound in my chest.

"No buts," I add before taking a deep breath. "When shit like this comes out, it doesn't even matter if it's true or not, it follows a person. Years later, people will look at me and wonder if I'm using and that sucks ,but you know what? It's on me. I fucked up, I do have an addiction, and that addiction could bring me down at any moment. You don't deserve to get caught up in that shit." I run my hands through my hair before looking back at her pained face.

"Fuck, Jordan, you could lose your job, a job that you love because of me. I'm sorry ...I can't let that happen. No, I won't let that happen." My voice is firm as I square my shoulders, waiting for her to reply.

Her eyes are glassed over, tears ready to spill at any moment. "You're doing it again," she says as her voice cracks.

"Doing what?" I growl back, rubbing my hands over my face, beyond frustrated with myself. I look back at Jordan as she blinks several times before softly speaking. "Making decisions—important decisions—for me. Deciding what's best for me without asking me what I want."

God, I fucking hate looking at her like this: in pain and knowing I'm once again the reason for it.

"I won't let my problems blow back on you. I love you too much to do that."

Something changes in Jordan. She straightens her back, brushes the tear that fell, and the light I always see in her beautiful blue eyes dims. "Get out." Her tone is harsh but her voice was soft.

"What?"

"Decision made. Now get the fuck out of my apartment." I'm looking at the woman I love, but she doesn't seem like the Jordan I know and it's all my fault.

"I'll call you in a few days and—"

"No!" she screams. "There's no need to call me, we're

done. Now, please get out of my fucking apartment," she says before turning away from me.

I know what I said, but I'm feeling exactly the way I did ten years ago. I allowed the words to come out of my mouth but that doesn't mean I really wanted them to come true, and just like last time, once I've said them, I start freaking out.

I'll just give her some time to cool down. Maybe then she'll see how this is what's best for her and her career. Instead of saying another word, I quietly walk to her door and leave.

Once I get back into my apartment, I can already feel it. Dread seeps into my system, dread of living a meaningless and lonely life without the only woman I've ever loved.

chapter 21

CHASE

I've been in my apartment for almost an hour now. I've already been sick twice. I want to run back over to Jordan's and beg her to forgive me, to tell her I didn't mean a word I said, but then I remember that I did mean it—at least, the part about not allowing my fuck ups to blow back on her.

By sticking with me, a drug addict, Jordan could end up losing a lot in her life, including a job she's told me before that she loves. *Why am I such a fuck up?* I keep going back to that day in the park when I allowed her to walk out of my life, wondering how different everything could be right now. When I think about it, I picture a life I've always wanted, with Jordan by my side, with a family of our own. And for a short period of time, I actually thought I could make that happen.

I'm going back and forth in my head about going back over there to make sure she's okay when I hear someone knocking, but the sound didn't come from my door. When I look out the peephole, I see Doug Taylor standing outside Jordan's door. After a few more moments, he uses a key, unlocks the door, and goes in.

A few minutes later, Doug is at my door. Shit. He's probably here to kick my ass for once again breaking his daughter's heart. I open the door and brace for his anger.

"Hey, Chase, is Jordan over here? She wasn't in her apartment and she knew I was coming so I figured she must have wandered over here."

"No, she isn't here. She was at her place . . ." I glance over at the clock and see it's been over two hours. "She was home a few hours ago."

A look of concern comes over Doug's face. "Did she tell you where she was going?" Instead of answering, I shake my head no. "What's going on, Chase?"

I let out a frustrated sigh. "Maybe you should ask your daughter."

"I would if she had taken her damn phone with her, so instead I'm asking you. I talked to Jordan less than four hours ago, and she not only knew I was coming up to stay with her, but she told me she would be home when I got here. You're her boyfriend and live right next to her, so I'm asking you. What. Is. Going. On."

Oh, fuck me. Doug Taylor might be a retired military officer, but he can still do scary quite well, even to an ex-football player.

"We aren't together anymore, Mr. Taylor. I didn't know she was leaving, but if I had to guess, she's probably with her friend Lacey."

Without taking his eyes off of me, he grabs his phone and starts calling someone. "Lace, is Jordan with you?" More anger flashes across his face before he adds, "Okay. Call me if you hear from her. She's not in her apartment but her phone is so I have no way of calling her."

Doug's body is tense and he looks at me like he wants to rip my head off. "You want to tell me why you aren't together anymore, because when I spoke with Jordan a few hours ago she failed to mention that. If anything she told me everything was fine, that she was going to head home to check on you. And you know what, Chase?" I swallow and shake my head as I take a step away from him. "I know my daughter. I know her well and I know when she's lying to me. And ...she ...was ...not ...lying. So tell me, why was everything fine a few hours ago and now no one knows where she's at?" Doug's teeth are gritted together as his eyes search mine for answers. Answers that I'm a little nervous to give him.

"Natural Cosmetics called a board meeting to talk to her about her relationship with me, so I gave her an out. I can't be the reason she loses the job she loves."

Doug's eyebrows lift while he's processing my comment. "Wait. You gave her an out or you broke up with her?"

I'm trying to decide how to answer when Doug cuts me off. "You son-of-a-bitch. You did it again." Doug's words echo my earlier thoughts. "Did Jordan ever tell you why she loves her job?" My eyes flare from hearing his question.

"No," I barely mumble out my answer before he starts up again.

"After you broke up with her, Jordan was a mess. She tried to act brave but we knew it was an act. She kept waiting for you to call her and tell her that you had made a mistake, but that never happened. Like you, she lost her way, she just didn't turn to drugs. But that didn't mean she was living her life the way a parent wants for their child. She wandered from one empty relationship to another until she eventually became a different person." My throat tightens at the idea of Jordan with random men.

"Chase, when you were teenagers, do you remember Jordan talking about Natural Cosmetics? About a future that was always hers if she wanted it?" Doug is waiting on an answer I think he already knows.

"No," I whisper.

"Exactly. Did you ever wonder why?"

Of course I've wondered why. Janette Taylor's parents were millionaires and in the two years I dated Jordan in high school never once did she mention it. I knew she was attending college at NYU, and that her grandfather had something to do with her receiving a scholarship there, but I didn't know any more than that because she never breathed a word about it.

"I met Janette when she was seventeen. I had just turned twenty and I knew better than to spend time with a teenager, but I couldn't fight it. Every time my eyes found hers, I knew she belonged to me. I had no idea that Janette came from money because she never acted like it.

"I made sure to keep my hands to myself until she turned eighteen, but then ...well, less than a month later, I asked her to marry me. I didn't have a lot to offer her but I knew I'd never love anyone else the way I love her. We married, I enlisted, and a year later we had a beautiful daughter.

"Janette's father wanted her to join him at Natural but I wanted to be the one that provided for my family, and Janette loved me enough to follow me anywhere I went. She had plans to work at Natural but it wasn't her dream. The day she met me I became her future, and it was the same way for me.

"When Jordan met you, it felt like history was repeating itself. You were younger than me, but I saw the way you looked at my girl. Janette and I knew you two were meant to be together the same way we were." I swallow and try to force down the acid building in my stomach, but Doug's not done with me yet.

"Jordan didn't talk about what she thought her future would hold, because once she met you, everything she thought she knew had changed. Hell, that's why I didn't threaten to kill you then, 'cause I knew. I knew you'd take care of her the way I took care of Janette. Only ...you didn't. You gave her something exquisite then you took it back and broke her heart. Since then she's been looking to find that again but something that special rarely happens twice."

Something exquisite. That describes my relationship with Jordan perfectly. Only I didn't grow up with Doug and Janette Taylor. I didn't get to see what two people in love looked like. Still, I knew. I knew what I had with Jordan wasn't just a case of teenage love, and I still fucked up my future with her. I might have had help. I might have had encouragement from someone running his own agenda, but in the end, it was still me that broke us.

"My daughter loves her job because she made that your replacement. She couldn't have you and she wasn't able to find whatever you two shared with someone else, so she gave up. She gave everything she had to that company because it made the lie she's been living that much easier." My chest tightens listening to him talk, but seconds later it gets worse.

"Chase, I don't think you understand this because of how your father usually spoke to people, including how he spoke to your mother, but you do not back a woman into a corner and refuse to give her an opinion. And you definitely don't do that to my girl." Doug waits for his comment to sink in before adding, "My daughter's heart will probably always belong to you, but that doesn't mean you'll always be the one holding it. Maybe if you stop trying so damn hard to protect her, you'll see it's you that's destroying her."

His last comment was just as painful as he intended it to be. "If I find you around my daughter again, it better be because you're begging her to forgive your stupid ass. And if by some miracle she does, you better plan to spend the rest of your life making her the happiest woman alive."

After giving me a look that would make a lesser man tremble, Doug turns around and walks out of my apartment.

Chase, don't lose the woman God meant for you over some foolish pride.

Oh. God. My heart tightens in my chest.

Something that special rarely happens twice.

When I close my eyes, I can see the tears she tried so hard to keep at bay.

Maybe if you stop trying so damn hard to protect her, you'll see it's you that's destroying her.

Oh. Shit. What have I done? I love this woman. I will always love this woman. A woman who has never given me a reason to walk away, but yet somehow I still do. All I've ever wanted to do was protect her anyway I could. But until this moment ...I didn't realize the person she needed protection from ...was me.

Jordan

Bang bang bang!

"Come on, door ...OPEN!"

I don't know how long I stood in my living room staring at the spot Chase was last in, but once I snapped out of my trance and grasped what happened—again—I grabbed my purse and left.

January in New York City is beyond frigid and my dumb ass forgot to put on a coat before I left. I made it a few blocks before the cold settled in and I realized I was walking down the street in the late afternoon wearing nothing more than a skirt and long sleeve blouse. When I looked up, I saw a bar called Nothing to Lose and, well ...I had nothing to lose. I went in and ordered a drink. I wanted to forget the horrible day I had, therefore I ordered a vodka tonic, hold the tonic. I expected the bartender to look at me funny but he didn't. He just poured my drink and left me be.

I don't know how long I sat there and drank but the sun had finally set and a different crowd was settling in the bar, leaving me to think it was time to go. Home, however, was the last place I wanted to be. I flagged down a cab and gave the driver the only other address I know by heart.

"Door, are you home? Please? I'm here and I don't wanna go. I got nowhere to go, anyway." I turn around and lean against Lacey's door then I slowly slide down until I'm sitting slash lying on the floor, my back to her door. I think it's possible that I had one too many drinks because Lacey's hallway is starting to spin. Moments later, I'm flat on my back, half-in and half-out of Lacey's apartment, staring straight up at my best friend.

"Where in the hell have you been?" Instead of answering, I find myself laughing. Looking at Lacey from this angle is hilarious. "What's so funny?" Again, I don't answer but my laughter hasn't stopped.

"Don't just stand there, help me pick her up." Before I have the chance to even consider who Lacey might be talking to, Jake's face comes into my vision.

"Is she drunk?"

"Wow, Captain Obvious, nothing gets past you."

"You don't have to be a bitch, it was just a question."

"I wasn't being a bitch. When you ask a stupid question expect to get a stupid answer, jackass."

"Jackass? That is not the name you were screaming a little while ago." At some point my laugher faded away, but after Jake's last remark, it returns in full force, causing both of them to stop and look back down at me still lying on the floor.

"Holy shit. You're fucking?" I curl up in a ball, still laughing at the fact that mine and Chase's best friends are screwing. "Fuck ...ing. Fucking. Fucking. Have you ever noticed how funny that word sounds? Fu ...ck ...ing."

"What the hell have you been doing, Jordan Michelle Taylor?" Lacey firmly ask as the two of them help me off the floor.

"I had nothing to lose at Nothing to Lose." Of course I burst out laughing again. Lacey doesn't find anything funny but I see Jake fighting off a smile. Once I stop laughing, I walk over to Lacey's couch and sit down.

"Earlier today, I had everything. Then I had nothing. Again. After having nothing, I decided I should take a walk, but then I got cold and I stopped when I was at Nothing to Lose."

Lacey's patience is gone. "How in the fuck does that tell me a goddamn thing?" she screams.

"Hold up," Jake says.

Thankfully, Lacey turns her evil stare back towards him. "Oh, shut it." Lacey looks back towards me. "Jordan, babe, tell me how four hours ago I got a call from your dad looking for you translates into you taking a walk in five-inch heels without a jacket or a phone?"

As Lacey's words settle in, I sober up quite a bit. Four hours ago? I've been drinking by myself for four hours? And holy shit, I forgot all about my dad coming into the city. Trying my best not to fucking cry, I look Lace directly in the eyes and give it to her straight.

"He did it again." Without another word, Lacey understands exactly what I'm saying.

"Oh shit," she says, giving me a sad look.

"Who did what?" Jake questions.

Lacey turns to him and sighs. "I think you need to leave." Even drunk, I can tell by the way Jake is looking at Lacey that he really likes her. And right now he seems shocked and maybe even pissed that she's kicking him out.

"Why? What's going on?" he tries again.

"Go ask Chase. He did this." I look up to see Lacey waving a hand in my general direction.

"What?" Jake's voice is soft, almost forgiving.

There was a time when I thought Jake Girard was an egotistical jerk, but once he melts a few of his outside layers, I was able to see there's a lot under the surface. A lot like Lacey. Maybe that's why they are having some sort of secret affair.

"Okay, fine. I'll go check on him." He grabs his coat but once he makes it to the door, he turns back towards Lacey and the brilliant smile he shines towards her has my heart completely sold on Jake.

"I'll call ya later."

Lacey, however, must not be as sold. "Yeah, whatever."

Jakes smirks then leaves. Now that we're alone, I can't keep my tears from falling. Lacey moves over and squeezes next to me, never once asking me to say a word. When I finally settle down, I accidentally do a weird hiccup slash burp that has me in another fit of laughter.

"If I recall correctly, I was told not too long ago that drinking away my problems probably isn't the best idea."

I start nodding my head in agreement. "You're right. Unlike you, I didn't actually set out to get drunk."

Lacey just rolls her eyes. "The end result is all the same. Plus, I agree it's a dangerous way to self-medicate."

We're both sitting on her couch, not saying a word. To me it feels like the day is stuck on repeat. Happy. Pissed. Devastated. Then lost.

"Do you think you can make it to my bedroom by yourself?" I slowly stand up then I start walking down the hall. "I'm going to call your dad and let him know you're okay."

I don't even answer; I just keep walking until I find her bedroom. I grab an old tee out of her dresser while tossing all of my clothing off, then I fall down on her bed and moments later everything goes dark.

"How's she feeling?"

"I don't know. She hasn't gotten out of bed yet."

"She's damn lucky I'm not able to punish her anymore

for the stunt she pulled." Shit. That's my father, and he's obviously not happy with me.

"If it matters much, I don't think she set out to get drunk and make us worry about her."

I hear an exaggerated sigh come from my dad. "I know. Yesterday was a flashback to a time we all would rather not remember."

I quickly dig around for a pair of shorts then I head out to Lacey's living room. "I'm sorry. God, Dad, I'm so sorry." He stands up and I run into his arms, where he wraps me up tight. All of the stress and anger from yesterday slowly releases.

My dad pulls away from me then looks me directly in the eyes. "You're going to be fine. No matter what happens, you'll be fine." I wish I shared the same confidence in myself, but with my parents and Lacey by my side, I'm sure I'll bounce back, just not to the person I was yesterday morning—while I still had a life with Chase.

"Come home with me. Your mother will be back tonight. Stay a few days and get your head back on straight."

When we were kids, I knew I loved Chase, but I didn't really know what I was missing when he left. We were just kids. We didn't get to spend every day together, we didn't get to practically live with each other, but now I know. I've basically been living with him for the last month. Getting my head back on straight now holds a whole new meaning.

chapter 22

CHASE

I waited for what seemed like forever for Jordan to return home. I wanted to tell her I was a moron and beg her to forgive me. I don't have a phone and Jordan left hers at home, which leaves me stuck doing nothing but waiting.

I'm sitting in the chair closest to the front door, hoping I will hear her return home when I finally fall asleep. I come awake when I hear someone knocking but it wasn't Jordan, it was Jake.

I swing the door open wide with a sigh then head back to my chair.

Jake steps into my apartment with a strange look on his face. He's watching me like he's waiting on me to say something, but I'm not about to tell a man that jumped on a plane and flew across the country to ensure my relationship to the only woman I've ever loved stayed intact from Carrie's lies that I fucked everything up.

"I don't share when I'm not asked to...often, but now seems very fitting." He swallows then gives me a serious look—a look I haven't seen on Jake but a few times. "Did I ever tell you about how I was engaged once?"

My whole body goes solid at his words. Jake is Mr. Carefree. Women are fun and the second they want more he's gone. "We were in college. I was in love, or so I thought at the time. Classic story, really. I come home early and catch her in bed with a teammate of mine. He was two years older and already looking to be a first-round draft pick, and I guess she didn't want to wait me out."

I have no idea why Jake has decided to share, but I know he's acting more serious now than I can ever remember him being. "I thought I was in love, but actually she was just a good looking girl that was trying to ensure she got where she wanted in life. Nothing about our relationship was real and I was too stupid to realize it at the time.

"She scarred me. Without a fucking doubt she left her mark, but that doesn't mean I don't want that. A woman, a healthy relationship, and, God willing, maybe a family that we'd share together. Now . . ." He nervously clears his throat. "Now I walk around with that scar, looking at a woman with guarded eyes. Fake? They're gone. Needy? Gone. Weak? Gone. Whether I realize it or not, I put every woman I meet through my own personal Jake Girard test, and you want to know something?"

"Um . . ." I barely mumble before he gives me his kill shot.

"You're girl passed. From the second I met her, she passed."

My eyes go wide at his statement. Out of all the days he would come back to my place and tell me this, it has to be today?

"Jordan has class and, yeah, that class might be worlds above yours, but for whatever fucking reason, you're the man she wants. So, why in the world do you continue to toss her away?"

"I..." I'm caught off guard by his question. I knew his demeanor was off when he came here, but fuck me. I did not expect him to already know how badly I screwed things up.

"I know. I fucked up. I'm waiting for her to come home so I can hopefully fix it."

A very sarcastic laugh rumbles from Jake. "Not tonight you won't, buddy. After whatever the fuck you did to her, she wandered around the city and finally showed up at Lacey's place wasted. Wasted. No coat, no cell phone, and she claims she took a fucking cab there."

Holy shit. How in the hell could she have been so stupid? My anger at myself heightens. She never would have gone out without me if I hadn't given her a reason to.

"Let her sleep it off. Then make sure you pull your head out of your ass and fix this. Most people don't get a shot at what you have with Jordan and you somehow managed to have it handed to you a few times. If you don't fix it now ...I doubt you'll get another chance."

After Jake shuts the door to my guest room, a light goes off in my head. Why in the hell was he at Lacey's apartment? To the best of my knowledge, the two of them have only been in the same room twice and neither time did either of them act like they were really fond of the other one.

I guess after Jake's announcement tonight I don't know him as well as I originally thought, but he's still a good friend; a friend that I'm going to start putting a lot more effort towards.

I need to purchase a new phone but right now, I'm being sneaky. Jake is in the shower but he left his phone in my guest room. I've watched him unlock his phone hundreds of times so guessing his password was easy.

I scroll through his contacts but I don't see Lacey's name. I was just about to give up when I see a contact that he called yesterday named Davis. I'm struggling to remember if that's Lacey's last name but I'm fairly certain it is. Plus, he called this person shortly after he left my place and I know at some point he was there.

The phone barely rings before she picks up. "Yes, you have an enormous cock, but no I do not have the time to put up with your obnoxious ass right now." Oh. Fuck. Yes, that is most definitely Lacey on the phone. She's never been my biggest fan and right now I'm only going to add to that.

"Hey, Lacey, it's me, Chase. I was hoping I could talk to Jordan."

The phone goes dead silent, to the point that I pull the phone away from my ear to see if she hung up on me. "Hello? Lacey?"

I can hear her clear her throat, then she gives me the hell I expected. "I'm sorry. When the caller ID says your arrogant ass friend is the one calling it threw me off. I have to switch from one pompous jerk to the other one. I apologize it took me a second. Now back to the question. Did you actually ask me if you could talk to Jordan? The same woman you once again just threw out when it suited you?"

Lacey loves to throw around her comments, but she's just

as arrogant and rude as any man I've ever met. But I've seen firsthand how much she cares for my girl and that's the only reason I've never called her out on her crap. That and it's helped that she hasn't had a reason to yell at me lately.

"I take it that was your rude and bossy way of saying no?"

I can hear her mumbling all sorts of crap to the point that I stop listening until she finally says something that catches my ear. " ...she's not here."

"Wait. What? Jake said she was with you."

"She was, fuck face, but that was last night. She left with her dad."

Her dad. Of course ...and I would bet my firstborn child, a child I plan to have with Jordan, that she's gone back to her parents' house because I know neither of them are at her apartment. I can't leave her alone to stew on what I said. I was wrong. I know that and it's time that Jordan does, too. If it's a requirement that I make a complete fool out myself in front of Doug and Janette, then so be it.

Jordan

Will there ever be a day when I don't love you?

My eyes startle open. I look around, remembering I'm at my parents' house, and then the reality of why I'm here sinks in.

I called Silvia yesterday morning, which was thankfully Friday, and told her I wasn't coming in until next week. If the board wants another meeting then they were going to have it without me.

I get up, grab the sweat pants and shirt of my mother's I wore around last night, then head down to the kitchen for coffee. As I pass my parents' room, I hear my mom let out a soft giggle. That right there is what I want. Not just someone to spend my life with, but someone that makes me laugh, someone who can't wait for me to come home at the end of the day, someone who looks at me like I'm their whole world, and someone that loves me enough not to give up.

I almost had that with Chase ...almost.

After pouring a cup of coffee, I put on a jacket and sit outside on their porch, looking at the bitterly cold water moving in the ocean. My thoughts from the day before, no matter how much I don't want to think about them, are on repeat.

If you aren't with me, then you'll be fine.

How could he say that? My breath catches as a lone tear slides down my face. Without him, how can I ever be fine? Today I'm going to allow myself to cry, then I'm heading back into the city, move if I have to, then I . . .

My thoughts shut down when I see movement out of the corner of my eye. I turn and seconds go by before I realize I'm holding my breath.

Standing on the edge of my parents' porch is Chase, and he looks like he spent the last day the same way I have: completely miserable.

I haven't said a word, but he slowly makes his way over to me then sits in the chair beside me, looking out at the water.

"The last time we sat here and watched waves together, it

was quite a bit warmer."

I don't give any indication that I heard him and after a few moments of silence, he tries again. "There are only two people in the world I would die for before I allowed anything to happen to them ...you and my Ma. Right now, Ma's life is shattered and there's not a thing I can do to fix it. Then you talk about the possibility of losing your job because of me. Well, I thought I could fix that. I never want anything bad to happen to you but in that moment, I wasn't able to see the big picture. That letting you go would hurt more. I'll spend the rest of my life a lonely bastard without you, but I struggle to remember that you love me the same way.

"My Ma, I know she loves me, but she didn't always show it the way your parents do. My dad controlled everything, including how we expressed our emotions. Sometimes it was easy to forget that she cared."

I hate that for him. Even now, as angry as I am, I hate that he wasn't loved the way every child should be.

"I'm sorry I freaked out. As much as I don't want to lose you, I don't want to hurt you, either. I might have been a professional football player, I might have the money I need to provide for you, but I also have it in my head that I'm not good enough for you. I'm a recovering drug addict that's been in the tabloids twice this week for shit that could blow back on you. And I did those things, the things that brought that kind of attention. I'm not innocent. I didn't get Carrie pregnant, but I still allowed her into my life."

I'm chewing on my lip, not really sure what I should say. "But I feel innocent when I'm with you. I've never done anything stupid or crazy when I've had you by my side. You ground me; you give me the peace I didn't even realize I was looking for, a peace I can only find with you."

He's saying everything I want to hear, but how long will this last? The past has shown that Chase handles things by leaving, and my heart isn't capable of withstanding yet another goodbye.

Chase stands up and reaches out, snagging my hand then pulling me to my feet. With his other hand, he takes my coffee and sets it down on the porch rail and then leads me down the steps and out onto the beach.

We start walking, to where, I have no idea, but my parents' house is quite a distance away when he finally stops and turns me in front of him.

"I don't deserve you. I don't think the day will ever come when I believe otherwise. But I know my life isn't worth a damn without you in it."

Chase is staring me directly in the eyes as he slowly drops down to one knee. My eyes go wide when I realize what he's about to do. "From the second I moved to New York, I've wanted to ask you this, but I was afraid you weren't ready. I was afraid if I asked too soon I wouldn't get the answer I wanted.

"I've learned a lot in the last ten years, most of it is what not to do, but still I learned.

"I learned not to depend on something to make it through the day. I learned trust and love don't always go hand in hand. And I learned that my life would never be complete without you in it.

"Jordan Michelle Taylor, if you give me the chance, I will spend the rest of my life by your side. I will spend the rest of my life building you up and never tearing you down. Together we will have the most remarkable family because it will be ours. My heart belongs to you and yours belongs to me, and it's time for us to make it official."

"Um." My mind is still spinning from his unexpected proposal. I look down at my hand and I see Chase has a large princess cut diamond set in a platinum band waiting at the end of my ring finger. He didn't just come here to ask me to forgive him and then decide at the last minute to propose. He came here to do exactly this.

"I was a jackass yesterday. I thought if I was gone, your problem would be gone, but I'm done with that. Together we're going to face problems, but the problems we'll face being apart are a thousand times worse. I know that now—hell, I knew that yesterday, but I freaked. No matter what happens, I'm never going to walk away from you again. We're a team and if you say yes, we always will be."

I should be mad, but at the same time, I don't want to hold on to my anger anymore. I should walk away, but I don't want my heart to be empty again, which is why I say the only thing my heart will allow me to. "Yes, but . . ."

A brilliant smile crosses Chase's beautiful face as he pushes the ring up my finger, then he jumps to his feet and lowers his mouth to mine.

"No, no buts. I get it. I'm done acting like a jackass. Good or bad, you're stuck with me. God, I love you so much, Jordan. I promise I'll spend the rest of my life making sure you're the happiest woman alive."

I've learned a lot in the last ten years, but the biggest lesson I learned is love isn't easy. Love isn't always the picture perfect, happily ever after that girls dream about. Love is often complicated, messy, and sometimes unforgiving. But if given the chance, with the right person, love can complete you.

That's what I've been searching for, the thing I've only

ever found with Chase. I don't need the perfect relationship. I don't need a fancy house filled with extravagant things. I want real, messy, unconditional yet powerful love. And I found that. Now, thanks to Chase, I'm going to keep it forever.

epilogue

CHASE

Six Months later...

From the time I was old enough to remember, my father was telling me I was put on this earth to do big things, and today is by far my biggest accomplishment. Today, I married my best friend, the woman I was put on earth to love and protect. And today is truly the start of our forever.

After Jordan agreed to marry me, our lives took a few bumpy turns. First, Jordan insisted that we go to counseling, both as a couple and as individuals. After all the hours I spent with Dr. Stein, I resisted the idea at first, but like usual, Jordan knew exactly what I needed. Following the Super Bowl, I did an interview where I told the public my personal story regarding my drug use.

My father had me convinced that I should go to my grave without ever talking about my addiction to anyone. However, between Jordan and our counselor, I began to feel a sense of relief.

For one, my story was out and not hanging over me like a black cloud. Another more amazing positive is how I'm using my experience to hopefully help others. I started The Drake Jones Foundation that allows college students and athletes that are struggling with addiction to seek—completely anonymous—counseling for drugs, alcohol or even to help with the undue stress that some feel they're under.

When I was at Ohio State, I thought about seeking help but I was worried the school or, God forbid, my dad would find out, so I continued to hide it, which only made it worse. The foundation Jordan and I started, which is currently already open in two major cities, doesn't require you to give your real name and is completely not-for-profit.

Before the foundation opened, I struggled with what to do regarding my role in Drake's death. I honestly didn't feel sitting in a jail cell for any amount of time would make a difference, other than hurt Jordan, but I still felt responsible. I decided to seek out Drake's family and tell them what happened, but what I found was shocking. Drake's mother was known for her own drug addiction. She died from an overdose when Drake was seventeen but not before he was addicted himself. For a very short period of time, Drake tried to straighten himself out, which is why he gave college a shot, but he was never able to stop using.

I now know from everything I've learned about Drake, he was going to need serious help if he ever kicked his addiction, help I wasn't able to offer him at the time. With no known living relatives I had no one to ask forgiveness from, other than myself. In my heart I don't think Drake would want me going to jail for what happened and I know I'll never put myself in a position to harm someone like that again. Opening the foundation in his name felt like the best way to not only give back but to keep Drake's memory alive.

My parents' divorce was final at the beginning of March. My dad started out fighting my mom but after the interview I gave he stopped and gave her whatever she wanted, which was only her independence from him.

When I was playing for the Cardinals, my parents purchased a home in Phoenix but they kept our family home in Florida. Ma decided to stay in Phoenix with a group of women she'd made friends with, while my dad returned to his families' citrus grove.

I haven't seen or spoken to my dad in almost eight months. I think one day I'll forgive him, but in the meantime, I've let go of my anger regarding him and everything he's done. I think deep down he's a good person that only wanted the best for me; he just went about it the wrong way.

Right now, however, my bride and I have just returned to our honeymoon suite in Honolulu where we were married.

"Thank you for today."

"Thank you?" Jordan is standing in front of me in the strapless white dress that she wore in front of our closest friends and family. I've been dying to get her out of this thing ever since I laid eyes on her. "You might have been mine for a while, but today you officially became mine, so thank you," I add with a huge smile on my face.

Jordan's eyes go soft. "I've belonged to you for almost thirteen years. Maybe I should be thanking you for finally becoming mine."

The lust and desire I see in her eyes are as strong as ever. I tug her close to me and my mouth finds her delicious neck. "Did you see them together today?" she says with a giggle in her voice.

Jordan's remark causes me to slow my assault. "Remember

what we agreed. No matter what trouble those two cause, we're not getting involved."

Jordan is referring to Jake and Lacey. Neither one of us are exactly sure what's going on with those two other than that they hook up quite often. If it's ever brought up in front of both or either of them, they laugh it off like they're just using each other, but Jordan believes differently. She is convinced that they are secretly in love with each other but are too afraid to admit it. Until today, I thought Jordan was exaggerating their feelings because she wants her friend to be happy, but I saw the way Jake looked at Lacey, and it was unlike anything I've seen from him before. Who knows, maybe there is more going on between our friends. Either way, it's not the topic I want to discuss on our wedding night.

"Agreed. We won't get involved in their relationship, but let's not worry about them right now. Tonight I just want to make my beautiful wife come as many times as possible."

Jordan's eyes find mine and I know she's on board with my idea. "That sounds like a fantastic plan, husband."

I brush her hair out of her face and stare into her blue eyes. "Stick around. I'm offering up a lifetime service just for you."

"That's all I've ever wanted. A lifetime with you."

The end

acknowledgements

First and foremost I want to thank my readers. Every friend and fan I've made along the way holds a special place in my heart.

I want to give a shout out to the ladies at S.A.S.S. who endlessly give up their time to help new authors get discovered. I'll never be able to say thank you enough to this amazing group.

Edee Fallon, I don't know what I would do without you. You are more then an editor to me. Our relationship has blossomed into a friendship, and it's one that means a great deal to me.

Juliana Cabrera, I don't think there's anything you can't design that I won't love. Juliana doesn't only design my wonderful covers she beautifully formats my books and answers my endless questions.

Katie Benson you have once again stepped up and read and reread Living With Regret. I love getting text from you, especially ones that have nothing to do with my books. I hope we have many more years of friendship.

I want to say a huge thank you to Judy Miracle with Wicked Babes Blog Reviews for beta reading for me. Your feedback was amazing.

I also want to thank Melissa from Booksmacked Book Blog. Not only did she do an amazing job helping me with the Living With Regret cover reveal, she's spent endless amount of hours helping me promote not only this book, but my others as well.

Colette Trainor, thank you for stopping what you were doing and reading for me. Your feedback helped and your review was amazing.

I want to give a special thanks to Mandy Stevens who tells everyone she knows that her friend is an author. Mandy, I've known you since we were only five years old and I think you are simply fabulous.

READ AN EXCERPT FROM

Beneath the lies
are emerald eyes.

Beneath the
LIES

RIANN C. MILLER

PROLOGUE

"Oh, my God, she canceled." Like normal, my mother's voice screeches over everyone else's. "That little bitch canceled less than ten minutes before we're supposed to leave!"

"Leeta! Not in front of the children." My mother's arms flap around wildly in anger.

"James, we have to go now if we're going to make it on time and we can't take them." Not that I need clarification, but her hand shoots out and points at my brother and me sitting on the sofa.

"I'll call a neighbor to see if I can find someone to come over."

Before my mother can start yelling again, a calm, peaceful voice speaks up. "I'll stay with them." Everyone in the room turns toward the beautiful lady with long black hair who moments ago was snuggled up with my brother.

"Mandy, don't be ridiculous. You don't want to stay home with three kids." My mother practically sneers her comment from across the room.

"Actually, Leeta, I was already feeling uneasy leaving Kate with someone I don't know. Now that you're asking random neighbors, I definitely feel uncomfortable. You three go and I'll stay here."

Uncle Marcus walks up to the soft-spoken lady. He looks at her in a way I've never seen my father look at my mother.

"Mandy, are you sure you're okay with this? I don't have to go—"

"No. No. No. I'll be fine. You go and enjoy the evening. You know how I feel about leaving Kate."

"Okay, it's settled. We need to get going or we'll be late," my mother yells, sounding every bit her normal, irritable self.

My dad picks up his keys from the table. "I left my car out front. We can just take it."

"No!" I watch the soft-spoken woman wince at my mother's crazy behavior. "Sweetheart, we should take the Mercedes. I had it detailed for tonight."

My father, who for the most part tolerates my mother's rude behavior, seems miffed at how she is acting. "My Jag is out front, Leeta. Like you said, we're already running late. There's no reason to take your car. Now let's go."

My mother is shocked stupid, apparent by her gaping mouth and wide eyes. She almost looks like she has seen a ghost. My father gives her a solid push on her back then my parents and Marcus quickly head out the front door. I stay in the same spot on the sofa, closely watching the woman we have been left with. She's smiling at the two of us, almost like she is happier to stay here with us than go out with my parents.

"The time change is really messing up Kate's sleeping schedule, but I bet she'll be up from her nap any minute. What do you boys want to do when she gets up?"

I turn my head slowly toward my older brother Tanner and see he is just as uncertain of what to say as I am. I'm only eight years old, but I don't remember my parents ever asking me what I want to do. As the two of us sit here not saying a word, I hear a little voice coming from a monitor.

"Just like I thought, Kate is awake. Stay here and I'll be right back."

Mandy pops up then takes off up the stairs, leaving both Tanner and I confused in her wake. I've never seen a person that acts concerned and caring before, which has my guard up.

"She seems...nice." I live in a world where people come and go, and the ones that stick around aren't usually nice unless they want something. I look over at Tanner, who seems just as unsure of this woman as I am, but I'm brought out of my thoughts when I hear her voice again.

"Okay, boys, I want you to meet my baby girl. This is Kate." I can hear the pride in her voice as I turn away from Tanner and back toward Mandy. She's once again smiling, only this time she's carrying a little girl on her hip. A mass of blonde, wavy hair covers most of her shoulder while the girl keeps her face tucked tight against her mother. "She's not quite awake yet," Mandy says in a singsong voice as she slowly rocks the little girl back and forth. Maybe Mandy is genuinely nice, or at least it's starting to appear that way. I watch as she starts softly singing a song that I can't quite make out.

With her smile still in place, she looks down at her little girl. "Kate, can you say hello?"

My eyes stay locked on the little girl as she slowly lifts her head. When her eyes find mine, I feel a jolt through my whole body. Her eyes look like emeralds—a shade of green I've never seen on a person before.

"Her eyes..." I mumble as I feel my heartbeat thumping inside my chest.

"Kate's eyes are very beautiful, but then again, I love everything about my little girl." Mandy's eyes dance back and forth between Tanner and myself, like she's waiting for one of us to say something.

"Well, what do you want to do? Play a board game? Go swimming? Are you two hungry? We can have an early dinner."

Without thinking, I blurt out, "Why are you being nice to us?" Mandy pauses for a moment, her beautiful smile fading into a frown.

"Why wouldn't I be nice to you?"

My eyes unconsciously narrow at her question, but Tanner speaks up to answer her. "Because people aren't nice unless they want something."

Mandy's eyes slowly drift shut. When they open again, I can see the fire in them. "Where I'm from, we're nice to everyone because you treat others how you want to be treated. I'm nice to you because I expect you to treat me the same way." Neither Tanner nor I say a word in return. That's definitely not how life works here.

"Maybe next summer you boys can come spend time in Colorado and we can get to know you better."

Mandy's warm smile returns, and at this point I'm positive I will go anywhere this lady asks me to. "Let me go get you guys a snack and then we'll go swimming. Can you boys watch Kate for me while I grab something from the kitchen?"

Mandy kisses the little green-eyed girl on the forehead before placing her in a chair across from us then walks off.

I look over at Tanner, but like normal, he's staring off, lost somewhere in his own head while he avoids our surroundings. I sneak another look at the little girl only to find her closely watching me. My heart speeds up again while I draw in a deep breath of air. I'm doing my best to shake off the strange feeling I have as I tear my eyes away from hers. Looking at her is the same as looking directly at the sun. It's hard to do for more than a few seconds. I lean my head against the back of the couch and close my eyes. While I'm doing everything in my power to avoid looking at this little girl, she hops down out of her chair and climbs up next to me. I didn't know this until she slips her small hand into mine and gives mine a firm squeeze.

I want to pull back. I meant to pull back, but her touch is soothing in a way I didn't know was possible. My heart continues to beat against my chest as my mind starts to relax. I'm sitting here staring down at our connected hands when I hear her start to hum the same tune her mother had just a few moments ago.

When I finally gain the courage to look up, I find those emerald eyes burning into mine, but it's the way Kate is smiling at me that I know I'll never forget. Like maybe... just maybe, I matter to someone.

Printed in Great Britain
by Amazon